Kill With Style

Hal Gulliver was also co-author of

THE SOUTHERN STRATEGY

KILL

WITH

STYLE

HAL GULLIVER

CHARLES SCRIBNER'S SONS

NEW YORK

Library of Congress Cataloging in Publication Data
Gulliver, Hal, 1935–
    Kill with style.
    I. Title.
PZ4.G972Ki [PS3557.U45] 813'.5'4 73-19262
ISBN 0-684-13727-5

1 3 5 7 9 11 13 15 17 19 H/C 20 18 16 14 12 10 8 6 4 2

Printed in the United States of America

Kill With Style

1 The New Life

I did not yet know it at that glancing quicksilver moment, lying half awake and wondering crossly what had made me stir, but it was going to be a big day.

A very big day.

Yes, indeed, it was going to be something to look forward to, a thrill a minute. In about an hour a cheerful, bright-eyed man was going to try and break my arm. It would not feel good at all. And I would find myself, before the day was over, checking out the quickest flight from New York to Miami. Hell, I didn't even want to go to Miami, a perfectly sound sentiment which remained steadfast even when I realized that I probably needed to go.

I groped for the pillow next to mine, vaguely discontent, knowing perfectly well that there was no one there, but groping away just the same. It is easy to get used to any number of things, among them the habit of finding a warm, reasonably friendly human form next to yours when you wake up in the morning. That was an old habit I had broken by use of a widespread modern technique. It is called divorce.

It was undoubtedly just as well that I did not anticipate all these gloomy things ahead at that moment, because I might have been tempted to pull the cover over my head and try to go back to sleep, refusing to answer the doorbell or telephone or talk to anybody at all, and that could have been a serious mistake. It might even have gotten me killed. At least the way it worked out I had a certain stupid chance to try to figure out who was doing what to whom though none of the whys seemed very clear for a while.

I was half awake because the telephone was ringing with a loud and terrible noise. That was what had first made me stir.

Now a man who stays up late at night should not own a telephone. It is absurd. It can cause him pain. I kept my eyes closed for several more rings, determined to ignore it, but the phone just kept right on raising loud merry jangling noisy hell.

Who hated me? I wondered. Who would call in the middle of the night?

I opened my eyes to look at the clock suspiciously. It was almost 9:00 A.M. All right, so it wasn't the middle of the night, it still *felt* like the middle of the night. It seemed altogether too likely that the telephone could keep ringing forever unless I did something about it, a grim thought. I sat up resolutely, blinking, and moved to the side of the bed and grabbed for the telephone.

"Hello," I growled in a hoarse voice, feeling greatly put upon by time and circumstance.

"Mr. Jim Roundtree?"

The voice speaking my name was feminine enough but a little metallic, boding no good. It was the voice of either an operator or of someone's secretary. In fact, it was both, as a second voice suddenly indicated, both an operator and a secretary, calling from New York.

"I have Mr. Roundtree," the first voice said brightly, after I grudgingly admitted identity. The hell you do, dear, I murmured to myself. Then came the second voice, the secretary's. It sounded familiar, tantalizingly so, as I heard her thank the operator, but it didn't quite hit me until she

said, in a friendly and altogether impersonal fashion:
"Hello, Mr. Roundtree, it's nice to hear your voice. Please
hold for Mr. Medlock."

Well, well, well, I thought. For a second I considered
hanging up and then decided to wait a moment to see just
what on God's green earth Medlock might want.

"Hello, Jim, how are you?"

It was the first time I had heard that smooth, deep voice
in more than six months. And . . . well, I decided at just that
moment that it wasn't worth it after all. I wasn't that curious
really. I didn't care what Medlock might want, and I didn't
want to talk to him.

I did take a moment to speak several clear sentences
into the telephone, mostly in the way of instructions to
Medlock about various things, but since some of the instructions related to portions of his anatomy and at least one I
was reasonably certain was physically impossible I did not
really think Medlock would follow any of the directions.

I hung up the telephone, wide awake now, and feeling
considerably better than I had in some little while. I felt
quite content with the world in fact. The telephone began
to ring again. No more than a minute later, which made me
smile, and I was humming softly to myself as I stepped into
the shower.

The telephone went on ringing for a long time. I
stayed in the shower under the hot water until I was sure
the ringing had stopped, then stepped out and began to
towel myself dry.

It was one of those days, as it happened, when I had
already decided not to go into the city. Not to go to my
New Office, as opposed to the Old Office, where hopefully
one day Medlock would trip on a small deceptive tear in the
thick carpet and with any luck injure himself in some ex-
tremely painful way. I had made the decision not to go to
work the night before. It had occurred to me while reading

a book I wanted to finish and sipping a little Scotch and staying up fairly late that today would be a fine day to stay at home.

It was not an unusual decision for me to make, not in my new career. It happened regularly. At least one day each week as a rule.

Hank's law firm didn't care any more. At first the senior partners seemed to hold certain unvoiced high hopes for me, despite my agreed-upon unorthodox working arrangement. That was my suspicion anyway, that they had taken me on some eight months before in this strange status only after looking over my Harvard law background and bright corporate record . . . bright right up to the point, at least, when one of the American growth companies of the decade (as one unusually bland company brochure had once phrased it) had fired the hell out of me.

The memory of Medlock's smooth voice on the telephone made me smile again suddenly as I remembered the instructions I had given him. I thought regretfully of something else I could have added. Good old Medlock had been right in there at the kill. Never missed a trick.

I fried one egg on the stove in the little kitchenette and ate it along with two pieces of toast, buttered and with grape jelly thank you, and finished my cup of coffee and felt considerably better.

Medlock's call was a curious thing.

I fixed myself a second cup of coffee and walked to the broad living-room window to stare out at the beach.

Not that I could really see the beach, but I knew where it was, just two blocks over, and I could imagine it. I was living for the time in a two-story wooden-frame house near the far end of Long Island, far enough from New York City so that I felt like the Voice of the Commuter when I drove in. But it was not too bad, better driving than that damned Long Island Railroad.

The telephone rang again, and I answered this time and heard what again sounded like the long-distance operator's voice asking for Mr. Jim Roundtree, and this time I hung up the telephone quietly, without any conversation with anybody.

I clasped one hand back of my neck, kneading the muscles slowly, and decided I did not especially like the thought that all of a sudden the old home office was trying desperately to get in touch. It was hard to figure. I am quite vain enough in placing a high evaluation on my talents and abilities, but it didn't stand to reason that they wanted to offer me my old job back. The parting of the ways had been too abrasive, not a damned bit friendly.

Ah, well, I thought, sighing and trying to put it out of my head.

The next thing that happened to me was strange. I have never put much stock in premonitions, and probably I had just had a little too much Scotch the night before, and too many other nights recently. I didn't really have a hangover or a headache, but I probably had not gotten quite enough sleep, and of an instant, despite the good breakfast I had just finished, I felt lightheaded and almost dizzy.

A blurred series of wild thoughts tumbled through my mind, most of them murky, like the passing glimpse of automobile headlights in a heavy rain.

It all came into focus on one principal thought: they were going to accuse me of stealing money. By they, I meant Troup-Kincaid, but Medlock would be behind it somehow.

The charge would be embezzlement, plain and simple. No, perhaps of some even more dire criminal fraud, probably embezzlement and stock manipulation. Or, more likely, since I had left the company, I could be conveniently blamed for whatever disastrous past decisions might have to be explained at the next stockholders' meeting. And it was just about the time of year for the annual meeting, I thought with a sudden sense of fear, or if not quite fear something close enough.

I shook my head impatiently, driving away the light-headed feeling.

The wild thoughts were foolishness, of course.

Once I sat in a corporate board room for a very important meeting. I was there for a special purpose, to answer just two questions relating to some things I had given study. There were six or seven other men in the room, all officers or directors of the company. They were balanced, fairly closely, on the knife edge of a decision, a question of whether to spend something like one hundred thirty million dollars on a particular project. They had already discussed it all thoroughly and had sought some other opinions, but the final decision came down more or less to the two questions. I knew it, and they knew it, and I had the somewhat eerie feeling that whatever I said would precisely tip the balance one way or the other.

As near as you can be certain about such things, they had in fact followed my advice.

A voice then in spending one hundred thirty million dollars. But embezzlement? No chance, just no opportunity. I had dealt in millions of dollars at one level, but not in the way of a man charged with locking up the drugstore cash register each night. I couldn't have taken a dime even if I'd wanted to. And it wasn't likely that anyone would try to make me a corporate fall guy for whatever reasons. No real opportunity. You need at least to be on the board or an officer of the company.

Premonition or not, I thought later that my instant's sense of fear or near fear had come close to truth. How does the bit go? Anybody not in a state of panic simply can't be aware of all the facts.

2 Opening Gambit

I was still staring out the front window when the blue car pulled into the driveway.

The car pulled in and then backed out again. I thought at first it was someone trying to turn around, but after the driver pulled out into the street again he seemed to hesitate, then this time backed the car into the driveway so that it was facing out. It seemed a curious way to behave.

This was all in early May. There had already been some warm and pretty days but it remained cool as often as not, sometimes even chilly at night. The morning had been cool and a little windy, though the sun was bright as if promising warmer hours ahead.

Even so, the man stepping out of the car in my driveway seemed to be pushing the season a little. He was wearing a light blue sports jacket, pale blue shirt, and white slacks and highly polished black shoes. He looked ready for Miami.

I finished my coffee, just a sip or two left in the cup, while watching the man walk up to the front door. He carried a black briefcase and wore black hornrimmed glasses.

He peered at the number, as if to be sure, and then rang the doorbell. I put my coffee cup down on the window ledge, not really hurrying to answer the door. It was curi-

ous. I was standing only a few feet away, and if he had
turned his head he would have seen me at the window, and
I had the feeling that he knew I was there watching him, but
he never turned to glance in my direction.

The stranger with the brightly polished shoes rang the
doorbell a second time and after waiting a second more
knocked stoutly on the door. "Mr. Roundtree?" he asked,
when I opened it at last.

There was something wrong about the man, though he
asked his question very politely. Maybe it was the white
slacks and pale blue shirt and light blue sports jacket and
what appeared to be an expensive tie. Or maybe it was those
damned shoes, which didn't quite seem to go with the rest
of the outfit. The man wore them all well but not as if,
exactly, he felt comfortable in them. Not uncomfortable
either, more as if he might be an engineer or something
similar (his face had a reasonably dark tan, early spring or
not), someone maybe who worked outdoors and who was
perfectly capable of wearing a coat and tie with grace but
who simply usually wore something else.

"What do you want?" I asked, not very graciously.

The man reached into his coat pocket, his hand moving
very fast, and the speed of the gesture made me anxious. I
was still standing in the doorway and I tensed my right hand
and shoulder, thinking how I could still slam the door.

His hand appeared again quickly, innocently, holding
out only an open wallet.

"I just need to talk to you for a moment."

He smiled and held out his wallet to flash an official-
looking card at me, not a badge, and not with a swift now-
you-see-it, now-you-don't movement. He held his wallet
up, open toward me, and held it absolutely still, patiently,
as if he wanted me to read every word.

Not that the card said much. It looked official enough
and identified the man as Anthony N. Stroud, insurance-

investigator type. I even looked at the small picture on the card. It looked reasonably like the man holding the wallet.

"This should only take a minute," he said.

"Come on in, Mr. Stroud," I said, moving aside and letting him follow me into the room, making the belated effort now to be polite. "I was going to have another cup of coffee. Will you have a cup? It's instant but not bad."

Stroud thanked me but said no thanks, he had just stopped for coffee a few minutes before.

I took my time fixing my coffee, letting the water boil and carefully measuring out the instant coffee and a little sugar and cream. The telephone rang again, which was fine with me, since I didn't intend to answer it any more that morning. It rang three times and stopped.

Then I heard a voice murmuring on the other side of the kitchen door and sighed. That damned Stroud was answering my telephone. Hell of a way for a stranger to behave.

There was a brief knock on the kitchen door and Stroud pushed it open.

"There's a telephone call for you, Mr. Roundtree," he said, as if he were a blasted butler.

"I'm not available for calls this morning, Mr. Stroud," I said.

He blinked and looked at me blankly for an instant, then disappeared back into the living room. I followed him out with my cup of coffee in hand. He was murmuring again into the blooming telephone and hung up as I watched.

"I said you weren't available."

"That's accurate," I said somewhat coolly.

"They said they'd call again," Stroud reported, and I didn't say anything.

I walked over to the window. There is a wide, heavy wooden table along one side of the living room, flush against the wall under the wide window on that side of the room. I use the table as a desk sometimes, a work space big enough so I can spread papers all around me in both directions and even look out the window occasionally while I work. Not that the view is so marvelous, just a reasonably scruffy side yard with one tall tree at the edge.

No, I take that back. The view is pretty fair and I like it. You can see green grass and sky and the single slightly twisted tall tree has a certain character. And I still knew that the beach was just two blocks away.

Stroud put his briefcase on the table and opened it up.

"I apologize for answering your telephone," he said, his eyes cautious, appearing a trifle apprehensive behind those heavy glasses.

"It's all right," I said.

"I wasn't sure you could hear that telephone in the kitchen."

"Don't worry," I said, "it's really quite all right."

There was something wrong about Stroud, damn it. I couldn't make it out, couldn't put my finger on it, but it was there. He sat down in a chair opposite me at the big wooden table and pulled a sheaf of papers from his briefcase.

"This should only take a minute or two, Mr. Roundtree," he said. "You left Troup-Kincaid last August?" I nodded, relieved in a way. I had been trying to think what an insurance investigator could conceivably want with me, since I had not been involved in any automobile accident or insurance claim or whatever, so it almost had to be something to do with T-K-I. Or with Barbara, I thought, with a sudden turn of the heart. Much to my preference that it have to do with the company.

"Do you remember a secretary named Barbara Ingram?"

The name almost made me jump, because I had just been thinking of a different Barbara, an ex-wife sort of Barbara.

I nodded at Stroud, startled, yet feeling relieved that whatever he was about, it had to do with the company. I remembered the girl Stroud meant, this Barbara Ingram, very well. She was a good secretary, matter of fact, a young almost pretty girl with short, curly dark hair. She had worked in the steno pool for at least three or four years, and I had used her several times, once for nearly a month when my own secretary was out having a baby. As I remembered, she had left Troup-Kincaid even before I had.

"She worked for me occasionally. I thought she was very competent. She left the company, I think, for another job."

"She left almost exactly three months before you did."

"That's about right," I said. "Is she involved in an insurance claim? What's this about, Mr. Stroud?"

"I'm trying to locate Miss Ingram. I was hoping you could tell me where she was."

I shook my head and Stroud looked disappointed. He hadn't really answered my question. "Why do you want to find her?"

"I don't know if you would remember," he said. "It's been over a year, and I don't recall your name coming up in any of the reports. But there was a thief loose in your offices."

"In my offices?"

"At Troup-Kincaid, I mean. Your company . . . your former company occupies offices on nine floors. There were robberies on six of the floors, yours included."

I had a vague memory of what he was talking about. There had been a series of petty robberies, things like breaking into a desk or lifting a girl's wallet out of her purse when she put the purse down somewhere.

"I remember," I said. "But didn't they catch someone?"

Stroud nodded, looking very gloomy about it all.

"They caught someone." He began riffling through the papers in his briefcase again until he found what he wanted. "Last June," he said, looking at a paper. "It was on a weekend. Night watchman heard something and caught the fellow cold. Man was trying to hijack three big electric typewriters."

"So what's your concern now?"

"Well, at the time, catching that one fellow seemed to solve the problem. The robberies stopped. Of course, he was only charged with trying to steal the typewriters, but it seemed likely that he'd probably been guilty of most of the earlier things too."

I sipped my coffee, deciding maybe I had been wrong about Stroud. He seemed a man intent on his work.

"So let me guess," I offered. "The robberies must have started up again. But what does that have to do with Barbara Ingram? Surely you don't think she had anything to do with it."

"It was last January, four months ago," Stroud said, sighing. "That's when they started up again. My belief now is that the fellow who got caught was just accidental, maybe never even been in the building before that weekend. I think whoever was doing most of the stealing plain got scared, decided just to lie low for a while. Then it all started up again."

Stroud shuffled through his papers some more. "You probably think this kind of petty theft doesn't amount to anything, but it does." He found the paper he sought and moved one finger along a line of figures. "The thief, whoever it was, stole goods valued at more than eight thousand dollars last year." He looked up at me. "That was really almost all in the first six months, before the fellow got caught with the typewriters. This year he's already close to seven thousand dollars in just over four months."

"Cost of living," I said. "Everything goes up." Stroud

did not seem amused, though he offered a small attempt at a smile.

"Yes, I suppose," he said. "Well, I hope to reduce this fellow's standard of living considerably. I think we've even got it fairly well narrowed down. That's why I need to find your friend Barbara Ingram. She could be a big help."

"She wasn't exactly a friend," I said, not liking Stroud's tone. "I didn't know her that well. She was a good secretary, and I liked her. But I don't know how you could reach her. And in fact, still you haven't told me how she could help you."

"I didn't mean to suggest anything questionable," he soothed, "just a manner of speaking." He began pushing his various files back together into his briefcase.

Stroud had thick, solid wrists, muscular wrists, I noted, watching him move his papers around. He was a heavier man than I had first thought, I decided, looking more closely at the way his shoulders and arms filled his light blue sports jacket. I stand just a little over six feet and weigh about 192 and I'm more or less an athletic type. Stroud, I figured, weighed at least as much as I did, maybe more, though he was not quite as tall.

"Oh, I'll find Miss Barbara Ingram," he said. "She left a forwarding address with the personnel department, but it was for the apartment where she was living at the time. She moved last December, around Christmas, and I've just been trying to run her down the easy way, figuring somebody she used to work with must have her new address. The way she might be able to help . . . seems she happened to come back early from lunch one day, and a man pushed past her, hurrying out of an office. Somebody had robbed two ladies' pocketbooks, almost certainly the man Miss Ingram saw. Wouldn't expect her to be able to make any positive identification exactly, but I've got a strong suspicion the thief has got to be somebody who works in that office building or has regular access to it. I thought she might help by at least giving me an idea of what the fellow she saw looked like."

Stroud had juggled all his papers together and snapped his briefcase shut.

"I was sorry, incidentally, to hear about your problems with the company," he said, "a shame. Several of the people I heard mention it think you got a rotten deal."

"Yes, it was a shame," I agreed, and to my own surprise I found I really meant it. I was ready to leave when the break came, but Troup-Kincaid had been good to me in a lot of ways. A lot of my time there had been exciting and enjoyable.

"I don't suppose you'd go back to the company if they asked you," Stroud said.

"Who knows? I just might. You never can tell," I said. I didn't mean that, not a word of it, but I didn't much like Stroud's question. Or his casual gaze, which somehow seemed very intent on my answer. Or the idea that had just occurred to me, that he could have asked me on the telephone if I had Barbara's address.

"Once you have left a place," Stroud said, "a job or a company or a city, it is often very hard to go back and start again." He laid his briefcase carefully down on one corner of the long table.

"Who the hell are you really?" I asked him. "Why did you come to talk to me?"

Stroud stared at me, his tanned face seeming a little too tanned, his eyes suddenly seeming too sharp and clear behind the glasses. I was willing to wager that he really didn't need glasses, and almost as if he had read my mind he reached up and took the glasses off and tucked them in an inside pocket of his coat. He glanced down as if his white slacks or black polished shoes might be at fault. "Everything I told you could be checked," he said. "It would check out, all of it."

"But it is a fake, isn't it," I insisted. "A great big phony."

Stroud's blunt, tanned face was without expression, except for the sharp, watchful eyes.

Don't know if you read science fiction, but Isaac Asimov once did a series of brilliant stories about the robots of the future and the problems such near-human creatures might have in relating to humankind. Stroud made me think of them. It wasn't that there was anything mechanical about him as he leaned over the table, controlled, leaning on his hands and heavy wrists. No, not that exactly, though maybe the impression came from his blank, serious expression as he stared at me, dark brown eyes earnest and a little puzzled. It made me think of Asimov and his robots as Stroud stared at me, very like a creature with all mental circuits functioning but not quite human, a creature that could not quite relate to me but was trying hard to understand.

Stroud, in any case, wasn't what he had pretended to be, clearly enough, though somehow I didn't even doubt what he had said, that his story might actually check out if I made only routine inquiry.

"You wouldn't really go back to Troup-Kincaid, would you?" he asked gently after a long moment.

"Who knows?" I said. "They might make me an offer I couldn't refuse."

"Please don't joke," he said. "All I want is for you to tell me you won't go back to the company, not even if someone asks you."

Stroud made me laugh, literally laugh aloud, I mean. The whole thing suddenly seemed so ridiculous. My laughter didn't seem to offend him, his serious expression not changing in the slightest.

"I think it's time for you to leave," I said after a few seconds, feeling serious again myself, serious and puzzled.

Stroud nodded as if in agreement.

What happened next came so suddenly that I wasn't sure for a second what in hell was happening.

We were standing by the long table under my window, Stroud at one end with his briefcase in front of him. I was next to the chair in front of the table. I guess Stroud reached for the front of my shirt, though I didn't at first comprehend the meaning of the gesture. All of a sudden I was being jerked forward across the wooden table, jerked so hard that my legs left the floor and I fell sprawling across the table with a mild bump.

Stroud let my shirt go at that point, I suppose, because by the time I began in confusion trying to sort things out I could already feel both his hands gripping my right arm as he twisted it behind my back, twisted it hard, in such a way as to make me gasp for breath and force my face down against the table.

It didn't feel good. It felt as if my face were being twisted down into the very grain of the wood.

It seemed unreal. If Stroud twisted my arm much more, I thought, he could probably encourage me to break my nose. I had fallen over toward the window, and though I was pinned and hardly able to breathe, I still had a nice view, at least with one eye. I could look out over the wide yard and toward that single tall, slightly bent tree. It still had character. I was not much interested in trees at that moment, however. I would have settled for one tall, even slightly bent policeman, with or without character.

One thing about Stroud, he wasn't a robot. Not an Asimov sort of robot anyway, since they had certain built-in limitations, the first one being an inability to deliberately hurt people. Stroud suffered from no such limitation.

"What in hell . . ." I managed to gasp out.

"I really came here as your friend," Stroud said.

I can tell, I thought, as he proceeded to twist my arm a bit more. The son-of-a-bitch was obviously crazy. He was trying to kill me. He was making my shoulder and arm hurt so much that they burned and ached with pain. I couldn't understand why my arm didn't break off. If it did, Stroud would probably beat me over the head with it.

"I wanted this to be friendly," said he. "Truly. You are not yourself a cooperative man."

Now, though this may sound silly, that was the time I began really to be afraid. It happened so fast, for one thing. But the more chilling thing was that Stroud wasn't crazy, or at least his voice didn't sound crazy. And if he wasn't crazy, then that meant he knew what he was doing, that he was deliberately trying to hurt me for God knows what strange reason.

He twisted my arm still another notch, and I really honestly couldn't understand why it didn't break. My face was pressed so tightly against the wooden table surface that both my eyes were pulled a little awry. I tried to blink and had trouble focusing my eyes. My face had broken out in perspiration.

"I'm really just thinking of your career," Stroud said pleasantly, taking his time, holding my arm in that twisted position with both hands. "Man leaves a big, cold, un-friendly company like Troup-Kincaid, ends up with a fine law firm, why he'd be a fool to go back, even if somebody asked him. Why, some of the people there don't even like you."

My arm hurt so much that I could barely understand what he was saying, but I understood the next thing he said.

"I'm a reasonable man," Stroud said. "All I want you to do is promise me that you'll say no if, by chance, some-body wants you to come back to Troup-Kincaid. T-K-I stock isn't doing well anyway, not the last few months. Hope you exercised your options and sold out. Now if you will prom-ise me that one little simple thing, I will let you go. If you promise me that, and you mean it, nod your head just a little

bit and I'll let you go. I certainly don't want to hurt you."
He just kept on talking in that reasonable voice.

I had one instant of panic, fearing for a second that I couldn't move my head enough to nod. Hell, I would have promised him anything.

Oh, but I managed, with an effort that made the sweat pop out still more on my face, to move my face up and down along the wood in what presumably seemed to Stroud to be a nod, because he let my arm go at once.

I lay there, still flat across the table for several seconds, feeling my heart pound and not really quite sure what to do.

Stroud reached inside his coat pocket and put his dark hornrimmed glasses on again and buttoned the middle button of his sports coat. He picked up his briefcase and fingered his tie, just as if he tried to break people's arms every day. Hell, maybe he did. Maybe that was how he made ends meet when insurance investigating was a little slow, hiring out to twist people's arms.

"I'm glad we could come to an understanding," Stroud said.

He sounded earnest and friendly and he straightened his coat some more and tucked his briefcase under one arm. Maybe he really was a robot.

There was some feeling coming back into my right arm and shoulder and neck. Normal feeling, I mean, instead of pain. I shrugged my right shoulder and stretched my arm and gave a groan aloud.

The groan was real enough, though I deliberately exaggerated it a little. There was also a real enough twinge of pain with each slight movement of my right shoulder, and I put my left hand on the table's edge, as if I really needed the support to stay on my feet. Truth was, I almost really did.

Stroud glanced at me with interest when I groaned. Just an honest craftsman taking an interest in his work. We were both now standing next to and in front of the long wooden table, facing each other, and by this time I had gotten my left hand and arm braced on the table the way I wanted.

The groan must have fooled him, I guess, because he really wasn't expecting my move. Stroud was very quick, quicker than I would have thought, and started to pull away and at the same time brought one hand across his body.

But it was too late.

I only threw a short punch, but I had my feet braced and used my left arm for leverage and came around hard with my right arm and shoulder solidly behind my fist.

He was quick and almost got his hand in the way, but I had started my move before anything of the kind occurred to him. He thought he had just plain hurt me too much, damn him, and he almost had. I hit him almost exactly where I wanted, just below the rib cage, with all the weight of my better than one hundred ninety pounds behind the blow.

It made a solid thwacking sound, and I felt the impact up through my arm and shoulder, almost painfully, but a much more satisfying pain than having your arm twisted.

Now, Stroud had hurt me when he twisted my arm and threatened me. Worse, he had embarrassed me by seeming to do it so easily. When I hit him, I was doing my best in my small way to injure him. I don't suppose I really wanted to kill the man, but I sincerely wanted to hurt him.

Stroud's reaction was not entirely satisfactory.

He didn't fall down, for one thing. Didn't even drop his briefcase, still wedged under his left arm. He *did* react all right, and his face screwed up in a strange expression. In fact, I thought his eyes went a little glassy for an instant. But only for a split second, the time it took for him to lean heavily on the table with his right hand.

Except for that, he didn't change position, and his hand

came away from the table very quickly and started in a new direction.

Some days I think I am an idiot; some days I am even reasonably certain of it.

I stood there waiting for Stroud to fall down, victim of the mighty Roundtree miracle punch, and next thing I knew his hand had disappeared inside his coat and produced this time not a wallet but what seemed to be an outsize large pistol, though I knew even when I first saw it that it was a fairly ordinary-looking .38 revolver.

Except that no pistol looks ordinary when it is pointed at you. They talk about combat soldiers the first time they hear a shot fired in anger. I had never heard a shot fired in anger and I wasn't shot yet, not in the first two or three seconds anyway, but I had also never had a pistol pointed unwaveringly at my abdomen in anger before either and I didn't like it at all. That particular .38 looked to me the size of a cannon pointing directly at my stomach.

We both stood there for a couple more seconds without anybody doing anything, then I heard a strange shuddering sound.

I was so caught up in the moment (maybe scared to death is a more accurate description) that I wasn't sure if the sound came from me or not. But no, it was Stroud, taking a long, apparently painful, deep breath.

"I came only to offer you helpful advice," he said finally, painfully, and then took another long breath. "It's been over three years since anyone hit me that hard. You caught me off guard."

"My heart bleeds," I said.

I had decided abruptly, again, that Stroud must indeed be crazy, that he was going to shoot me in any case, and that I would go out like a man. That is, while imitating bad lines from old movies. That's what men are supposed to do under pressure, isn't it?

"My heart bleeds," I repeated.

"Oh, shut up," he barked at me, seeming really angry for the first time. He took another one of those long breaths and shook his head slowly from side to side, as if he were really trying hard to be patient with me. I decided I wasn't going to help. He was either going to shoot me or not but either way I didn't like the bullying son-of-a-bitch.

"I don't know if you're a real investigator, insurance or otherwise, but I'll bet I know your specialty," I said. "Your specialty is probably beating up women. And young boys, probably nine and ten year olds."

He blinked his eyes at me. His eyes were patient, incredibly patient, but they were cold and mean and very unfriendly.

"Why don't you really shut up," he said in a quiet tone. Then, softly, as if the idea had infinite appeal: "The last time a man hit me that hard I shot him."

I thought a bit forlornly of throwing myself at him, lunging and ducking and taking my chances. He seemed to be holding the revolver casually, almost carelessly. But his finger was on the trigger and the gun still pointed directly at my middle at a distance of perhaps five feet. It was no contest.

"Not unreasonable that I shot him, actually," Stroud droned on, as if reading my thoughts. "I mean, after he hit me, he ran outside this lodge and found an ax and when I shot him he was trying to cut me into firewood. Not unreasonable to shoot a man who wants to do that."

"You lead an adventurous life," I said.

He hesitated and shook his head again. "Don't put your hand on the ashtray," he said wearily. "I mean, really don't."

I had inched my left hand in the direction of a heavy ashtray near my corner of the long table. It had bounced almost to the edge when we were struggling on the table.

I put my hand now carefully back at my side, wishing a lot that I had an ax. Where are all the axes when you need them? Probably lying around outside lodges somewhere. It occurred to me that if he shot me at that instant, those could be the very last words I'd ever hear from another human being: *Don't put your hand on the ashtray. . . .*

That struck me as being plain silly. Anyway, I concluded, if Stroud had any intention of shooting me at all, he probably would have already done it.

That crazy man then proceeded to point his damned pistol at my right kneecap, *aiming* it at my right kneecap.

"My strong inclination," he said, "is to shoot you somewhere that would be very painful and might make you limp the rest of your life. But that would be yielding to an impulse, a reckless impulse, even though it has the charm of most reckless impulses. I am a serious man, Mr. Roundtree. My advice to you earlier about not returning to Troup-Kincaid was offered seriously and even, I may say, in a not completely unfriendly way. That is, it would certainly be for your welfare to follow that advice."

"What makes you so sure Troup-Kincaid wants me back?" I demanded.

Stroud didn't answer. He still had his briefcase under his left arm. Before I knew it he had abruptly shoved his pistol back inside his coat and was heading for the door. I followed him, after an uncertain second, and watched him move through the door and toward his car without even a glance back at me.

"Take it and shove it in your ear," I muttered aloud, but mostly to myself and mostly in confusion. I'm not even sure he heard me. He didn't look back as he pulled the blue car out of the driveway and sped away.

3 Old Friends Are Best

I didn't like any of it, not at all, but I wasn't sure quite what to make of it.

There was a small bulletin board next to the wall telephone in the kitchen, and I searched around for a moment to find a ballpoint pen, then jotted down a note on the corner of a newspaper clipping on the bulletin board.

I didn't like being bullied and I didn't know what to do about it at that moment, and both feelings were frustrating.

The late-morning sun looked warm and pleasant through the kitchen window. I pushed the window open. It felt warmer than the day before. Maybe Stroud had known what he was doing and hadn't been rushing the summer season at all. I decided to put on swim trunks and a heavy sweatshirt and walk over to the beach for a while and think about what had happened.

I wasn't really gone very long, long enough to jog up and down for a time and then take a quick dip, and when I got back, there was another visitor in a different car parked in the driveway. But this time I recognized the car. It belonged to Hank Carmichael, and he was sitting patiently enough behind the wheel, reading a copy of *The Wall Street Journal*.

"I could have used the Marines a little while ago, but

now you're too late," I said, having walked up almost to the
car window before he glanced in my direction and saw me.

"You know the Marines' biggest problem?" Hank
said, peering at me nearsightedly just as if he knew what in
the world I was talking about. "The Navy is supposed to
take us places. That's the Navy's main function in life, but
the damned Navy is always late." He shook his head in
rueful sadness. "Otherwise, we would have been here in
time."

"Come on inside," I said, grinning. "This is an unac-
customed honor. I am awed and impressed."

Hank had been out to visit but only on weekends. The
fact that he was here in the middle of a working day meant
that it had to be on business, though I couldn't guess what.
I hadn't telephoned in to let anyone know I wouldn't be in
the office that day, but I couldn't think of anything I had
been working on that was urgent, nothing that wouldn't
wait at least until the following day.

It had been Hank who had maneuvered my unusual
working arrangement with his law firm. I suspected sometimes that he was a little disappointed that I had proved to
be dead serious about *not* getting serious in trying to carve
out my own spot within the firm, but he had never said so,
at least not to me.

Often I stayed overnight in the city, working late into
the evening at the office, then getting a hotel room and
coming to work early the next morning. Hank's law firm
had no complaints about the length of my working day on
the days when I went to work. It was usually quite a long
day. But that fitted in fine with my idea that I ought to spend
every third or fourth day doing something else, often, specifically, being lazy.

I wondered now, a bit guiltily, if Hank had been trying
to call me one of the times that morning when I didn't
answer the telephone, maybe about something important

enough to make him finally drive out to the beach house in search of me.

I had come to love that blasted house, I must admit, even if it was almost too far out for convenient commuting back and forth to the city. I suppose it really had been built originally as a summer beach house, though it was a solid enough old frame dwelling. It belonged to a friend of mine at *The New Yorker,* a man with no doubt more foresight than I'll ever have, who had bought house and land in the early sixties, when property values were about half what they are now. When he was working on a magazine piece, he would frequently leave the city on a Wednesday afternoon and work away at it during a four-day weekend. And he would work hard, though it was likely there would be at least three cocktail parties during the four days.

I had first met him there at the beach house at one such weekend party. Friendships always amaze me. My friend at the magazine was a reasonably good friend, I'd say, a man whom I might have called if I'd needed help of some kind. Yet there must have been a dozen people I knew better in New York alone, Hank among them. Yet somehow, my *New Yorker* friend was the one who called me the week after I was fired. Don't know how he'd heard, but he called and expressed sympathy and finally insisted that I borrow his house out at the end of Long Island. Said he would be going to Europe for a few months and pretended I would be doing him a favor. The way he insisted made me think that he knew I had some family problems, along with having just been fired, but he never made reference to that, for which I was grateful, and I, after appropriate moderate protest, accepted his offer with some gratitude.

Turned out, he really was going to Europe for six months to a year to work on a book. Last postcard I'd gotten had said he probably wouldn't be back in New York until the end of the summer.

"What brings you out this far?" I said to Hank.

"I figured you might be down on the beach," he said, which I translated as meaning he probably had tried to call and hadn't been able to get me.

"Yes," I said, "and before you even tell me what you want, I need a favor, as usual. But only a small one."

Hank nodded and raised questioning eyebrows.

"I need to check an automobile registration. It's from this state, a New York tag. You could probably get it checked quicker than I could."

"Sure," he said, "give me the number." I herded Hank toward the small kitchen and showed him the number I'd written down on the bulletin board. It was the number I had hastily scrawled after watching Stroud's blue car move out of my driveway.

"Let me call the office," Hank said.

Two or three of Hank's senior partners had gotten particularly friendly with me after the first few weeks. They sent me down to Washington for the firm once, on what had amounted to a high-level lobbying job. I had done well, if I do say it. I think they really had wanted to make me a partner, at least if I had ever seemed willing to work at it a little bit. But I had failed to take the hint or rise to the bait or whatever, and I had been pretty consistent about staying home from work every third or fourth working day. It was the kind of thing that upset senior law-firm partners, made them think a man lacked something in high purpose and firm dedication.

But then, on that score my conscience was clear. I had given Hank fair warning from the beginning.

"Look, old comrade, upon whom I impose," I told him, "I don't want to be in your prestigious law firm exactly. Your partners, at least the two I've met, appear to me to be a little like lean and aging and very successful dinosaurs. But I need some money, some regular income for a while, until I can sort some things out, decide about some things. Now as you damned well know, I am one of the very best and most astute corporate-type attorneys you've ever encountered."

"You are modest too," Hank interjected dryly. "I've always liked that."

I grinned at him. "Just find me a way to earn a little cash, old son. I will solve your tax problems and stroke your old municipal bonds. Up to a point, I'll do good. I'll solve your hard and knotty legal problems that nobody else in the firm wants . . . or that everybody's bored with."

Hank at first glimpse seems a tall, rather grimly earnest man whose heavy, somewhat round face usually wore an expression of unshakable high seriousness, at least right up to the point when, as now, he cocked an eyebrow at an old friend and smiled a slight mild smile. I had always placed a good deal of confidence in that wry smile.

"What you mean," Hank said, "is that though you are a corporate dropout, so to speak, you want my proud and prestigious law firm to pay you a lot of money. But you don't want, really, to be part of the firm. And . . ." Hank's eyebrows lowered as he considered his words judiciously. "And," he repeated, "you don't want anybody to fuck with you."

"You phrase it admirably," I said, "delicately but admirably. You sum up my request with precision."

Hank chuckled, then frowned. He sighed after a moment and bent forward and closed his eyes and wrinkled his forehead and ran one finger along the bridge of his nose, slowly and reflectively. It was a regular performance.

I remember that we had just finished lunch, and while Hank meditated, I signaled the waitress for two more cups of coffee.

Hank opened his eyes after what seemed a long, thoughtful time. "You are a demanding, no-good fellow, and I am fond of you," he said, shaking his head.

I remember feeling myself stiffen just a trifle. It was a

matter of being super sensitive, and I knew it at the time, but I couldn't help it. Hell, I had just been run off from one job, even if more or less by intention, my own intention, and that same week I had been through a hellish, grueling session with an attractive lady and her lawyer, both of whom took a decidedly uncharitable view of my being unemployed, it being particularly inconvenient for the lady just at the time when she was working out the style in which she wanted to live as my ex-wife. And even with an old friend like Hank, my minor-league reflex action when he hesitated was that Good Old Hank was about to give me the polite line, you know, certainly-nice-to-have-seen-you, old classmate, and I-certainly-wish-I-could-help kind of line.

That was not the case, I was sure, Hank being one of those rare people you sense somehow will invariably go out of his way to be helpful, even under the most trying circumstances. My own quick, instinctive reaction was a bad sign, a sign of the kind of tension I'd been under. It had built up more than I realized.

"So what do you think?" I asked Hank, after his long silence.

"I am just considering," he said absently. "It is a matter of tactics." The waitress made and poured us both more coffee. "I think we should try to have lunch, tomorrow or the next day, with my oldest living law partner, Robert Murray Baldwin. Name mean anything?"

I shook my head. "Only vaguely," I said.

"No matter. He doesn't practice much any more, but he still about half runs the firm on a lot of things. The great advantage of your meeting him before talking to anybody else is that he's likely to think it all sounds like a good idea, and if he does the other senior partners would certainly go along," said Hank.

"Do you think he will go along? Suppose your Robert Murray Baldwin doesn't buy the idea?"

"I don't want to seem immodest," Hank said, in a tone full of cheerful vainglory, "but Mr. Baldwin regards me as the prime example of vigorous young blood in the firm." I raised a skeptical eyebrow without saying anything. "Of course," Hank admitted, "the average age of partners, junior and senior, is about sixty-one."

"You are at least my age," I said. "I know some law firms where tottering old men of thirty-four are already falling by the wayside."

"Granted," said Hank. He stared at me quizzically. "Don't underestimate Mr. Baldwin because of his age. He must be eighty-one or eighty-two by now, but he's not senile and he's not stupid. He's a friendly man, articulate and very shrewd. He's likely to ask you two or three pointed, if polite, questions." I nodded. Hank sighed. "Speaking of it," he said, "what in hell happened anyway?"

It was my turn to sigh.

I was in effect asking Hank to get me a job, at least on a temporary basis, and old friend or not he had every right to ask the question. It wasn't even that I minded talking about it, though some of it, at least the reasons for some of it, still seemed a little confused in my own mind.

Hank shrugged almost at once, before I could answer, as if to say it really didn't matter.

"I do think you ought to know that I've heard at least two or three versions," he said.

He sat back in his chair and stared for a moment at a point about a foot over my head, striking a judicial pose. His hands were folded together in a perfect church-steeple structure, fingertips touching. All he needed was a white wig and he could have hired out as an English judge.

Hank chuckled aloud, suddenly and briefly, in a small eruption of great good humor, destroying his judicial image. "This is true, 'fore God. I must have talked to at least six of our law school classmates in the last two or three weeks, all with something to say about you, he said. "Now, for an analysis of those varied calls . . ."

"Spare me," I said. "I'm your old and valued friend."

"No, no. Very interesting. I said there were six, right? Of the six, at least two thought reasonably well of you. Not close friends, I wouldn't say, but remembered you and seemed sorry you had had bad luck. One didn't remember you at all and just mentioned it in passing, an item of interest because you were in our class." Here Hank paused to look at me directly and grin. "The other three, I think it fair to say, have hated your guts since law school. I think possibly you had earned their honest hate. I think probably you had gotten the top three or four job offers they each had coveted."

Hank fascinated me in spite of myself. It is hard not to listen attentively when someone describes what other people think of you.

"How did they know I'd left Troup-Kincaid? Been fired, that is. Why would they care?"

"Be serious," Hank said. "You were named general counsel . . . when? More than a year ago. When you were thirty-two. There were some business news stories here and there. That's right young to be in that league, with a corporation as large as T-K-I. Made a lot of people notice your career."

"I earned it," I said without any false modesty. "I earned it but I was lucky too. Henry Winston had wanted to retire for five years by that time, I suppose, and it happened that I had just the kind of expertise on anti-trust law that T-K-I needed."

We had gotten sidetracked then in other talk, and Hank had never asked again about how and why exactly I had been fired. Oh, once, several months later, I told him most of the story, at least in abbreviated form, but he had been persistent in keeping his curiosity under control. Or maybe, more likely, he really didn't care that much about the details. Why should he?

That had all been eight months ago now. I had needed a job and I had come to Hank, and that had been good enough, that I needed his help, and my strange working arrangement with his law firm had turned out to be reasonably satisfactory to everyone. Particularly to me.

I owed Hank a lot, I thought now, as he finished his telephone call and came back from the kitchen into the living room.

"It may take a couple of hours," he said. "You know young Lawrence? I asked him to run down that car-tag number. He likes these cops-and-robbers things."

"Thanks," I said.

"That's the good news," Hank said. "Now for the bad news. I haven't told you why I came out here."

"Give it to me all at once," I said. Hank seemed a little grim, and I couldn't imagine what he was leading up to. I felt sure his other law partners were satisfied with my work, that they thought I had been valuable to the firm. There was no pressing crisis in any of the cases on which I was currently working, nothing I had neglected, certainly nothing likely to have blown up in the past few hours.

More things had blown up in their fashion, gotten out of control, than I knew about at that instant, but I would know soon enough.

"Maybe you'd better sit down," Hank said.

"Now you're being protective," I told him.

"All right," he said, "all right, the simplest way to tell you is to tell you. You're working for Troup-Kincaid again."

"Sure I am," I said, feeling the grin spread across my face, yet not entirely cheerful with it as I remembered Medlock's effort to telephone and that damned Stroud's curious threats. Hank did not smile back. I decided to sit down after all, looking at Hank's long, solemn face and waiting for him to say he was just joking.

"Hank, that is crazy, what you just said," I insisted firmly, when he didn't say anything. He started to speak, but by this time I wasn't sure I wanted him to tell me.

"I don't know what is going on, Hank," I said, "but Troup-Kincaid's executive vice-president, Harrison Medlock, tried to telephone me this morning. I didn't talk to him. I don't even like the bastard. Then some wild man dropped by and twisted my arm and threatened me, said he wanted me to promise that I wouldn't go to work for T-K-I again. Going back to Troup-Kincaid is about the last thing I intend doing, but when I didn't immediately confide that to this gentleman he started twisting my arm, literally twisting my arm. It felt like it was going to break."

I stopped talking, all but out of breath. "Now Hank, now you," I went on, "now you pay me a visit all of a sudden, and you tell me that yes, indeed, I am working for Troup-Kincaid again. What are you talking about?"

"Fellow just walked in and twisted your arm, huh?" Hank said with a cheerful show of interest. "You mean all that handball and weight lifting and running around the track doesn't help a bit? He just walked in and twisted your arm?"

At the moment I didn't think it was especially funny, but I understood why Hank did. I had tried to get him to play handball with me, alleging that he would become weak and frail before his time, and that his hair would turn gray and fall out if he didn't get some sort of regular exercise. He sounded positively pleased that Stroud had twisted my arm.

"This man who gives you such pleasure and who threatened me also waved a pistol around," I said. "He indicated that if he weren't such a serious and responsible citizen he'd be inclined to shoot my kneecap off."

That bit of news restored the solemn expression to Hank's face, and it was his turn to sit down. He asked me to describe exactly what had happened, and I did in some detail. "I can't make any sense out of it," he said when I finished.

"I can't either," I said, "though there somehow seem to be strange and wondrous things going on with Troup-Kincaid." I frowned and stared hard at Hank. "But the most wondrous and strange of all is what you just said. What did you mean that I'm working for Troup-Kincaid again? That's not true."

Hank stared at me and sighed. "It is true, in a manner of speaking," he said. "That's what I drove out here to tell you. Your old corporation hired your new law firm. First thing this morning. Old William Q. Wexler Senior himself, illustrious board chairman, called Jim Burns about it."

Burns, on most things, was the operating senior partner of the firm.

I thought about it. Well, it would be rare for Wexler to telephone anybody on company business these days, let alone fooling with hiring some legal work done. Wexler the Senior was an active man and still probably owned the biggest single block of T-K-I stock, but his son, Bill Wexler, Jr., had taken over as president of the corporation five or six years before.

The older Wexler spent most of his time these days flying all over the damned world in his private jet aircraft. Henry Winston, one of the few people at T-K-I for whom I still had a friendly feeling, once alleged to me that all that flying around Wexler Senior did came purely out of jealousy and frustration. T-K-I had come to own a lot of companies and a lot of things, said Winston, but the older Wexler had always wanted to own an airline and the company had never been exactly in a position to buy one when somebody was selling.

Wexler was a Texan originally, like Jim Ling of Dallas, though really of an older generation, and he had not lived in the state for years. But he had observed with interest as Ling put together his conglomerate in the 1960s with what, until the credit crunch, seemed some of the fastest financial footwork going. It had almost given Wexler another heart attack, Winston maintained, when Ling had acquired Braniff Airways (no matter that Ling had probably paid too much for it) in a $500 million package that involved Ling in also buying a bank, a car-rental company, and several insurance companies.

"All right, Hank," I said, after thinking about it for a moment. "If Wexler Senior called Jim Burns, that's a big thing. Big thing for the firm, I mean. Congratulations."

"Burns was beaming, absolutely beaming, and talking about hiring half a dozen new young lawyers. Wexler talked to him about some manufacturing plant in New Jersey. Seems there was a stock tender offer before T-K-I bought it, and one of the principal stockholders died about that time, and in some confused way everybody is suing everybody else. You know about it?"

"A little," I said, nodding. "It would take half a dozen lawyers a good year to unravel. But, Hank, that doesn't have to involve me. Let old Wexler and Troup-Kincaid hire your firm. But that doesn't mean me." Something in Hank's curious expression concerned me. "Does it?"

"You're part of the deal," he said. "Wexler wants you to fly to Miami, either tonight or first thing in the morning, a special assignment of some kind. He asked Burns to let you be on loan from the firm to Troup-Kincaid. Not for very long, he said. He said it would take probably only a few days, no more than a week."

"Lord God," I said, and I did not mean it as an irreverent (or irrelevant) expression. "What did Burns say?" I tried. But I could already guess.

"He told Wexler that he couldn't see why not. Especially if it were only for a few days."

I started to just shake my head and tell Hank that I wouldn't do it, but then I remembered Stroud, the man's even voice as he twisted my arm and told me what a reasonable man he was. That was a factor. If I refused to go to Miami, that would be presumably exactly what Stroud wanted. Somehow Stroud had already known when he came to see me, when he threatened me, that Wexler wanted me for something, that Troup-Kincaid in this indirect fashion would be offering me a job again.

There was something else too. We were sitting in the living room, Hank and I. My Scotch glass from the night before was on a small table at one end of the couch, near the reading lamp. I stood and walked over and picked up the glass and sniffed at it. It smelled stale, not bad but not good, just the way a drink glass with melted ice and a little whiskey left in it smells the next day. It was the staleness I wanted to savor. It fitted with the way I was living, in somebody else's beach house and in somebody else's law firm (even if I did earn my way).

"I'll go to Miami, Hank," I said. "But I want to ask you something first. Suppose I said no. Suppose I asked you to call Burns right now and tell him I wouldn't do it. What would happen?"

Hank considered the question.

"He wouldn't fire you, if that's what you mean, certainly not if you told him about the man who came to see you. That would give him pause. It would make the whole thing have a ring of funny business. In fact, if you don't want to go to Miami, it would be better if you called him yourself right now. Burns is not a fool, and he tends to be a cautious man. But I must also tell you," Hank said, and shrugged, "his initial reaction was that it was a compliment to you that Wexler wanted you for special duty of some sort even though you'd left them in not entirely friendly fashion last year. He figured, I think, that the Miami thing might relate to some legal matter you were already familiar with."

"What is it about? Did Wexler explain why he wants me in Miami?"

Hank fished around in his inner coat pocket and came out with a piece of paper. "I don't really know much. Wexler wants you to be at the Miami airport by noon tomorrow. A man named"—he looked at the paper—"Medlock . . . will meet you."

"Wonderful," I said, thinking of Medlock's smooth voice before I hung up the phone on him that morning.

I was really tempted to call Burns at the office, while Hank was there, and tell him that the whole thing indeed had a ring of funny business and that I had no intention of going to Miami, particularly not to meet anyone named Medlock, who happened among other things to be a man I didn't like.

"All right," was what I said aloud, thinking that life was too short to die curious and the only way I would ever find out what this nonsense was all about was to go ahead and go to Miami. It was a thought I would remember in the next few days, along with the old saying about curiosity and cats.

"You have a current passport, don't you?" Hank asked.

"Passport?"

Hank was still peering at his piece of paper, apparently with my instructions on it. "Yes," he said. "You'll need your passport in case, I suppose, you take a trip across the big waters. And you'll need to pack enough clothes for about a week. Some sports clothes, bathing suit, and be sure and bring a tuxedo." He glanced up at me. "Sounds as if you're going on a Caribbean cruise. What have you done to deserve a vacation?"

I shook my head, somehow by now in a fatalistic and

good-humored frame of mind. I really didn't want to go to Miami, and I really didn't want anything else to do with Troup-Kincaid. That was an era of my life that was over, at least one that I wanted to be over. Yet I apparently would be on my way to Miami in a few hours, again in the employ of T-K-I, at least for a time. And somehow the whole thing left me cheerful and feeling alive and chipper. "You know, Hank me lad," I told him, "I am a modern-day John C. Pemberton, Lieutenant General John C. Pemberton, that is to say."

Hank looked at me doubtfully.

"Wait a minute," I said. I went into the bedroom and returned with the book I had been reading late the night before, *Never Call Retreat,* one of Bruce Catton's superb volumes on the American Civil War. I had almost finished reading the book before falling asleep in the early-morning hours, and I remembered the passage I wanted, one near the beginning of the book.

"Here it is," I said to Hank, after thumbing through pages for a few seconds. "See, John C. Pemberton, he was commander of the Mississippi Army of the Confederacy."

I read Catton's description of Pemberton aloud to Hank: " . . . A transplanted Yankee whose morals were above reproach but who could neither reassure civilians nor inspire soldiers, a man dedicated but wholly without good luck." It made Hank smile. "That is the story of my life," I insisted. "I am a man dedicated but wholly without good luck."

"Don't know about that," Hank said, "but it's probably just as true as the part about your morals being above reproach."

Hank was in a good mood when he left. So was I, until I stretched my arms over my head, getting my suitcase down from the bedroom closet, and felt a painful twinge where Stroud had twisted my shoulder.

4 General Earl Van Dorn Who?

Hank met me at Kennedy Airport early the next morning, as he had promised he would. He had a thin manila folder with him and after he watched me check my bag he asked me about two or three minor items from the office, things I knew about, none of them pressing. Then he gave me his card with the office telephone number on it, and with both his and Jim Burns's home telephone numbers written on the back of the card.

"We're your shock troops," Hank said. "That's just in case you need to call out the troops some time other than during office hours."

"Thanks."

"Oh, by the way," Hank went on, "got something on that car license number. Not that it helps anything. It was a rented car, man named Stroud according to the rent-a-car office records, same name he gave you. He turned it back in yesterday afternoon."

"Probably just as quick as he could after he drove into the city from my house," I said.

"Probably."

We shook hands, Hank looking more worried and solemn than usual. He had joked about it the day before, but I think my story about Stroud threatening me really bothered him. Hell, it bothered me too. But I didn't know what to do about it, except to go to Miami and try to find out what was going on.

"One other thing," Hank said as I turned to go. "You once told me more or less how you came to be fired." I nodded as Hank hesitated. "Go ahead," I said. "You can't hurt my feelings."

"Let me see if I have it straight," Hank said. "It could be important. See if this is a fair way to describe it. You made an ass of yourself at a company reception, somewhat consciously, in the sense that for assorted reasons you didn't really give a damn. You insulted some people and you left, finally, with someone else's wife, a willing enough companion, I gather. On the day after all that, you had a huge clash with somebody . . . who?"

"Medlock, the executive vice-president."

"Oh, Lord," Hank said. "The man you're supposed to meet in Miami? That does make it nice. All right, so you had a fight with Medlock, not just about your undoubtedly outrageous behavior the night before, but about some other things too, and before it was over you were cleaning out your desk. That about cover it?"

I sighed, not because Hank's recital offended me but because it all seemed long ago, even though it had been less than a year, and I just didn't care especially to think about it, though I knew I would see good old Medlock and no doubt some other T-K-I people in Miami in two hours or so when I got off the plane.

"That's about it, Hank, why?"

"Only one thing," he said. "I was trying to figure last night, after what's just happened, Troup-Kincaid suddenly entering your life again from two different directions, if anything that had happened when you were fired could have any bearing on what's going on now."

"Don't see how." I shook my head.

"Is there anything of significance you didn't tell me?"

I thought for a moment. "Only one thing, the name of the woman at that reception." Hank lifted one hand and shook his head, as if to say that couldn't possibly have anything to do with anything. Then he froze: "Not Mrs. Medlock?"

"No, no, Helen Wexler," I said. "Mrs. William Wexler. Junior, of course, but still . . ."

"Dear God," Hank said, "you mean the wife of young Wexler, the wife of the president of the company?" He made a small whistling sound. "When you decide to commit corporate hara-kiri, you don't fool around, do you." It was a statement, not a question, and I didn't have anything much to add to it. I promised Hank I would telephone the office from Miami, and he walked me to the gate for my airplane and we said goodbye.

"One thing I'll tell you," Hank said just as he turned away. "Dedicated and luckless you may be, but you don't resemble Lieutenant General Pemberton nearly as much as you do General Earl Van Dorn."

"Who the hell was he?" I said.

"He was also a commander of the Confederate Mississippi army. Go look it up in your Bruce Catton book."

I smiled at Hank's retreating back. I couldn't remember anything about a General Van Dorn, but whoever he was that was Hank's kind of humor and one-upmanship. He had undoubtedly looked up the reference after I had belabored him with General Pemberton the day before, and though I wasn't sure, I had the dire suspicion that the comparison with Van Dorn would not reflect well on my character.

The flight to Miami was uneventful. I had picked up *The New York Times* and *The Wall Street Journal* and tried reading for a while. Vietnam was still a mess, one way or the other, even though American troops were out now. Con Edison was warning again of new brownouts and blackouts

that summer if everybody kept their air-conditioners on all
the time. New York police were trying to locate more than
two million in narcotics, seized as evidence in a raid, which
had mysteriously disappeared after it was in the hands of
police. Things in the Middle East seemed even more uncertain than usual. A woman had shot her husband and her
husband's mother and two children and a stranger who
came to the door and then shot herself and nobody knew
why. It looked as if there might be another strike of city
workers about something or other. The Mets had won two
games in a row and the sportswriters were making mild
pennant talk.

I was tired. I had tried to get a good night's sleep the
night before, but the memory of Stroud's brief, unpleasant
visit kept me awake. Not because it frightened me, though
once I dozed off and came bolt awake in the fearful belief
that he was in the room getting ready to twist my arm again,
but mostly from just a baffled, frustrated kind of feeling that
it didn't make any sense at all.

It didn't make any sense for me to be flying down to
Miami on a morning flight either but why not? Nothing in
my life had seemed to make a whole lot of sense for a while.

I tried to take a nap during the last hour or so before
Miami but without any luck.

Miami International Airport has a kind of Airport
Bland look to it. Not depressing but not very thrilling
either. You can't keep looking out the window at the warm
sun and blue sky every second. Yet the sun felt good getting
off the plane, hot and bright and cheerful (used to know a
girl like that). Inside, I found it less cheerful as I got my one
suitcase, then wandered upstairs.

Medlock would meet me, according to the instructions
I had gotten through Hank, near the Delta Airline counter
in the main terminal lobby.

There was no sign of Medlock or anybody else I'd ever

seen before, just a pretty good long line of people waiting to check their bags. I stood back about thirty feet from the Delta counter, put my suitcase down, and waited. What was I doing here? And who the hell was General Earl Van Dorn?

5 Medlock's Move

I spotted him before he even started to move toward me. Not Medlock, nor anyone else I knew, but I recognized the man nonetheless. I saw him just as he, staring at me from about fifty feet away, decided that I was his man and began moving toward me.

He was youngish, though probably at least thirty, and he was dressed for the part. Don't know how to describe it, exactly. A bit modish. He was wearing one of the colorful shirts and broad matching ties that were still fashionable that spring. Good expensive suit. Could have been almost any well-dressed young executive type. Except I was sure I was right. He just plain had the look.

He smiled as he neared me and started to hold out his hand in greeting.

"Don't say it," I said quickly, holding up my hand in a stop signal. He frowned at me warily. I was not behaving properly, not according to the ordinary script of things, and if my guess was right this man would be one who put a high value on the conventional script of things.

"You're one of them, all right," I said to the man. "You've got to be."

"Are you Mr. Roundtree?" he asked, very correct now. He no longer held his hand out in greeting.

"That's right," I said. "And I already know who you

are. You're one of Medlock's Minions. You've got to be.
You look the part."

The young man was not dumb; few of Medlock's
young men were. He cocked his head and looked at me
keenly with intelligence and a distaste he tried to conceal
with a polite pretend smile but which came through loud
and clear.

"Admit it," I said loudly, so that a gray-haired lady
(not elderly gray-haired, blue-gray haired) in the Delta
counter line turned around and stared. "Admit it," I said,
"you are one of Medlock's boys. He probably brought you
in from one of the regional offices, God knows from where,
some time in the last year. If you'd been in New York
before then, I'd know you, at least by sight."

"I'll admit anything you say, Mr. Roundtree, if you'll
just stop yelling," he said quietly. I glanced at the Delta
line. Two or three other people had turned around to watch
us curiously. I felt good, exuberant even.

"I may even stop yelling," I told him, "just to
be friendly. But why shouldn't I enjoy myself? Believe me,
I'm not here out of just sheer old love for Troup-
Kincaid . . ."

My use of the company name in such offhand fashion,
even in a lowered voice, did not sit well with my new
acquaintance. It all but made him flinch and he looked
appropriately pained.

This in turn gave me a new thought, brought me up
short. I looked him over again with care. I knew what I
meant by the term Medlock's Minions. It was a term I'd
coined myself and used occasionally, not actually to Medlock personally but in such context that I was reasonably
sure it would get back to him. It was used as a joking phrase
sometimes, even among people who admired Medlock.
Medlock hated it. It referred simply to the kind of bright
young men he pulled in around him. Usually they really

were bright, if sometimes in a somewhat limited and conventional way, and though I'm sure he would have denied it, Medlock seemed to want them to dress the way he did, talk the way he did, and think the way he did.

You may have heard the story, one that sounds apocryphal at first, about the young engineer at IBM who went to work one day wearing not a colorful way-out shirt but a light blue shirt instead of his usual white shirt and tie. He was sent home by his supervisor, who gave him the word: Don't come in again without a white shirt. He decided not to come in again. Now, I used to think that story was myth, until someone I knew swore to me that it was really true. It's changed now, I understand, but for a long time IBM really played that kind of game, making all the people there appear in the same conventional garb, just like computer cards bouncing out of a machine all in a row.

Well, the Medlock's Minions thing was similar, though a little more subtle than just insisting on white shirts. He liked his young executives, the "comers" he liked to call them, to dress in a kind of up-to-the-moment current style, a bit modish fashion, as he did himself, and if you watched it you could tell them after a time. Or at least you could tell the ones, young men and women too, who aspired to catch Medlock's eye.

The young man meeting me had picked up my suitcase and started me off in a new direction. Something hit me after I had used the "Medlock's Minions" phrase he had seemed startled for an instant, as if he had never heard the phrase.

He was trying to aim me somewhere toward the other side of the terminal, but now I stopped him.

"I just figured something out," I said, peering at him with what I hoped was a shrewd gaze. I really was enjoying myself, in this case a bit unfairly, since the young man had done nothing to offend me, but the thing was I didn't give a damn about Troup-Kincaid any more. I had sort of thought I still did, in a way, but I didn't. So, I fixed the young man with my Shrewd Gaze: "You aren't based in New York, are you? You quite likely have caught Medlock's eye, bug boss type that he is, but you haven't made it to New York yet. He got you here to Miami to help out with whatever the hell is going on, which means he thinks well of you, and maybe you're just at the point of going to New York. If you are lucky, that is. Am I right?"

He frowned and didn't answer and continued to look pained. "We have to go this way, Mr. Roundtree," he said, urging me to start walking again. He was still holding my suitcase in one hand (maybe that was one reason he was impatient, it was heavy enough) and eager to get me to somewhere else and away from the crowd at the Delta counter, and I had started to walk again, at least a step or two, but then I stopped once more and did a near-cruel thing. I jerked my arm out of his hand and repeated, "Am I right? You're not based in New York."

He stopped right next to me. He had to if he was going to direct me anywhere. "I am based in Jacksonville," he said quietly and with a certain dignity.

"That's wonderful," I said, trying to remember what T-K-I owned in Jacksonville.

He had done pretty well up until then. Now he glared at me with an expression of great purity, pure intense dislike, while I tried to remember about Jacksonville. It was not anything really big, I suddenly recalled, I mean, not anything like a whole plant or company, just part of something else, something we had to keep our eye on . . . oops, that Troup-Kincaid had to keep its eye on.

But I remembered.

"You're an accountant, aren't you?" I asked, starting to walk again in the general direction in which we had been headed. He nodded. Suddenly he grinned and looked over at me curiously, his animosity gone.

"Is the pattern all that obvious?"

"Yes, indeed, sir," I said, "it often is."

"I'll keep that in mind," he said.

The young man led me to a small, open bar on the main floor of the terminal. Not much of a bar, presumably there for people wanting a quick drink before making a flight. It had been a year or two since I had been through the Miami airport, but I felt sure there were other, more comfortable lounges.

Medlock was sitting at one end, with empty stools on both sides of him. He gestured expansively at me, just as if we were long-lost comrades, and waved me to one of the stools. There was plenty of room, so I sat with one stool between us, half turned along the bar to face Medlock.

"I'll check his suitcase," the young man said to Medlock, then headed off in some other direction with my bag.

I followed him with my eyes, mistrustfully, but I really didn't care. It wasn't my idea to be in Miami at all. As long as I was playing somebody else's game, I would play it. They could take my suitcase and steal it or sell it or throw it in the Atlantic ocean if they wanted.

"Well, Jim," Medlock said. "Well, it's good to see you, believe it or not. I'm sorry I couldn't get through to you on the telephone yesterday."

"I enjoyed talking to you," I said. "At least I enjoyed my end of the conversation."

"Now, Jim," he said. "Now, Jim. You said some discourteous things, but I don't blame you. You've got some reason to be angry with me. I don't deny that. Let me get you a drink."

I still didn't have the least idea what all this was about, but I liked the way it was going so far. Medlock was often a fierce, blunt man, and I had spoken unkindly on the telephone. His determinedly friendly attitude made me think that for some reason he needed my help.

He gestured at the bartender. Medlock was already

drinking a martini and he ordered another. I ordered a Bloody Mary. Actually, in a funny way, it was good to see Medlock again. He was a pleasant and friendly man, an intelligent man, even an interesting man sometimes. I came very close to liking Medlock. I had been around him a few times on informal occasions, and he couldn't have been more charming, more agreeable. He was a good storyteller too.

Trouble with all that was that it was a social thing, part of Medlock's personal corporate-image sense, part of getting along, of not making any enemies by accident. Medlock made his enemies on purpose and when it was unavoidable.

I had already been with Troup-Kincaid when Medlock became executive vice-president, about five years earlier. He had been the chief fiscal officer of a company T-K-I was taking over, in his early forties then, and considered a quite competent company officer, a "comer," to use his own favorite word.

Wexler the Senior, then T-K-I president, had tapped Medlock for the job of executive vice-president, had in fact created the position for him. Wexler was already beginning to have some health problems and a lot of people, me included, thought one reason he'd done it was so that he could let himself be kicked upstairs to become chairman of the board, thus permitting his son, a man already roughly Medlock's age, to become president of the company.

Which is exactly what happened about six months later, the inner-office theory being that Wexler the older wasn't really too sure his son could run T-K-I and wanted a tough, competent operating officer like Medlock in charge of most decisions. That was the way it had worked out. Wexler the Junior was a reasonably able man, no dummy by any means, but he was far less fascinated with corporate doings than his father.

"It's just like the Army," I once heard Medlock say. "There's usually a commander, someone who aspires to a benign Eisenhower sort of image, in this case Wexler Senior or Wexler Junior, take your choice, either one, someone considered a grand fellow, a grand old man even, who gets his picture in *Fortune* and makes statesmanlike comments on how our plants will all have the latest antipollution equipment installed by year after next, and then there's got to be an executive officer, someone who can make things work."

It was apparent at this point in the recital where Medlock fitted into this scheme of things.

"There's always a grand old man, and then there's always the son-of-a-bitch who makes it go. I like to make things go."

He had said all this good-humoredly and cheerfully and as if making fun, but I had believed every word, thinking it an accurate self-appraisal, even though Medlock didn't really intend for it to be taken too seriously.

But I had watched him operate. In appearance he was a somewhat soft-looking man, reasonably trim and always well dressed, but inclined just a bit to put on weight, so that his face tended to seem a bit full and round and his middle a bit heavy. It was deceptive. He was a genuine decision-maker, a very efficient man, not inhuman or cold like a computer, a man in fact who took seriously the idea that a business executive needed to allow for the human foibles and frailties around him.

Yet Medlock embraced this generous sense of human understanding and compassion only when it applied to those people whom he valued within the company framework, and if it were a cost matter, a matter of combining two divisions, or of closing a regional office, or of firing somebody, even of firing a hundred people indirectly by eliminating their jobs, he was capable of acting quickly, too quickly, I thought, in a ruthless and efficient fashion.

"I really am glad to see you, Jim," he said, after we got our drinks. "I need some help in the worst way, and I've always admired your ability and judgment. You ought to know that."

"Even when you fired me," I said, lifting my Bloody Mary for a long sip. "Cheers."

"You know what I mean," he said. "I fired you only because you gave me no choice, none at all." Medlock peered into his martini, no doubt saddened at the thought.

"That just isn't true," I objected mildly. "You wanted to fire me."

"Now, now, Jim, let's not fight old battles," he said with an expansive wave of his hand, as if it had been years before, instead of just a few months ago, when he fired me. "I don't know what was troubling you or why exactly you were so angry. The other thing could have been straightened out. But you as much as told me you didn't want to work for T-K-I any more. You all but said you wouldn't finish that report, not even when we had to have it under some deadline pressure. What else could I do?"

"That wasn't it," I flared. "You could have taken the report, it was complete enough."

"Let's don't quarrel," Medlock said swiftly. "Bad of me to mention unpleasant things now. I need to talk to you, at least for a moment, and Mr. Wexler wants to see you too."

I turned from the bar, surprised, and looked around and across the terminal floor. "Where in the world is he?" When Medlock referred to Mr. Wexler I knew he meant Wexler the elder, now chairman of the board. He called the younger Wexler, Bill, by his first name.

"We have to go to him in a minute. He wants to talk to you. It's important, very important." Medlock hesitated, staring at me as if he wanted desperately to be friendly but was not sure how. "Look, Jim, don't misunderstand what

I'm about to say. You should know, odd as it sounds, that old Wexler finagled Winston and me into hiring your law firm on that New Jersey estate thing, which God knows is tangled enough so that maybe some new legal talent could help on it, but we hired the firm really solely just to get you down here."

Well, at least that answered one question.

"I didn't know how important I was to old Troup-Kincaid," I said. "It is a touching and new experience."

"You'll understand more in a few minutes," Medlock said. "But listen to me, we've got to join Wexler in just a moment, and there's not all that much time before your plane." He glanced at my wristwatch, then at his own watch. I didn't even bother to ask what plane he was talking about. I was afraid he would tell me.

"Let me try to say this quickly," Medlock said. "You'll be working for T-K-I this next few days, no question about that, even if it's just through your law firm. But I want you to be working directly for me too. I need your help. There are some things going on that I neither like nor understand. My honest guess is that somebody, some pirate, is trying to take over the company." I must have looked at Medlock strangely, because he lifted one hand in a helpless gesture. "I know that sounds ridiculous. But you haven't been around these last months."

He stopped talking, not so much to let his words sink in, but because the young man last seen with my suitcase had reappeared and walked up to whisper something to Medlock.

Medlock nodded. "I need just another moment. We're almost through talking." The young man handed me an airplane ticket, baggage receipt attached.

Be nice to know where I was supposed to be going, I thought, and opened the ticket, an Air France ticket. Well, well, well, quite an itinerary. Puerto Rico, Haiti, Antigua, and . . . destination Martinique. Martinique? I'd never been there but knew it was almost to South America, not too far from the coast of Venezuela.

"I've never been to the French West Indies," I said to Medlock. "It ought to be nice this time of year."

"Gorgeous," Medlock said.

Hank had almost guessed right. I was going to take a Caribbean cruise or something close to it.

"We've got to go," Medlock said, glancing at his watch once more and leaving some money on the bar for the check. "But let me finish what I was saying." The young man who had given me my ticket had withdrawn to a discreet distance out of earshot.

"You'll be working for the corporation in any case, for Troup-Kincaid, but I want you to consider working for me too," said Medlock. "That sounds like I'm trying to bribe you," he went on hurriedly, defensively, "but I don't mean it that way. I don't want you to do one single thing that's unethical or against anybody, certainly not against the company. What I do want is that you let me know what you find out, just as soon as you find it out, and before you talk with anybody else about it." He shook his head grimly, a bit fiercely, and his expression reminded me that Medlock was in his way a strong, decisive man, one accustomed to getting his own way.

"Right now I don't trust anybody," he said. "Not Wexler the Senior or Bill Wexler. Henry Winston is about 323 years old, and I can't believe he would be mixed up in this, but at the moment I don't even trust Henry."

Medlock seemed genuinely agitated, more so than I'd ever seen him, but I found it hard to feel a whole lot of sympathy.

"Medlock, even if I wanted to help you," I said, "I don't know anything about anything."

"You'll know the basic story, as much as I know, in just a few minutes," he said. "We've got to go see Mr. Wexler.

We've got to go. What I need to know is, will you try to help me? Damn it, Jim, you know me. I can be a worthwhile friend, a good ally."

"Why do you want to trust me when you don't trust anybody else?"

"I think you're honest, Jim." Medlock hesitated, then added flatly: "And you've been away from the company, that's the big thing. I know we had our differences, but you've been away. The things that have happened have all been in the last couple of months." Medlock paused, then plunged on with what seemed still further reluctant candor. "And I need to trust you. Old Wexler wants you to go to Martinique on a one-man fact-finding expedition. You'll hear all about it from him in a minute. But I need you, I need your help. I need you to let me know what you find out as soon as you find it out."

"I've never really been bribed before, Medlock. What can you offer?"

"Damn it, it's not a bribe," he began angrily, then paused as my question registered at a different level.

"You used the word first," I said cheerfully. "What can you offer."

"What do you want?" His eyes narrowed, the anger gone, as he appraised me. He had been worried for a second, but now he thought he was dealing once more with a situation he understood. "Would you want your old job back? General counsel? At a higher salary? You know we've never named anybody to the slot since you left. Henry Winston is still there to look over people's shoulders, and we were in no hurry about it. Misunderstandings occur. I could say, after your no doubt sterling performance this week, that I was very wrong to fire you. I could apologize and urge it on Winston that we bring you back. He would certainly go along. He protested to Bill Wexler when you left, said then that I'd acted hastily."

This last interested me. I didn't know old Henry had done that.

"I wouldn't want to work with Troup-Kincaid in New York again," I said. "Too near you, Medlock."

"There are other possibilities," he asserted, confident now, refusing to be insulted. "You could go to the West Coast."

I shook my head. "What I really need is cash, just plain old money," I told him. "I'm reasonably content with the law firm where I am now but I've had some expenses."

"I was sorry about your divorce," Medlock said carefully. He stood there, looking at me, and I could almost hear the wheels going around in his head.

"I think we could do something about cash," he said. "Your law firm will be paid directly, of course. But suppose we made you a special consultant in addition to that? I think I could guarantee putting you on the payroll somewhere as a consultant for a full year, at say three thousand dollars per month. Wouldn't that help your financial problems?"

Medlock was in a position to do just what he proposed, put me on as a consultant. Three thousand dollars per month for a year added up to $36,000. Yes, that would be a great help.

"My, my, Medlock, you must think you need me a lot," I said, "though of course it's only company money."

Medlock frowned at that but didn't say anything.

We shook hands solemnly and started away from the bar, guided by the young man who had brought my ticket.

6 $50 Million Bundle (in Small Bills)

Wexler the Senior was waiting in a VIP room just off the main terminal. There was no lettering on the solid wooden door, it seemed only an office of some kind, but inside it was beautifully furnished, more like a spacious living room than anything else, with a thick expensive rug, two sofas, and half a dozen square, comfortable easy chairs. The paintings and prints on the walls looked as if they might be originals.

There was a table in one corner, covered with all the needed ingredients for opening up a small corner bar, including glasses and two huge silver buckets of ice cubes.

The wide-glass picture window was directly opposite the door, with a clear view of one set of runways. A jet was coming in for a landing just as we entered, as Medlock and I entered, that is. The young man stayed outside, presumably guarding the entrance and ready to run errands on demand.

"Jim, it really is good to see you," a voice said.

That was about the same thing Medlock had said at the bar, and I didn't put much stock in it. I did believe it now from Henry Winston, who was standing near the window when I came into the room and who turned to greet me.

"It's nice to see you, Colonel," I said.

Winston is tall and very thin and has fully white hair, which gives him an even more pronounced aging-patrician

look than he already has. I liked him very much. He was
a bit reserved and so much older than I that we had not
gotten to be close personal friends exactly, not even when
I reached the level of dealing professionally with him as an
equal. But he had always been helpful and encouraging.

Winston was a good attorney, even brilliant. He had
been general counsel of the corporation until he was nearly
seventy, and then they had almost refused to let him retire.
I had succeeded Winston and been given the title more than
a year before I left Troup-Kincaid. But even then he had
stayed on as an unofficial counsel emeritus, a kind of high-
level adviser, and of course he was on the T-K-I board of
directors. He was a very gentle, courteous, and courtly
man, but he knew the law and he was fierce and unbudging
in defending his client's interest.

"I am very glad to see you, Jim," he said, somewhat
formally, "but I wish it didn't have to be under these exact
circumstances. We've got some troubles, I'm afraid. You
remember Mr. Wexler?"

"I do indeed," I said, shaking hands with Wexler the
Senior, who grunted hello when he stood up to greet me.

Wexler was a broad, healthy-looking man with a deep
sun tan. He was certainly younger than Henry Winston,
probably several years younger, but he looked younger
than that. He had to be close to seventy himself by now, but
he could have passed for a man in his fifties. Oh, not if you
looked close; there were appropriate lines on his face and
neck, lines that revealed his age pretty accurately. But he
was in good physical trim, a heavy-set healthy man, balding
a bit and with a little edge of gray in his thinning brownish
hair.

Wexler had been laid low by a heart attack, a severe
one, about six or seven years before, well . . . in fact, not
too long before he let himself be moved up to chairman of
the board so that his son Bill could become president of the
corporation. Not that health had been much of a factor in

his moving-upstairs decision. He had reportedly recovered completely from the heart attack, and Wexler Senior was one of these men who, after the wings of the angel of death brush close, pay respectful attention. He had always been an active and athletic man, given to tennis and golf and swimming. After his heart attack he had gradually begun such exercise again and he had lost weight, about twenty pounds.

And he had done another thing. He had ripped out the three offices next to his on the executive floor and had ordered a small gym and steam room installed. He had started seriously taking good care of himself after the heart attack: exercise, rest, the right food (and not much of it). Wexler was a widower, and after his wife's death he had gained a certain moderate reputation for drinking whiskey and chasing young ladies. He reportedly still believed in both pursuits, but since his heart attack, in far more sedate fashion than before.

Hell, it occurred to me, a man who lived the kind of careful yet enjoyable life he did ought to look healthy.

"Good to see you, Roundtree," he said. "I was sorry when Medlock ran you off last year. Some days he's got less sense than others." Medlock was standing next to me and sputtered and made near-gurgling noises. "Oh, be quiet, Harry," Wexler said, before Medlock could speak. "I'm cultivating the young man."

He stared at me good-humoredly. Then, to Medlock again: "You do the honors. What'll you drink, Jim?"

I asked for another Bloody Mary, if they had the makings. Medlock glanced at the table crowded with bottles and assured me they did. Wexler was drinking from a big square glass with a lot of ice and what looked like a lot of bourbon. He had been sitting in one of the square armchairs near the window, looking out over the airfield, and he urged me over to the chair next to his.

"Aren't you going to speak to me, Jim?"

I knew the voice by God, and I will admit that hearing that voice without warning sent a certain chill through me, an unexpected quickening of feeling. Maybe thrill is a better word than chill, though either will do.

I literally hadn't even seen her. She was sitting in another of the big chairs, one turned facing entirely toward the window. She probably wasn't visible at all from the door, and I had walked nearer without noticing the long, tanned legs that were just barely in view in front of her chair, stretched out in an indolent and probably calculated pose.

"Hello, Mrs. Wexler," I said, taking a step toward her chair. "You're hiding. I didn't mean to ignore you. It's just like old home week here."

"You called me Helen the last time I saw you," she accused.

"The last time I saw you and called you Helen, it got me into considerable difficulties," I said.

"Oh nonsense. Bill swears that all that had nothing to do with Harry Medlock's firing you." She smiled at me, then took a second to glare over at Medlock, who sipped his drink and appeared resigned to people talking about him as if he weren't there.

Helen Wexler held out her hand and I took it, she holding my hand and reaching over with her other hand to give mine a squeeze before letting go. "I am glad to see you. I tried to telephone after you left the company, just to tell you I was sorry, and you never returned my call."

I didn't remember ever getting a message to call her, and it was something I would remember, but looking at her affectionate, warm, calculating smile I couldn't really make out if she was lying, whether she had really tried to call me, or if she was just saying that now to annoy Medlock or even Wexler.

"My bad-tempered old father-in-law wanted me to

leave before you got here. I wouldn't hear of it," she said.

"Not so old, Helen, not so old," Wexler objected, staring at Helen, his daughter-in-law, with mixed admiration and affection and lust, and also what seemed to me to be genuine disapproval.

She really was a strikingly beautiful woman, with long dark hair and widely set frank brown eyes, good skin, and a good tan. She had perfect white teeth and a good-humored, absolutely dazzling smile. She was expensive and had expensive tastes and looked it, and she could have passed for almost any age from about thirty-three to, oh, say thirty-seven or thirty-eight. I happened to know she was actually forty-two, one year younger than her husband Bill. The sleeveless little red summer dress she wore had probably cost God knows how may hundreds of dollars.

Helen Wexler was not, as far as I know, an especially unkind or vicious or cruel person. On the contrary she was usually charming and friendly. It was just . . . well what? I suppose that she was spoiled absolutely rotten. She did exactly what she wanted to do pretty much without exception. She had come from a wealthy family before marrying a wealthy man, and the things that money couldn't do for her she was able usually to persuade people to do for her because they liked to make her smile or because in some cases, God help them, they fell in love with her.

I figured her husband, Bill Wexler, to be in that second category, and I figured that he (or any other man) could trust Helen about as far as he could throw her. Now, Helen was of medium height and had a trim, pretty figure and was firmly built, a tennis player like her husband, and probably weighed at least one hundred twenty-five pounds. I figured on that basis I could lift her and throw her roughly twelve feet, and I was perfectly willing to trust her at least that far.

Her saving grace and one reason I liked her was that she really was so extraordinarily self-centered that it became almost silly, and she herself had intelligence and humor enough to appreciate that, even to make little jokes about it occasionally.

"Maybe we'll have a chance to have a drink in the islands," Helen said. "You can explain the difference to me between the Windward and Leeward Islands. I never have understood it."

"Oh, goddamn it, Helen, leave him alone," old Wexler roared. "That's the only reason I didn't want you still here, because you put on a show. Do me a favor, go try to reach Bill one more time in San Francisco. He may have called the office since we checked."

Helen stood up and stretched and tossed her long hair and looked probably almost as cool and tanned and desirable as she intended to look, and each of us, the four men in the room, paid her the compliment of undivided attention.

"I'll leave, which is what you really want," she said to Wexler Senior, "and I'll try and reach Bill again, but I'll bet he is just Lord knows where by now and just planning to show up in Martinique tomorrow." She leaned closer to pat her father-in-law on the cheek, a gesture he apparently hated and pulled irritably away from. Helen chuckled.

"All right, scat," Wexler said. "Try the San Francisco office again and any place else on the coast you can think of. I really need him, Helen, I've got to talk to him."

Wexler sounded so intense, so solemn, that it had an effect on Helen. She went quietly at last, promising to do her best to track down Bill.

Wexler sat back down again and urged me into the armchair next to him, both chairs facing the broad window. We sat for a moment in silence while he sipped his bourbon.

"You ever screw her?" he asked.

I looked at him in reasonable amaze. This was his son's wife he was asking about after all, striking and attractive lady though she was.

"Only on Tuesdays," I said, after a moment. Then, when his eyes seemed to brighten, I said, "You are the real thing, Mr. Wexler, a genuine dirty old man."

Henry Winston, who had frowned severely at the question, now smiled. "He's got you pegged, Will."

Wexler grunted, not seeming to take offense. He was still a handsome man, but after Helen had left the room he had slumped down in his chair and looked depressed and gloomy, more his full age than before. He wore a dark, conservative suit but with a white-and-pink striped shirt and a broad red tie. He fingered the edge of the tie as he sat pushed back in his chair, sipping a little whiskey out of his glass. He might conceivably, I thought, begin looking his full age before too long.

"There isn't going to be much time, not if Roundtree is going to make that Air France flight," said Medlock, glancing at his watch.

"There's time enough, Harry, just calm down. Here, get me another drink," said Wexler, handing his glass to Medlock.

I was beginning to get weary of everybody being so mysterious.

"What is this all about, Mr. Wexler? Why did you want me to come to Miami?"

He didn't answer until Medlock had fixed his drink and handed it to him.

"Show him the file, Henry," Wexler said.

Henry Winston held a flat brown envelope, a T-K-I company envelope, and he handed it over to me. Inside were four sheets of ordinary white typing paper, each with a sentence or two made up of what appeared to be words clipped from newspaper headlines or from magazines, some of the words on rough newsprint, some on slick magazine paper.

"INSIDERS, BEWARE," read the first line on the first sheet. "God Knows What You Do!," said the second line on the same sheet. Then, a final line: "A 43,900 Swindle!"

I couldn't understand what it meant, if it meant anything, and after puzzling over it a moment I started to look at the next sheet.

"No, wait," said Wexler, "let's take them one at a time, so you'll know what they are, or at least what we think they're about." I was sitting next to Wexler, and Henry Winston had walked over and stood with one hand resting on the top of my chair. "Henry," said Wexler, "you've got the finely honed legal mind. You explain."

Winston leaned over my shoulder and put his finger on the first word, "INSIDERS."

"This particular one will make sense when I tell you that officers or directors of the corporation sold about that number"—he moved his finger down to the figure 43,900 on the sheet—"shares of T-K-I stock in the first quarter."

"What kind of 'swindle' does it refer to?"

Winston shook his head. "I can't imagine what that part means. There is no swindle involved, not that I know anything about, not even any accusation of dishonesty on anybody's part. The stock sales were all perfectly legitimate, all reported to the Security Exchange Commission just the way they're supposed to be. There's only one curious thing. The letter was sent to Mr. Wexler . . . let's see, when exactly, Will? The last week in February?"

Wexler nodded. It occurred to me that Henry Winston was the only man I knew who called Wexler Senior by his first name.

"As it happens," Winston said, "almost all the insider sales of T-K-I stock for the quarter were in January and the first week of February. I sold two thousand shares myself, looking forward to income tax time."

"Well, it's obvious isn't it?" I began. "Some disgruntled stockholder type was attacking you affluent insiders. . . ." And then I stopped. "My, my, my. The letter came in February. It really was an insiders' message wasn't it?"

I felt foolish for not seeing it at once.

"That's the curious thing, of course," Winston said mildly. "Even though this looks like a crank letter, no one outside the company could have had any way of knowing that exactly 43,900 shares had been sold at just that time. The figures weren't secret, of course, they're accumulated routinely for the SEC filing."

"But at the time the letter was received those figures weren't public either," I said.

"Someone who knew where to look could find them," Winston said, shrugging. "Someone with the company or even a stranger, a message boy who wandered in at lunch time, if he knew where to look. We've checked since. There were at least three filing cabinets where these figures were easily accessible, none of them closely watched."

"But a stranger would still have had to know where to look," I said, and Winston nodded. "Are the figures exactly accurate?" I asked.

Winston frowned. "Actually, there were a few more sales in March, and one board member bought a few shares, and it about balanced out, so that the total figure at the end of the quarter came out almost exactly."

"Almost exactly, hell," Wexler said. "That 43,900 was the exact figure when I got the letter. I added it up myself. At first I didn't even make the connection. My secretary showed me the letter, then filed it away. She remembered it when the second letter came."

I moved the first sheet aside, to look at the second letter.

"Wait, there's one other thing," said Wexler. I didn't know what the other thing was, but it gave Wexler a harsh expression, made him look mad as hell, in fact. Winston and Medlock both knew what it was about and kept their facial expressions carefully neutral, but I had the impression Henry wanted to smile.

"Within a few days after the first letter came," Wexler

said, "each of the directors or officers who had sold stock got a package in the mail. You know what was in it? A duck! A real duck, a dead duck!"

"You mean as in 'you're a dead duck'?" I asked.

"I don't know," Wexler said in an abrasive voice. "It's insane. Who knows what it was supposed to mean?"

Winston yielded to temptation and permitted himself a slight smile, then wrinkled his nose and shook his head, as if he could recall the actual smell with distaste. "You wouldn't believe it, Jim. Mine was wrapped so carefully that when I first opened the box, there was nothing. I started to open up the wrapping paper, and the odor hit me. Terrible!"

Wexler pointed now at the second sheet of paper. "Look at this one."

"Clean Desk Often Means a Cluttered Mind," read the one sentence on the second piece of paper.

"The letter came after the fact in this case," Winston said. "We walked into the office one morning and there was garbage, literally trash-can garbage, banana peels and broken bottles and just generally messy stuff, all over our desks."

"Dog shit," Wexler said, and I peered at him, not sure if that was a comment or what. "I swear it," he said, "there was dog shit on my desk."

"Not every desk was involved," said Winston.

"Not yours," Wexler said, as if it were an accusation.

"I know," Winston shrugged. "I had taken some files out late the afternoon before and I left them scattered over my desk. They weren't disturbed. There were two or three other desks like that, desks that for some reason had been covered with files or whatever. Nothing bothered or touched on any of them."

"Just the clean desks," I said.

"Every one of them on two floors," Wexler said grimly.

"You weren't even in the city, Will. It was all cleaned up by the time you heard about it," Winston said.

"That's all very well," Wexler grumbled. "But I got a full report and I still don't like it. First dead ducks, then garbage and dog shit all over my goddamned desk."

Medlock pushed forward, a fresh drink in his hand, and his flushed face made me think maybe the alcohol was getting to him, but his words were clear and unslurred and spoken with sincerity. "I'll tell you one thing," he said. "There may or may not have been any dog mess on your desk, but if there was I wish to bloody hell your secretary had had sense enough to keep it a secret."

Wexler glared at him.

The third letter seemed to me even more cryptic than the first two.

"If God had Intended Man to go to the Moon, he'd have laid a ROAD," it read, and this time the words were spelled out, in what looked like individual letters all clipped out of the same magazine. Then, in addition, down at the bottom of the sheet, this message: "Bye, Bye, Martin."

"I don't understand this one at all," I said.

"That was when we finally called the police," Winston said. "But what can they do? They told us what we already know, that it looked like someone who knew a lot about the corporation was playing games with us. Except this last one wasn't a game. There was a man killed."

"A man named Cornelius Martin," said Medlock. "Did you know him?"

The name had a slightly familiar ring but I couldn't really place it. I shook my head.

"He was an engineer, a very good one, and a plant manager for the last two years. You know, near Los Angeles," Medlock said.

And I did know where it was—that is, I knew the plant. Maybe I'd seen Cornelius Martin's name in connection with it, but I couldn't quite remember.

"I don't understand how Martin and the Los Angeles plant tie in with this."

"We're trying to tell you, damn it, hard as we can," snapped Wexler impatiently. He was a feisty old man. "Christ, look at that," he said, standing up from his chair. He was staring out the window at the airfield. One jet was landing and one was taking off, and they were about to cross paths.

There was no danger of the two planes crashing together, they were well separated, but from our angle it looked almost as if they were going to collide. The hot Miami sun was reflected, brightly silver, from both planes. "They're beautiful," Wexler said after they had passed and the optical illusion that they might hit each other was gone.

Wexler stood looking out the window and the sun caught his forehead, glinting in his thinning, reddish brown hair. He had a strong profile, a strong face. He was getting old and he didn't like it and he was a man who would not go gently or gladly into that night. I didn't blame him. I didn't much want to go either.

"Tell him about Martin," he said to Winston, not turning from the window.

"That message ending 'Bye, Bye, Martin' came just after we had gotten a NASA contract," Winston said. "Martin was production manager where they would . . . well, still will . . . make the component for the permanent space station. It's just a small electronic component and not a very big contract, a sub-contract really. But it might be important. It's the very first space-agency contract of any kind we've ever had, even on a very minor scale. We missed out on the Apollo flights."

Wexler frowned into his drink and turned from the window to sit back down in his chair. "I tell myself," he said, "that space is the future, the technology of things to come, that there'll be the exploration of the planets, the space shuttle. We need to have some small toehold in it, I think, but I wouldn't want to get too far into it, not into really depending on government contracts."

"It's too easy to get in a box," Medlock said in agreement. "Look at Lockheed right now, after all the flak they caught on the C5A contract, and that's a damned good airplane too, and the company is still trying to come back. Or look at Boeing after Congress cancelled out on the supersonic transport. Seattle seemed like a ghost town for a while."

"What happened to Cornelius Martin?" I asked.

Winston and Medlock and Wexler all got very grim faced. It was Winston, again, who finally spoke. "Technically, he was killed in an ordinary automobile accident two days after that letter came. It was an accident. That was how the highway patrol marked it down."

"Even Medlock still wants to believe that," Wexler said bitterly.

"No, no, I don't any more," Medlock responded. "Not after your man from Detroit. He made a believer out of me. But it still seems so far-fetched. It's hard to believe that *those*—"and he gestured at the stack of letters—"could translate into, well . . ."

"Into a murder," Wexler finished for him when Medlock hesitated.

"All right, call it murder," Medlock said reluctantly. "But it doesn't make any sense, and it's so hard to be sure, even if the brakes were suspicious."

Wexler glared at him, then sighed.

"I'm sure enough," he said, "too goddamned sure." He turned to me urgently, as if it were vital that I be convinced too. "I got a man flown from Detroit, an expert who knew that model car inside out. The car was a total wreck, so there's some slight element of doubt. But he said it was ninety percent certain that the brakes had been tampered with, fixed so that they might give way at high speed."

"What did the highway patrol say?"

"They were impressed," Winston interrupted, "but not overly. The accident is down in their follow-up report as a suspicious accident, which just means the traffic section passed on the report for possible criminal investigation. But that was in early April when Martin was killed, more than a month ago, and they haven't found anything."

"Maybe there isn't anything to find," Medlock said stubbornly.

Nobody said anything else for a moment or two.

There was only one sheet of paper left, the last letter in the file. When no one said anything else about Martin, I reached for the last letter and pulled it to me.

"Man Lives not by Bread alone," it read.

"The source of the quotation is easy enough," I said, "but what does this one mean?"

"That one is Will's personal message," said Winston. "He'd better tell you about that one."

Memory of what had happened obviously still made the elder Wexler angry as he started the story. But he told it well, with a good sense for detail.

Wexler had been in Las Vegas two weeks before, just for a weekend, because some old friends of his, a man and his wife, were going to be there. The first night he was there the couple had come to his hotel for a drink and they had gambled in the hotel casino for a while. Then they had gone back to the hotel where his friends were staying for dinner, then to a show in the same hotel. The little friendly get-together had broken up about 2:00 A.M., said Wexler, and he had started walking back to his own hotel, only about four blocks away.

The two young men grabbed him about one block from his hotel, somewhat roughly, though without really hurting him, and they had shoved him swiftly into an alley near a building.

The two men were both muscular and husky, said Wexler, and seeing that he was outnumbered he stopped struggling after they forced him off the main street. "There was no point in anybody getting hurt, I figured, not for a few hundred dollars," said Wexler. He offered no protest when the men took his wristwatch and wallet, not at least until one of them counted the money and said something like, as Wexler remembered it, "That's not much cash for a great big old tycoon like you."

That had scared him, sent through him the fear that the two men knew who he was and that it was a kidnap attempt, that they intended to abduct him and spirit him away somewhere.

He tried to break free then, but they had a good hold on him. As he struggled to escape, one man held his arms and the other hit him, hit him in the stomach and knocked the breath out of him entirely. Then the same man slapped him back and forth across the face.

Much later, in retrospect, Wexler said, it seemed apparent that they were not really trying to hurt him.

The two men released him suddenly, and he fell down, the breath knocked out of him and seeing stars and flashes of light from the slapping back and forth, his head ringing. At the time he thought fleetingly that a policeman or someone else must have come along and frightened the two men away. But no one came. He wasn't really hurt or even unconscious, and after a moment, as he came more fully to himself, he realized that his wallet had been poked back into his side coat pocket.

He checked the wallet and found everything there, not even any of his money taken.

He was not far from his hotel, and when he got there only minutes later he found an envelope waiting for him at the hotel desk, an envelope with his name on it and the folded sheet inside with the message, "Man Lives not by Bread alone." He asked the message clerk and the man remembered that someone had left it there earlier that evening but he didn't remember who.

"Somebody was just trying to scare me," Wexler said, "to show me they could hurt me or rob me if they wanted to."

"I thought you always had a security man with you," I said to Wexler.

"I usually do," he nodded, "but not always. Nobody has ever really tried to kidnap me, though I've often thought of the possibility. It's an ugly possibility. That night I had a security man driving my car." He shrugged. "When we went to dinner, I turned him loose. Why not?"

The idea hit me, of course, that the two young men in Las Vegas roughing up Wexler were at the least spiritual cousins of Stroud, and that Wexler's experience was in a way not too different from Stroud coming to my house and twisting my arm.

"Let me tell you about something," I said and proceeded to describe the whole sequence of Stroud's visit and what he had said and what had happened.

Henry Winston stared at me with intent interest, his pale blue eyes narrowing as he listened. He asked me twice to repeat the description of Stroud but finally he shook his head, as if to say, whatever his train of thought, it finally had not led him anywhere.

Medlock and Wexler both listened to my account with puzzled, impatient expressions, Medlock seemingly with especial exasperation.

"I tell you, sir," Medlock said to Wexler when I finished, "you ought to call the Martinique meeting off. We've got enough problems with the board. We don't need something that's going to blow up while we're there."

"I hope it does blow up," Wexler said flatly. "At least

that might tell us something, who and what we're up against." He finished his drink broodingly. "Somebody knew I was going to try to get Roundtree down here, and they knew it at least by yesterday morning, in time to get that man Stroud out to Roundtree's house and threaten him. That probably means somebody, whoever it was, had to know about it the night before. I had only talked to two people about Roundtree by that time. They're both in this room." He pointed with his empty glass. "You and you," aiming the glass at first Winston and then Medlock.

Winston looked disturbed and gazed at Medlock for a second, then he chuckled. "Only one thing wrong with that, Will."

"What's that?" asked Wexler.

"Somebody else must have known," Winston said. "It may well be true that we're the only two people you talked to, but there has to be a way someone else knew about Jim. I know I didn't have anything to do with the man who went to see him and who threatened him." He glanced at Medlock. "I don't think Harry did either. You've known us both too long, Will. I'm quite sure it's wise in something as confusing as this to be suspicious of everybody. But, having said that, I don't really believe you think either one of us had anything to do with the things that have happened."

"Don't be too sure what I think," Wexler declared sourly. But then he sighed and pushed out his lower lip, as if to concede that what Winston was saying was perfectly true.

"You're right of course, Henry," he said. "I can't really believe you or Medlock had anything to do with it all, especially not with Martin getting killed. But it's like all the other things, those stock figures and the NASA contract. Somebody knows an awful lot about what Troup-Kincaid is doing. That information is coming from somewhere."

Medlock appeared about to say something, but there was a knock on the door and he went to answer it.

He talked to somebody for a moment through the slightly open door. "Your plane starts boarding in just ten minutes," he said to me. "Your suitcase is already checked, and you have your ticket, right?"

I nodded, patting my coat pocket where the ticket was. "What do I do when I get to Martinique?"

"A car will meet you," Medlock said. "You'll be staying at a hotel just outside Fort-de-France. It's a nice hotel, a new one. That's where the board of directors meeting will be held, but not many of them will be coming in before tomorrow some time. This'll give you a little extra time to sniff around and to make contacts with board members as they come in."

"You know everything that we know," Henry Winston said. "Will thinks—and I agree—that whoever is doing these things, it somehow involves scheming in connection with the corporation, with T-K-I, and it's as likely as not going to surface at this meeting of the board." He hesitated and glanced at Wexler, who nodded, and Winston pulled out a long envelope. "Here's a copy of the agenda for the board meeting, plus a memo from me about several different items, plus a report on a hotel venture the board will be considering."

"That's when the fighting starts," Medlock said, grinning, as if the prospect of the kind of fight he understood cheered him considerably, "when we start talking about the hotel project."

"You just want me to move around and see what I can find out, then," I said.

"That's right," Wexler said.

"He's got to hurry if he's going to make his plane," said Medlock. "They're boarding in just a minute." He touched my shoulder, edging me toward the door. "Don't worry if it seems like we're not giving you a whole lot of instructions. At this point, you know as much as we do. Anyway, we'll all be down in Martinique by the time of the board meeting, day after tomorrow. The meeting will last two days, so there'll be time to talk some more." Medlock had his hand on my arm and squeezed urgently on the last phrase.

I started for the door, but Wexler stopped me with a movement of his hand. He stood up from the armchair near the window, his empty drink glass in hand, and walked over to me.

"You both go on," he said to Winston and Medlock. "I know he's got to catch a plane, but this will only take about three minutes. I want about three minutes alone with Roundtree before he catches that plane."

Medlock frowned and started to object, changed his mind when Henry Winston pulled at his arm, and they both walked out. Wexler went over to fix himself another drink and I followed him to fix myself one, this time a little Scotch over ice instead of a Bloody Mary.

"Medlock is right about one thing," Wexler said, once we were seated in the two big armchairs facing the window and the airfield. This was a nice life, I decided, looking out at the hot Miami sun on the nearest runway, while sipping a drink in, as they say, air-conditioned comfort. I didn't much care if I caught the flight to Martinique or not.

"I agree with Harry," Wexler went on, "that somebody maybe would like to take over the corporation. There are some members of the board who never liked the way I ran things, and they don't much like the way my son and Medlock have done some things either. Given a shot, they'd vote for new management. I just mean, if I can, to keep them from having the shot."

Wexler groped in his coat pocket for his leather cigar case, a handsome black leather case, opened it and pulled out a cigar, and then aimlessly stuck it back inside the case and pulled out a different cigar.

"I know one thing that Medlock and Winston don't know," said Wexler. He pulled out a sheet of paper. It had words pasted on it just as those other four sheets had. The words came from an old song, "Where have you been, Billy Boy, Billy Boy, where have you been, Charming Billy?"

"It came two days ago," Wexler said. "I haven't been able to get in touch with my son, Bill, since it came. He was supposed to be in San Francisco that day. I tried to call him right after I got the note. Within five minutes, I'd say. It didn't hit me for a minute or two. I'd been in the office for a while, then went to a meeting, and I found the envelope and the note on top of my desk when I came back. I opened it and didn't really pay attention for a few moments, even though it was the same clipped-out words pasted on." Wexler ran down, as if he had a lot on his mind. He frowned at me.

"That's when you tried to call Bill," I said.

"He was in San Francisco, just like he was supposed to be. He had checked with the office that morning. I called and found he'd checked with our people just before noon. As far as I can find out, nobody since then, nobody, not the office or his wife or anybody else, has heard from him since that morning. That was forty-eight hours ago. I can't locate him."

"Have you called the police?"

"No, no." Wexler shook his head. "Bill was on the West Coast to see several people, and he'd already seen them by the time I called. The office there had no reason to expect him to stay around. He told his wife that he might get back a day or two early but that if he didn't he'd meet her in Martinique. Bill and Helen are supposed to host a cocktail party for the members of the board.

"What do you think has happened, Mr. Wexler?"

"I think it's one of two things," he said. "The first is that he's been kidnapped. Oh, there's a third possibility, just that he's gone crazy in some unlikely way. I don't believe or accept that one, but it is theoretically possible. Kidnapped is more likely. I've kept the letter about Billy Boy in my pocket since it came, thinking there would be another letter, a ransom note or a telephone call. So far, there's been nothing." Wexler turned to me, almost balefully, taking a long drink from his bourbon glass. "Do you know what I'm worth?" he demanded.

"I would think quite a lot." I resisted the impulse to smile.

"I could raise fifty million dollars cash on short notice," he said. "I figured it up. There are some things in trust I can't touch, and I couldn't just unload as much Troup-Kincaid stock as I've got. I'd have to borrow money with the stock as collateral and make arrangements to sell off the stock gradually, so it would pay off the loan and the interest both. But, after doing those things, I think I could put together fifty million dollars."

"That's a lot of money."

"Maybe sixty million," he said broodingly, "depending on the market. I'm willing to pay it." He looked at me squarely. "I'll pay it in ransom to get my son back. You let that be known if you can find anybody on Martinique who can give me back my son."

"That's a lot of money," I repeated somewhat inanely.

"Yes, that's a hell of a lot of money," he said. "You've got to catch your plane," and we both stood up and I drained my glass and started for the door. "I'll tell you what I really think," Wexler said harshly, and his tone stopped me.

He stared at me with a bleak, fierce expression. "I think they've killed him. I think they've killed my son. I don't know why or what's going on but that's what I think."

He paused. "And if that's true, Roundtree, I'm going to find out who's responsible, even if it takes all of that fifty million. I don't care who it is. I'm going to find them and I'm going to destroy them."

7   Thinking Things Through

I had a jolt when I finally got on the plane.

I had stopped for a minute at the newsstand, realizing suddenly the flight was a full seven hours, and I wanted some things to read and I had my hands full of newspapers and magazines and a couple of pocket books, and I hesitated at a point not very far down the aisle, juggling my papers a bit and deciding whether to claim my proper seat right there or to push on a few more steps in hopes of finding a window seat still free. It didn't seem very filled up toward the rear of the plane.

A man in an aisle seat, I realized abruptly, was staring at me. He was sitting no more than ten feet in front of me.

It was Stroud. He stared at me in a decidedly unfriendly manner, not making any effort to turn his head or conceal his identity.

I moved along the aisle until I stood right next to him, not certain for the life of me what to say to him. I had the feeling I wanted to yell for a stewardess to call the police, but that idea seemed almost silly when we were both on a plane moments away from takeoff. I thought calling the police might even be a bad idea, at least if my prime concern was in trying to find out what was going on. I decided not to say anything at all, settling for an unfriendly return stare as I started on past.

"It's a bad time of year for traveling," he said.

"You go to hell," I said, and found a seat three rows behind Stroud. At least the son-of-a-bitch was where I could keep an eye on him.

The young man from Jacksonville, Medlock's aspiring follower, actually had walked me to the plane, explaining that normally the flight left at 2:45 in the afternoon and would get me to Fort-de-France in seven hours, but that would make it 10:45 there because their time was an hour later than Miami time usually, except that now it was May already and we were already on Daylight Saving Time, so that it was 3:45 when the plane left and that meant it would still be 10:45 at night when I got to Martinique but not with the hour's difference, so I wouldn't have to change my watch or anything.

The young man was just full of information. I thanked him politely.

I settled into my seat by the window as we taxied up the runway for the takeoff, waiting clearance from the tower. I peered back at the terminal building, trying to see the window of the VIP room where maybe Wexler Senior was still sitting, but I wasn't sure which window it was.

The hot Florida day, the sunshine, seemed to me to look unusually tropical, maybe because I knew the plane's direction. I could almost see island maidens in the haze at the edge of the runway. We were scheduled to land briefly in San Juan, and Haiti, on Antigua, and then on Guadeloupe before getting to Martinique. The last time I'd been on a plane seven hours at a stretch it was on a nonstop from New York to London. By comparison this was a real puddle jumper.

It was a long plane ride. It would give me time to try to think through the things that had already happened.

Stroud was sitting three rows ahead, though even the back of his head was hidden by his seat. He was the first thing I wanted to think about. He was deeply involved in whatever was going on, presumably working for some-body, the people (whoever they were) trying to do something (whatever it was) to Troup-Kincaid. This line of thought exasperated me. If you considered, I didn't have the vaguest notion of what was really going on. Stroud, for instance, may have only guessed that I would be on that particular flight. Or he may have known in advance. It was an Air France flight—and this was a small point, but I'd checked—there was only one flight per day. If Stroud had known enough to know that I would end up working, even if through the law firm, for Troup-Kincaid again even before I knew it . . . well, in some certain fashion he surely would have known about the upcoming T-K-I board meet-ing in Martinique and that I'd be on my way there.

Maybe he could have guessed about the flight, maybe not. But he had guessed accurately that I would not yell for the police. After all, what could I prove? I could say he had come to my house and threatened me, including twisting my arm and pulling a gun, but I had no witnesses. My word against his.

But who could tell? Maybe Stroud had been surprised to see me too, figuring I would be on the flight the follow-ing day, which after all would put me on Martinique the day before the formal board meeting.

All this got me back to what Wexler Senior had said, that he had spoken only to Henry Winston and Harry Med-lock about contacting me and wanting me to be a kind of informal troubleshooter at the Martinique meeting. Stroud had certainly known about that in advance. How had he been told? Was Winston or Medlock the villain?

It was hard to believe, but I gave it some thought. I liked and admired Winston, but he was a brilliant, austere, often remote man. There were private possibilities with him, personal reasons, for all I know, that would not be readily apparent as motive. And yet Winston was of an age, just past seventy now, not showing it much and still lean and strong and alert, but with a strong hint of that fragile, almost translucent quality some thin old men come to have.

It was almost impossible to imagine Winston as villain, and I turned in my mind to a candidate I viewed with relish: Medlock.

I didn't much like Medlock, hadn't liked him much really before he fired me, and didn't like him now. He was too single-minded, too ruthless at times. I thought he was a prick, with few characteristics of redeeming social significance. And yet it was a bit hard to cast Medlock as villain either. He lacked imagination in one way, in that his imagination and abilities were so totally absorbed in a conventional, successful corporate career.

I could imagine Medlock in the Machiavellian middle of a corporate fight between Wexler Junior and Wexler Senior, if that were possible, winner take all. I couldn't imagine him quite being involved with all those curious anonymous notes, or with two thugs roughing up somebody in Las Vegas, and least of all with a man named Cornelius Martin getting killed in California maybe because someone had deliberately tampered with the brakes of his car.

I sighed, giving up Medlock's possible villainy reluctantly. I would keep an open mind, but offhand it seemed to me that Winston and Medlock were both unlikely villains.

The anonymous notes to Wexler Senior had a certain crude humor about them, almost deliberately heavy-handed, as did some of the other things, the dead ducks in the mail to corporate insiders and the garbage only on the clean desks. But there wasn't much humor in Martin's death or in Wexler being roughed up a bit or even, it occurred to me sourly, in Stroud trying to scare me. I tried to find a thread, however slender, that made sense of all the incidents. I decided after a time that I simply didn't know enough.

The only thing almost really clear was that somebody involved knew a lot about Troup-Kincaid, about the inner workings of the company, and it stood to reason (if there was any reason to it) that the most likely candidates for villain would indeed be at the board-of-directors' meeting in Martinique.

I got out the map in the little tourist guidebook furnished by Air France in the back of the seat ahead of me.

I still had a somewhat hazy idea about Martinique, its exact location, I mean, remembering only that it was in the French West Indies. Good God, I thought, looking closely at the map, it seemed only a tiny way from Venezuela. Hell, that's where it was, more or less, seeming just above the broad, curving shoulder of South America. It was at the very tail end of that line of islands that were as near the United States as Cuba, moving down roughly parallel to the line of the coast of Mexico and Central America a few hundred miles to the west.

By the time you followed that line to Martinique, South America was just a short jaunt away.

I gave up thinking about Martinique. Maybe I was going to be there in a few hours, but as far as I was concerned that bloody island was light-years away.

I also gave up thinking about Troup-Kincaid and whatever was going on. A stewardess, as pretty a young girl as they are supposed to be and often are not, was coming down the aisle, and I gestured to stop her and asked if there was still any Scotch aboard the airplane. She admitted there might be and smiled nicely and after a minute or so brought me a drink.

One of the books I'd picked up at the Miami newsstand was a paperback edition of Bruce Catton's *Never Call Retreat.*

I wanted to see what Hank had meant at the airport, his parting shot. I had told him the day before that I resembled the late lamented General John C. Pemberton, as described by Catton, a man dedicated but wholly without good luck. He had checked the reference just to make mischief and told me I reminded him instead of another Mississippi Army commander, General Earl Van Dorn. I barely remembered the name, let alone what Hank was trying to say to me.

I found the reference after a time, just after the stewardess brought me my second drink of Scotch. Despite my intentions to forget about it all, my eyes kept turning to the airplane window and I kept gazing at clouds and blue sky and down sometimes at the big waters, my mind still trying to get a hook into what the hell was likely to go on at this Troup-Kincaid board meeting, who was doing what to whom.

Ah, well. Back to Van Dorn. He had commanded the Army of the Mississippi just prior to Pemberton taking over, and though he was described as curly-haired and alert and one of President Jefferson Davis' favorite officers, he hadn't had much luck either. The Yankees had "whupped" him at Corinth, and a lot of Mississippi people apparently blamed him for all their woes. A certain Senator Phelan said that people believed the worst about Van Dorn's private life, including "horrid narratives of his negligence, whoring and drunkenness, for the truth of which I cannot vouch; but it is so fastened in the public belief that an acquittal by a court-martial of angels would not relieve him of the charge."

Turned out, alas, Van Dorn's military feats improved a bit later, but as Catton put it, in the spring, "unacquitted by angels, he would be shot to death by a Tennessee civilian who considered himself an outraged husband."

I frowned, wondering for an instant if Hank had meant

that as a direct reference to my encounter with Helen Wexler at that reception and my difficulties thereafter. But no, I felt sure Hank meant to insult me only in more general terms.

The thought of Helen Wexler cheered me. She had suggested we ought to have a drink and talk about the Windward and Leeward Islands. I flipped through the little tourist book, fully intending a swift boning up.

8 Papa Doc's Turf

Stroud and I talked once before the plane reached Martinique.

We both got off to stretch our legs when the craft stopped in Haiti. It was the only time it occurred to me to leave the plane, and I guess really the only time we stopped anywhere long enough. The sun was beating down maybe not much harder than in Miami, but there were some pretty good offbeat tropical props to go with it. The airport seemed out in the middle of nowhere, with low, rolling hills in the near distance which in themselves had no particular reason to look sinister other than that I'd probably read too many stories about Papa Doc and voodoo ceremonies. The late dictator had been succeeded by his son; I wasn't clear where that left the voodoo magic.

The airport terminal building was not large but of modern solid construction. Brown-skinned people in assorted dress, most looking healthy if poor, crowded impassively up against a rail on the open second floor of the low, two-story building, as if waiting for someone, but none of them moved, or made any gestures especially, as the several passengers disembarked. Maybe coming down to watch the planes land was a major holiday excursion on some sunny days in Haiti.

There were some police or soldiers about—I wasn't

quite sure which, from their uniforms—and several other more or less official-looking people who stared at me and the half-dozen other passengers getting off.

The airstrip was wide and long and modern and paved, and I'm sure in a week there were a lot of planes in and out, but it wasn't doing much business at that moment. We were the only big plane in sight. The grass was well kept along the small walk in front of the terminal, and without either of us really seeming to plan it Stroud and I fell into step as we neared the front of the building. He had slipped on a pair of dark glasses, and with his deep tan looked right at home in the glaring sun, as if he were a field engineer on his way back out to a construction job.

He grinned at me, and God knows why, I gave him a rueful grin back.

"I don't suppose you threaten people in public," I said.

"There's a little bar in here, not much of one, but it'll do. I'll buy you a beer," he said.

We passed one thin, somewhat elderly, brown-skinned gentleman carrying a cane and dressed in very dapper fashion. He wore dark glasses too and stared expectantly at me and at Stroud.

Stroud nodded and smiled at the man, not so much as if he knew him but more in a generally friendly way.

"You are visiting Haiti for a few days?" the man said. "May I get your names? It is for the newspaper."

"Just passing through," I said. Stroud smiled and nodded and didn't say anything.

"You know that fellow?" I asked when Stroud and I had passed out of earshot and into the shade of the building.

"Not really," he said. "I've seen him before. I don't think he knows me. I was down here once on business, back in . . . oh, years ago now. He puts out a little weekly newspaper, and he really does list the names of tourists coming in, at least if they sound even slightly important. He also works for the government and passes along any information he runs into that might not be listed on somebody's passport."

The little bar wasn't much, as Stroud had said, more of a counter, but the service was quick and it was easy to get two cold beers. We found a place to sit down, and I wondered what kind of business had brought Stroud to Haiti probably while Papa Doc Duvalier was still alive and kicking, before they finally gunned him down and his son and the rest of the family took over.

Thought of the dead dictator made me wonder what possible kind of business Stroud might ever have had in Haiti.

"What are you anyway, Stroud, some kind of hired gun?"

The way it came out, the sound of my tone of voice, I mean, it sounded almost like a friendly question, you know, like two men who had just met making casual conversation and discovering both had been in the Army and one asking where the other had been based. I didn't quite feel that friendly, but after all we were drinking a cold beer together. We both took a long swallow of beer before Stroud answered.

He smiled. "I thought I told you. I'm an insurance investigator. On vacation at the moment, though, just your regular old ugly American tourist off for a few days of sun and fun in the French West Indies."

"You're not an ex-CIA guy, are you?" I tried. It was a shot in the dark but I was thinking of the kinds of people the CIA had hired when they were putting the Bay of Pigs invasion of Cuba together. Some of them had ended up later as arms runners for hire, professional soldier-of-fortune types.

Stroud reacted with a frown. "You ask too many questions," he said. He didn't react very much, however, not as if the question had really touched a nerve, more just as if he didn't care about answering any questions about himself.

"Why are we even being friendly, if you don't want to talk?" I said.

Stroud sighed. "Call it a temporary truce, Roundtree. Call it anything you want. You are spoiling my cold beer in scenic Haiti."

I sighed too.

"Look at it this way," Stroud said. "I tried to persuade you to stay out of this. You wouldn't pay attention. But it's not personal. You might even decide to believe what I said in New York, that I was actually trying to give you friendly advice."

None of this convinced me very much of anything, except that probably Stroud wasn't after doing me any harm before we got to Martinique and maybe received new orders. And who was giving the orders? That's what I needed to know.

In the few minutes before we got back on the plane we finished drinking our beer and got to talking about baseball, and Stroud even asked me a polite question or two about corporate law practice, what kind of problems I generally had to fool with, said he'd thought once about being a lawyer himself.

We got back on the plane and took our separate seats, and I wondered some more about Stroud. Maybe he had no intention of doing me any harm on the plane, but it was dead certain he was heading for Martinique in some connection with the Troup-Kincaid board meeting. I had a thought I didn't like especially. Stroud acted so confident, so thoroughly professional, that it occurred to me he might have a professional reason for encouraging our cold-beer friendly conversation (wary though it was).

Maybe Stroud thought he was picking up helpful information, not about any secret things but just about me, the way I drank a beer and made small-talk conversation.

Suppose Stroud felt relatively sure that he would have to do something with me on Martinique, maybe even kill me. A professional could always use as much information as possible.

9 Planter's Punch and the Congressman

The islands of Guadeloupe and Martinique are so close together that it seemed I hardly had time to undo my seat belt after Guadeloupe before the plane was circling again for the landing on Martinique.

Stroud left the plane ahead of me rapidly. We didn't speak.

There was no red tape to amount to anything. I got my suitcase somewhat aimlessly, because at about that time it occurred to me that I wasn't sure what I was supposed to do next. Stroud got his bag hurriedly, and without a backward glance moved out and grabbed a taxi, one lined up with several others in the warm evening. We were on time. It was about 11:00 P.M. I wasn't sure what I was supposed to do exactly, but I was fairly clear that somebody had made some sort of arrangement.

I was right, I didn't wait long. A man I knew, Troup-Kincaid lawyer type, moved across the way to greet me, fellow named Johnathan Pettigrew. I became general counsel for T-K-I only after he had gone out to the West Coast. We had worked together earlier for a brief time, and after I became general counsel I became technically his boss, but he actually was out in California right up until the time I left T-K-I, so we never had that boss-type relationship exactly. I was glad to see him, friendly face and all that.

"Hello, Jim," he said, grinning, as we shook hands. "I left the party just to come fetch you."

"What kind of party?" I asked.

"The hotel is doing big things for us tonight," he said. We got my suitcase and went outside, where I discovered Pettigrew had a car and driver waiting. I was just as glad there was a hired driver, since Pettigrew seemed to have sampled the good liquid things at the party in fair amount. He wasn't really unsteady but he was bright-eyed and too full of smiles.

"The hotel isn't too far," he said as we both piled into the back seat. "Nice to see you, Jim. I hope you haven't come to get your old job back. I've had my eye on it."

His seeming candor made me chuckle, though then I reflected it was a fairly shrewd probe on his part. He probably had as good a chance as anyone on Troup-Kincaid's legal staff to become general counsel, unless, of course, they decided to go outside the corporation. That's what they had done with Henry Winston. Henry had been a highly successful attorney in a small (but distinctly blue chip) New York law firm before Wexler the Elder had talked him into coming to Troup-Kincaid.

I doubted if Pettigrew had the vaguest notion of why I had come to Martinique, except apparently to attend the board meeting. Somebody had probably phoned from Miami after my plane left and asked that I be met. But my being there at all was bound to give rise to instant speculation, especially with someone like Pettigrew, who knew the history well. He was just trying to find out whatever he could.

"I don't think general counsel is big enough for my talents," I told him. "I was thinking more of Medlock's job. He has a bigger office, and I've heard his stock options are better."

Pettigrew frowned. He was willing to pick my brain

but he didn't really want any part of that kind of subversive talk.

"I hope it's a good party," I said.

He brightened. "You'll see. About half of our board members are here, and there are a couple of other meetings. The hotel just decided to have an open-house kind of reception."

It didn't take long to get to the hotel, and the driver dropped us at the front entrance. I could hear the music a long time before we got to the entrance. There was a small musical group posted just inside the lobby, a steel band, small in number but loud and boisterous, with a calypso beat.

"This is only the outer edges," said Pettigrew, after he got my suitcase out of the car and gave the driver of our car some parting instructions. "Wait'll you see the swimming-pool area back of the hotel."

The outer edges, in quieter times known, no doubt, as the hotel lobby, were crowded with people, some dressed formally, more evening dresses than tuxedos, and some dressed in sports clothes in fairly casual fashion. There were several pretty waitresses of light brown skin, all, I assumed, natives of Martinique, since their West Indian features were a little bit different from those I was accustomed to see in brown.

The waitresses wore colorful blouses and one in a mostly red blouse offered me my choice from a round tray with several glasses.

"Do you speak English?" I asked, probably a silly question in a big hotel like that, but bear in mind I had been on the plane for seven hours.

"My French is better," she answered in perfectly good English and held the tray toward me. "Would you like a drink?"

"What are they?"

"Planter's Punch." I thanked her and took one. Pettigrew had gone to the reservation desk with my suitcase and returned now and gave me a key.

"You're in 302," he said. "The bellboy will take your bag upstairs. Come on, let's go out by the pool."

He led me through the lobby and out onto an enormous patio area at the rear of the hotel, with tables and umbrellas covering the open spaces. The view was out over the wide bay, and it was beautiful.

It was a clear night. The stars were out, and across the water, probably several miles across, there were lights visible here and there along the curving shore of the other side of the bay.

Pettigrew led me down a stairway to the patio and toward the far side.

There was a swimming pool to the right, a nice one. No one was swimming but there were lights on the side of the pool, under the water, and several dozen gardenias were floating on the water. It was pretty.

I spotted several people I knew, all from Troup-Kincaid, and a lot of people I had never seen before. There were more people out here than in the lobby, but there was more space too, and it seemed more relaxed. It was warm, with a slight breeze, and while I could still hear the steel band somewhere behind me, the sound was about right for my taste, subdued and not too distant but not too loud either.

The hotel was built on solid rock, overlooking the sea, and there was a sudden drop just beyond the patio. The ground fell off at a gentle slope for a few feet and there was a guard rail and then a drop of, oh, it seemed fifty or sixty feet down to the water.

Off to the right was a long, gently descending path. It went at an angle away from the hotel and then cut back in a sharp horseshoe curve that led down to the water.

"It's beautiful here, isn't it," Pettigrew said as we looked out over the water. He gestured at the several fair-sized yachts anchored not too far out. "How would you like to own one of those?"

"Be nice," I said, and I meant it at that moment. I'm not what you would call a seafaring man; indeed, I'm one of those barely able to tell a rowboat from a schooner (I know the schooner is bigger), but the boats in the bay looked expensive and comfortable and as if they had well-trained crews capable of taking you halfway round the world, which they probably did.

"That's my choice," Pettigrew said and pointed out to a superb vessel, one that looked like what I vaguely imagined was a nineteenth-century sailing ship, one with three tall masts and tons of canvas sail. The ship was at anchor, of course, and none of the sails were up, but at that distance I could see the bulk of canvas folded near the masts.

"They really sail that thing," I said, "like with sails unfurled and all that?"

"Sure," said Pettigrew. "It's got big engines too, but those sails can make it move. I watched this afternoon. You'll get a chance to see. It belongs to one of our Frenchmen. All the Troup-Kincaid people are invited for an afternoon of it. There's supposed to be a lovely beach across the bay, and I think the plans call for us all to go over after the board-of-directors' session one morning and drink whiskey and eat good food and swim, in roughly that order."

"That sounds fine. But what Frenchman belongs to the ship?"

Pettigrew peered at me curiously. "I thought you were down here for the board meeting. That's what half of it is about."

I sighed, sipping my Planter's Punch. "Johnathan, at the moment I am again working for good old T-K-I, but I was pressed into service on rather short notice by Medlock

and Henry Winston and Wexler the Senior, and I ended up
down here almost before I knew it. Don't play games, just
tell me what Frenchman we're talking about."

I thought all of a sudden of the memo or several ones
Henry Winston had given me in the envelope in Miami; I
probably should have read them on the plane. I promised
myself I'd read them through, or at least skim them before
I went to bed that night.

"Well, the Frenchman is going to run our hotel."

"What hotel?"

Pettigrew sipped his drink. He enjoyed knowing
things I didn't and was in no hurry to tell me.

"Troup-Kincaid may go into the hotel business right
here on Martinique. If the board approves it this week, that
is. It takes a lot of money to start a big luxury hotel."

It didn't surprise me, though hotels were a new kind
of project for T-K-I. When I was still with Troup-Kincaid,
I got so I could almost spot the timing for a brand new
venture of some kind. If earnings started building up a bit,
and they had been up most quarters for a long time, then
the first thing that would happen would be a token move
to reduce either our short-term or our long-term debt.
Then, before you knew it, the profits coming in would be
channeled toward something new, and before it was over
the start-up costs of whatever it was would kick our debt
back up higher than it was before. Of course, that part
didn't make any difference if most of the projects more or
less ended up making a profit too, and that had been the
usual track record. If something didn't make money after a
reasonable time, which also happened, why then the company moved quickly to sell it off or liquidate it for whatever
could be salvaged.

Wexler the Senior had built up a pretty sizable corporation that way (the word conglomerate had both come into
and gone out of fashion while he was doing it), and even

though he had now stepped down from most operations, Medlock and Bill Wexler Junior had continued pretty much in that pattern.

"What was it you did with hotels?" I asked Pettigrew, because I remembered something but could not quite place it.

"The little hotel school," he said. "You know, below San Francisco."

And I remembered. It was a small but reasonably profitable little school for training staff people to work in hotels. Troup-Kincaid had bought it several years before from another company. God knows why, since it was smaller than anything T-K-I usually fooled with, but it may have been that Medlock or somebody was already thinking about hotels.

"You do their legal work, I guess," I said to Pettigrew, and he nodded. "If Troup-Kincaid builds a hotel on Martinique, could that school train people to work in it?"

"Might be possible," said Pettigrew, "but I think what they've been talking about is some sort of management contract with the Frenchman . . . he's supposed to have superb background in the hotel business . . . and that would, I guess, mean that he would hire the staff, probably some from France and some local people here on Martinique."

We stood just near the edge of the patio, still gazing down at the ships in the bay. There was only a sliver of moon, but the stars were bright. It looked as if you could reach out and touch the gently shifting vessels.

"Gentlemen, gentlemen, I want to speak to both of you," the booming, familiar voice said from behind us.

It was a member of the T-K-I board of directors, a tall, balding man named Arthur Hinrichs. He was in his fifties somewhere, an impressive man who dressed well and moved well with people. His hairline was getting pretty far back now, and the top of his head was as suntanned as his face. He wore glasses and his dark eyes were bright and alert behind them.

"Jim, it is especially good to see you," said Hinrichs, shaking hands with both of us.

"Hello, Congressman," I said.

Hinrichs was from New Jersey and had actually served in Congress for two terms, then had lost an election in a try for the U.S. Senate. He owned a construction company and some real estate and had gotten out of politics in favor of making money after his loss in the Senate race. Henry Winston always called him "Congressman," though I'm not sure anybody else still did, and I had picked up the habit.

"It is good to see you, Jim," Hinrichs repeated, beaming at me. "I hope this means you are back with Troup-Kincaid."

"Just for a while," I said, "probably not long."

"He's a new troubleshooter," Pettigrew said, and both Hinrichs and I gave him a quick glance. My impression from the airport came back, that Pettigrew had had enough to drink already. He smiled cheerfully at both of us.

"Trouble? Trouble? We're not going to have any trouble on a beautiful island like this," insisted Hinrichs, all good humor. "Both of you boys come over to my table for a minute. I want you to meet someone. We'll get you another drink on the way."

Hinrichs was exuberant and hard to resist. I decided the Planter's Punch was fine but switched to Scotch at our way stop at the bar.

"Meet these people," commanded Hinrichs, in a nice way, when we got to his table. It was one of the round tables on the patio, with half a dozen chairs circling it.

I recognized Hinrichs' wife, a plump, rather serene-appearing dark-haired lady, who nodded at me.

We were nearing the table, not quite there, when Pettigrew nudged me and murmured, "You're going to meet our Frenchman,'' so that I guessed at the man in the white suit who stood up and smiled.

He was a tall man, a little bit stocky, with completely white hair, prematurely white obviously, since he couldn't have been older than forty-five. He was not handsome, really, rather a broad blunt face, but he stood up most graciously when we approached and, as if at his signal, the two other men at the table stood up too.

"This is Mr. Martel, Charles Martel,'' said the Congressman, "and these are his associates.'' The other two men were already standing, one about Martel's age but a bit heavier and softer, and the other a thin, somewhat younger man who smiled nicely with very white teeth and shook hands with a firm grip.

Martel made introductions while the handshaking was going on, Pettigrew and I and the two Frenchmen, and I didn't catch the names very well, except the flow of several syllables, and that the thin, younger man's first name was Jean.

"Mr. Hinrichs used to be a Congressman, you know,'' said Martel. "He was explaining to us about the New York mayor's race. It is fascinating for me.'' Martel spread his hands over the table, moving them out in a gesture that ended up with his hands cupped and wide apart, as if he were getting ready to reach out and gather the whole table into his arms. "Fascinating. I have read American newspapers, but I have never lived in the United States at all. Jean here lived in New York for three years. You still have friends there, no?'' Martel stared at Jean with an ironic smile, and Jean made no comment but flashed those white teeth in a good-natured smile. "Roger only cares about money,'' Martel said, nodding at the heavier man. "He couldn't be less interested in politics.'' Then Martel turned his attention back to Hinrichs. "Congressman Hinrichs tells wonderful stories.''

Maybe Martel believed every word that he said, but it struck me it was as if he were pushing the hotel project and he wanted members of the board of directors on his side; he certainly knew what he was doing with the Congressman routine.

Hinrichs was in his element.

"I was just talking about John Lindsay, Jim," he said to me. "I was in the House with John for one term before he ran for mayor of New York City. Charming man, and bright, even if I didn't always agree with his politics." Hinrichs shook his head. "Never understood why anybody would want to be mayor of a big city these days anyway. Too many problems. The mayor gets blamed for everything, and a lot of things he can't control. I used to send John notes every time they had a big garbage strike or something he was catching hell about, tell him that what he really ought to do is move New York City over to New Jersey and start over."

We all chuckled, and I resisted the impulse to ask the good Congressman, ex-Congressman, that is, if Lindsay had ever responded to his allegedly humorous notes.

"What do you think, Mr. Roundtree?"

The question came from Jean, who was gazing at me politely. I gazed back just as politely, indicating with raised eyebrows that I wasn't too sure about the meaning of the question. "Congressman Hinrichs," Jean went on, "was saying to us that he thought Mr. Beame would win the New York mayor's race this year. Do you think the same?"

I shook my head. "I just don't think it makes much difference who gets elected. Nothing much will change."

Jean frowned as if about to disagree, but Martel spoke first with that gentle, ironic smile. His wide, blunt face became almost handsome with his smile.

"You are cynical, Mr. Roundtree," he said. "Jean does not agree with you about politics. He went to law school while he lived in New York, and I think sometimes he wishes he had stayed there and gone into politics himself.''

The Congressman looked a little shocked at the suggestion that it didn't make any difference who won an election.

"Abe Beame is a capable man, I think" he said. "I like him, even sent him a few dollars, not this time, I confess, but the first time he ran for mayor."

"I don't say it never makes any difference who gets elected," I said. "Just in some cases, and in this particular one it won't change New York City much no matter which of several candidates wins. In some elections, it makes a lot of difference."

Jean smiled with those white perfect teeth and looked content. "I agree," he said.

Martel smiled too, that small ironic smile. "It must, though, be quite a trick to decide when an election makes a difference and when it does not. That is true of other things, certainly."

Martel seemed to me suddenly an immensely likable man. I don't mean that I decided I liked him. I wanted to know more about hotel projects and where Bill Wexler, Jr., was and some notion of what the hell was going on before I decided any new acquaintance was a great fellow, but it struck me that Martel was one of these people who seems immediately charming and pleasant and who yet in some way utilized those attributes for his own advancement, not necessarily in an unscrupulous sense.

A dark-haired young lady, quite pretty, came to our table and Martel looked serious when he saw her. She leaned down and said something to him in a low voice. He nodded and she turned and went away again.

"I must go," he said. He glanced at his watch. "It is late here. In Paris it is much later than here, but I have one partner who thinks nothing of working through the night. He wants me on the telephone."

Martel stood and smiled and gave us all a slight bow.

My glass was empty and I wanted a drink, so I excused myself and headed for the bar.

The Congressman was right behind me, his glass just as empty as mine.

"Jim, it is good to see you," he beamed, as we stood by the bar on the patio.

His plump, dark-haired wife had followed him from the table. "Arthur," she said to the Congressman, resting her hand on his arm for a second. "It's after midnight, I think I'll go up to the room." He nodded and she smiled pleasantly at me. "Don't keep him up talking too late," she said.

The Congressman and I got our drinks, but he seemed in no hurry to go back to the table. I glanced over that way. Martel had gone to take his telephone call and Pettigrew seemed deep in conversation about something with Jean and the other Frenchman.

"Don't you like Martel?" the Congressman said.

"He certainly seems a likable man," I said, feeling the question encouraged a positive answer.

"A good man, I think, good credentials," the Congressman said, nodding vigorously. "He's perfect for a big hotel venture like this." Hinrichs frowned. "I don't understand how anyone can be against it." He stared at me, his bright, dark eyes hungry behind his glasses, his tanned, balding head catching a small reflection of light. I had a sudden impression of what he must have been like on a congressional committee, determined and persistent.

"I don't know much about the project, in honesty, Congressman," I said.

"I thought Pettigrew said you were here as a kind of troubleshooter," Hinrichs said. "This hotel project is the only thing on our agenda that's even the least bit controversial."

Hinrichs stared at me as if I really were a witness

before a congressional committee and he was intent on wrenching the truth out of me.

"Sorry, Congressman," I said, "I really don't know much about it." I found myself for the second time that evening regretting that I had neglected to read Henry Winston's memos about the upcoming board meeting while on the plane.

"Wall, no matter," he said, relaxing. "I can't imagine that the board of directors will fail to approve it, but you never know. You're with a New York firm now, Jim?"

I admitted it and we finished our drinks and got into another half-hearted discussion of New York City politics, me finding myself in the unlikely position of defending Rep. Bella Abzug, whom I don't even like but who was also not on the personal favorite list of the Congressman, and when he all but suggested that she was probably a communist, I found myself saying that was nonsense and defending the lady in at least semi-gallant fashion.

The patio was thinning out a little bit, though there were still several dozen people here and there, and I could still hear the steel band from the front part of the hotel.

Martel's table, where I'd left Pettigrew chatting with the two Frenchmen, was empty now. I thought I saw one of the Frenchmen, the heavier one, talking with a man and woman several tables further away, but it was in the shadows and I couldn't be sure.

I wasn't sure if I qualified as an official troubleshooter or not, but I decided I wasn't making much progress in finding out anything. There had been, in addition to the Congressman, two or three other Troup-Kincaid board members scattered about on the wide patio when I first came in with Pettigrew. I didn't spot any of them now, so there was no chance to get into conversation with someone else who might know something or other.

I had one other question for the Congressman.

"Mr. Hinrichs," I said, "I happened to see Mr. Wexler the Senior in Miami just before coming down to Martinique, and he seemed to think Bill Wexler might be already on his way down here from a different direction. You haven't seen him this evening, have you?"

The Congressman shook his head. "I'm sure he'll be here. Let's see, there's some kind of ceremony in front of the hotel before noon, some local officials and speechmaking, I think, and then there's a short bus tour around the island and a board-of-directors' meeting at five. Let's see . . ." Hinrichs was fumbling in his coat pocket for a letter, which he pulled out and studied. "That's what I was trying to remember. Tomorrow's Thursday and that first board meeting at five is just the preliminary session, mostly for handing out reports and things. It won't take long, and Bill and Helen Wexler are hosting a cocktail party for the directors right afterward. The real board meeting won't be until Friday morning."

"But he's not here yet," I said.

"No, no, haven't seen him," the Congressman said. "You know Bill. He'll probably get in just in time for the cocktail party."

"Yeah," I said, "I know Bill," remembering the note, *Where have you been, Billy Boy, Billy Boy, where have you been, Charming Billy?* I wondered if Billy Boy would ever make his own cocktail party.

10 A Friendly Frenchman

The Congressman got one more drink and seemed disappointed when I told him I thought I would call it a night.

I started threading my way through the tables and chairs on the patio and had almost reached the swimming pool when I saw Stroud.

At least I believe it was Stroud. The man, whoever, was standing just inside the hotel lobby but right at the door leading out to the steps that descended to the pool and patio area, and as I happened to glance that way, the man turned and stepped back inside, out of my view. I was sure enough that it might be Stroud, so that I hurried up the steps and into the hotel.

No sign of him, and I thought I might have been mistaken.

There were still people in the lobby and still two young ladies moving around with the trays of Planter's Punch. They were strikingly pretty, both of them. I was to read later when I got around to it that the girls on both Guadeloupe and Martinique were considered among the most beautiful in the world. The two waitresses in the hotel lobby both had brown skin the color of light walnut wood and high cheek bones and slim, pretty figures.

The heavier Frenchman, Roger whatever his name was, was coming in from the patio area and he stopped me.

"Ah, Mr. Roundtree, I think everyone is giving up, is saying enough for the night."

His English was not as good as that of Martel or the younger Frenchman. But he seemed relaxed, good-humored. He wore glasses, which edged down along his nose until it seemed they would fall off at any moment. It gave his round face a Santa Claus look of cheerful mischief.

He gestured at one of the pretty waitresses with her tray of drinks. "Won't you have one more drink with me? We hardly had a chance to talk earlier."

Why not? I thought, and we both reached for a last Planter's Punch.

"I don't sleep well any more," he said conversationally. "It is a sign of age, I am sure. I feel rested when I wake up in the morning, but I have a hard time going to sleep. I think one more drink will help me sleep very nicely."

"Have you been to Martinique before?" I asked, and he nodded. More than once, he said, the last time with his son and daughter. The girl had just completed college, and the boy had just finished military service. It was a vacation to give them all a chance to see something of each other. His wife, he added, unfortunately had died years before and as best he could he had tried to serve as both parents.

"I have a question to ask you," he said. I nodded. "Let me say first that I make quick judgments about people." He shrugged and smiled. "It is a necessity in business. Usually my judgments are good. For instance, I observe two young men come to my table, you and Mr. Pettigrew. I judge that Pettigrew is probably a fool, and that you are not."

"You flatter me," I said, "but you are a bit hard on Mr. Pettigrew."

"Perhaps, perhaps," he said, dismissing Pettigrew with an airy wave of his hand. "But I could tell Mr. Hinrichs held the same opinion."

His question, he went on, concerned the building of the hotel on Martinique. He was an old friend of Mr. Martel's and he knew that Martel had the intelligence and skill to run a hotel magnificently and since he was planning to put some of the necessary money into the project it was important that he know that, but there was one other thing that troubled him and he would value my view. It was obvious that the success of a big new hotel rested with attracting tourists in goodly numbers, and in the modern world this had to mean American tourists to a great extent, despite all the talk about the shrinking dollar. Did I think, he asked, that American tourists would come to Martinique in those numbers? It worried him, he said, that the other islands like Bermuda and Puerto Rico were relatively so much closer to the American mainland. What did I think?

"Sure they'll come," I told him. "Why not? More people have money to travel. Martinique is a beautiful island, and it's not that far these days. It's getting so that it's fairly ordinary for a family to fly to London or Paris for a week or for two weeks."

Roger smiled at me, his eyes twinkling through his glasses, like those of a friendly uncle, his round, plump face suddenly seeming relieved. "I trust Martel's judgment," he said, sighing. "But I become nervous always just before investing money."

"That is a good time to be nervous."

This made him laugh and he clapped me on the shoulder like an old friend and said that between the last Planter's Punch and my intelligent opinion, which he valued highly, that now he would go to his room and be able to get a good night's sleep and maybe it would be his good fortune that we would have a chance to talk some more the next day.

I said fine and wished him pleasant dreams, and he started for the elevator.

I already had my hotel-room key, but I checked with the desk to see if I had any messages.

There was one. "Call me before you go to bed," it

read, and it was initialed H.W., the same way Henry Winston used to initial his office memos.

The clerk guided me to a house phone, and I rang Henry.

"I thought I left you in Miami," I said, "What the hell are you doing here?"

He chuckled dryly but without much humor. "I didn't expect to be here until tomorrow," he said. "William decided that we all should fly down today in the company plane, so we did."

"You made good time."

"We probably started a good two hours or more after you left, but one advantage of a company plane is that you fly nonstop. You were island hopping. We were here almost by the time you were. Have you been able to talk to anybody yet?"

"Only the Congressman," I said, "and he doesn't seem to know much."

"I haven't gone to bed yet," Winston said, "just getting unpacked. Come up for a drink."

Winston's hotel room was not overly large, fair sized, but it had a small balcony just outside a French window, and a table and two chairs on the balcony looking out over the water. The angle and the way the hotel was built made it impossible to look out over the patio, but we could still hear the steel band faintly and it was the same bay and boats shifting gently in the water.

Henry had loosened his tie a little bit and hung his coat over the back of a chair, but otherwise he looked as cool and formal as if he were ready to begin a board-of-directors' meeting.

He gestured at the top of his dresser. There were three bottles, one of rum, one of Scotch, one of bourbon.

"Courtesy of the management," he said. "I've got some ice."

He mixed us both drinks, his just Scotch over the ice cubes with almost no water at all, and we both walked out on the narrow balcony. Henry stood at the edge, for a moment, staring out over the water. There was enough light to frame his thin, handsome face, his white hair. Henry was getting old but he looked like a U.S. Senator from a New England state ought to look or maybe like a U.S. ambassador named to a post that took considerable polish and brains at the same time, regardless of how much money you had contributed to anybody's political campaign.

Henry seemed grim.

"I talked with Wexler on the airplane," he said. "There's something he's worried about that he hasn't told me."

It wasn't a question, and I made no comment. Henry was undoubtedly thinking, as I was, of the few minutes Wexler the Senior had spent alone with me just before I got on the plane.

"Don't tell me anything you don't think you should," Winston said to me, "but I'm not dumb, Jim, you know that."

I sighed and sipped my drink. Winston wasn't dumb and I trusted him, but I didn't think I ought to tell him something that Wexler the Senior could have told him if he had wanted to do so.

"I can make an educated guess," Winston said. "When you left Miami, I don't think William had any plan to fly to Martinique that same afternoon. He would have told you to wait and fly with us."

"Did Helen Wexler fly down too?" I asked.

"She did, though I suggest that you not give yourself undue concern about that lady's whereabouts," said Winston, a little sharply. "But to go on, I don't think William had any intention of flying this evening when you left. He seemed intent on getting in touch with Bill. You heard him ask Helen to try the West Coast again, and she did. He made several long-distance calls himself and muttered and fumed a lot."

We were sitting on the balcony outside Winston's room, and nobody said anything for a minute. I was thinking about Stroud and wondering if he really was in the hotel, and I was just getting ready to tell Henry about seeing Stroud on the plane and our conversation, when he turned to me.

"You know what I think?" he asked.

I shook my head.

"William thinks his son is in some kind of trouble, that Bill is in a mess of some kind. It is the only reason I can imagine that William would be so desperate to contact his son on short notice, especially when he can anticipate seeing him no later than tomorrow in any case, at the board meeting. I think he made us all hurry back to our hotels and pack our suitcases and fly down today because he hoped frantically that he would find Bill here at the hotel when we arrived. That was the first thing he did when we got here, checked to see if Bill had gotten in. And, though it is hardly likely that Bill would stay in any hotel other than the one where the board meeting is to be held, the second thing he did was to have someone start checking all the hotels on Martinique, even some in Fort-de-France, where, shall we say, it is inexpensive enough so that it is inconceivable that Bill Wexler would ever stay there under any circumstances."

"What do you want me to say, Colonel?"

"I want you to tell me what Wexler told you in Miami," he said, in that boring-in inquisitor's voice, as if he were back in the courtroom and dealing with a reluctant witness.

"I can't, Colonel," I said, not happy about it. "You understand I can't."

He didn't say much after that. I told him about Stroud and said I would try to find out somehow if he really was staying in the hotel. We finished our drinks and Winston walked me to the door of his room.

"I am glad you are here, Jim," he said, but the thin, bleak smile he offered didn't make him seem very glad about anything.

"One thing, Colonel," I said. "Your educated guess of a moment or two ago confirms in my mind that you are a perceptive and astute observer."

That made him smile a little more cheerfully but not much.

"There are one or two things I wish I could tell you, Jim," he said, "but it is not clear to me yet that they have anything to do with the curious things going on, and they are rather personal things for the people involved. They may have nothing to do with this. One thing you can do, though. Be as nice as you can to Helen Wexler when you see her tomorrow. She is under a great strain."

I was tempted to tell Winston that such an assignment was the most pleasant suggestion anyone had made recently, but he might have misunderstood. So I said yes, certainly I would, and he smiled almost as if he meant it and we said good night.

11 Things That Go Bump in the Night

It occurred to me as I left Winston's room that I had been on Martinique and in the hotel for several hours and had yet to get by my hotel room.

I wondered gloomily on the way down the elevator to the third floor and room 302 if the bellboy had indeed delivered my suitcase to the right room.

It was there all right, unopened on top of the luggage table. My room was similar to Henry's and I had a small balcony too, but the view wasn't as good. There were, however, the same three gift bottles on my dresser, one of Scotch, one of bourbon, and one of rum. There was even ice in the ice bucket. I decided I might grow to like Martinique.

I was sleepy but I wanted to read through the memos about the board meeting and especially about the hotel project. So, first I unpacked moderately, then took a hot shower and brushed my teeth, and then fixed a tall glass of Scotch and water, not too heavy on the Scotch.

The envelope Henry had given me before I left Miami had a cover letter about the general agenda, probably the same letter the Congressman had pulled from his pocket, because it included a bit about Bill and Helen Wexler's cocktail party and the other scheduled things, then an eight-page memo in summary form with short paragraphs about a whole series of things, including some current earnings figures, and one or two items that required action by the board, but most of the paragraphs were there for information only. The few things needing a board vote weren't very controversial.

The last things in the envelope was a two-page memo about the proposal to construct an enormous luxury hotel on Martinique. Or, as I examined it, I realized that it was really two separate one-page memos that had been stapled together.

The first page was a blunt, bare-bones summary of the hotel proposal itself. The hotel and yacht basin would cost close to thirty million including the land, on which there was already an option. There were some technicalities, but basically the French officials on Martinique, with the support of the appropriate officials in Paris, were enthusiastic and saw no problem that could not be worked out.

The rationale was that travel and tourism were going to be increasingly important as more people over the world had more money and more time. There was a likelihood that it would be five years before the hotel could be expected to be making any money and begin repaying the initial investment, but by the same token, Martinique was a magnificently beautiful island, less well known and less developed for tourists than some other places and yet likely to experience substantial growth in tourism, so that in a few years the hotel venture might seem an inspired investment.

Moreover, the memo concluded, a French businessman of splendid credentials, one Charles Martel, who already owned and operated one hotel in Paris and three other hotels outside Paris, was willing both to invest his own money in the project and thus share the risk and also sign a management contract, making him responsible for hiring the staff and the quality of service in the hotel.

"Frankly," the memo ended, "we would think hard

about recommending such an investment if a man as successful in hotels as Mr. Martel were not willing to take an active role."

It was not signed, but it was presumably a summary by the Troup-Kincaid headquarters research staff of a much longer report. I had seen that kind of memo before. It was typically the kind sent to board members before a meeting, with the longer report and research to be examined later, usually at the board meeting itself.

The second page was a different kind of memo, a very confidential one written by Henry Winston to Wexler the Senior also about the hotel project.

It was mostly a brief summary of how Winston thought the nine members of the board might react to the hotel proposal. It was difficult to analyze, Winston said, because at first Medlock had seemed enthusiastic and Bill Wexler had seemed cool to the idea. Then, in the past several months, the positions of the two men had almost reversed: Medlock now seemed to feel that five years might be a long time to wait for the hotel to begin repaying the investment, especially if there were better investment possibilities around, and now young Wexler had appeared to get interested in the project and almost certainly would recommend approval.

"So it's hard to predict, since the board will no doubt ask the views of both the executive vice-president and of the president. And you know our board. They can be decidedly independent minded," the memo concluded.

That was the exact truth. In fact, old Wexler had seemed to want to have that kind of board of directors.

There were nine members, including Wexler as chairman. There were two members, Henry Winston and a realtor from Houston, who had known Wexler since they were young men together, inclined more or less routinely to vote with Wexler the Senior on almost anything. Of the other six, there were three as likely as not to vote against Wexler on any real controversy on which there really were divided opinions.

Most board decisions, needless to say, were unanimous. It wasn't often there was a real split. But when there was, the initial split was usually three and three and with three swing members who could go either way. One of these three swing votes was the congressman Arthur Hinrichs. The other two were lawyers on the board because of their ties to the group of banks which generally loaned Troup-Kincaid more money than anybody else.

The two money lawyers were pretty objective and a little conservative, which is exactly why the banks wanted them on the board. Hinrichs, as a rule, voted with the money men, so that on any really split issue, the board usually ended up with an informal 6–3 split, which somebody would make as a formal unanimous motion and it too would be recorded 9–0 in the board's minutes.

Wexler the Senior had seemingly two general feelings about such controversies: first, he was inclined to support his son, Bill—after all the president of T-K-I now—and second, he nonetheless believed it healthy if Medlock or some members of the board opposed his son and that it was up to his son to make his case. Wexler the Senior had sometimes ended up on the short end of those 6–3 votes when it was likely that if he had really raised hell and torn his shirt he could have turned it the other way.

There's probably a third thing to be said about Wexler the Senior in such dealings. He was willing to be outvoted and not get overly excited about it. "I don't run things any more, I know that," he would say gruffly at such times. But there was one thing he was not willing to do. He was not willing to be taken for anyone's damned fool.

I put the memos away and finished my Scotch and wondered about a lot of things.

I couldn't see anything wrong with the hotel project, not on the face of it. But it was the one thing that involved controversy at the board-of-directors' meeting, at least the one obvious thing, and that made it in my mind automatically to be viewed suspiciously.

I hadn't seen the surveys and the T-K-I research reports but I was willing offhand to bet that they were all right, that they included good information without any tricky parts. The one thing that struck me most in Winston's memo was the bit about how Medlock had started out enthusiastic, Wexler the Younger not overly enthused, and that then, in a matter of months, the two had almost exactly shifted position.

I knew both Medlock and Wexler Junior well in this corporate decision-making context. I remembered cases in which either had shown some flexibility, totally changed his mind in one direction or another. Yet I couldn't remember a case when they had almost exactly reversed position. It was curious.

Winston's memo wound up with the rather neutral conclusion that the board of directors would probably split on the idea of putting thirty million into a hotel and yacht basin on Martinique and that it might go either way.

At the bottom of the memo was a note clearly in Wexler Senior's sprawling handwriting. "I have no strong feeling, Henry," it read. "What do you think?"

There was no other notation on the memo (or at least on my Xeroxed copy of a memo), no indication of what Henry Winston had replied.

I was weary and tired of thinking about memos and mysteries. After standing on the balcony a moment and breathing deeply of the warm fresh air, I turned out the light and went to bed.

It didn't take me long to go to sleep.

It was a dreamless sleep, far as I can remember.

It didn't take long for me to get waked up again either. It was after 4:00 A.M. when the banging and bumping on my door came. I came awake reluctantly and glanced at my little travel clock, which read just 4:18 A.M. I had been asleep two hours maybe but no more.

The loud knocking was at my hotel-room door. I went to the door and asked who it was and thought I heard someone mutter.

I don't suppose I would have answered the door but something in the bumping and banging was irregular, as if two or three children were banging at random. This doesn't make sense, I suppose, but I don't think I would have opened the door if the knocking had been loud and steady and regular.

So, like a fool, I called, "Who is it?" one more time and got no answer and opened the door.

It was a mistake.

It was Stroud at the door, wearing the same suit he had worn on the airplane hours earlier, looking solid and mean. He lunged for me with one outstretched hand as the door swung open.

I stepped back and tried to bring up my fist to hit him anywhere I could, but I felt fearfully that it was too late.

Stroud's body fell against mine.

Fell was the word.

He couldn't stand up. My wild swing fortunately only brushed his shoulder and then I was trying to hold him up. He was muttering something, and as I pulled him inside the room his forehead brushed against my cheek. His face was covered with sweat, far too much for the moderately warm night.

My first thought was that he had been shot or stabbed or whatever. After all, he was a rough customer in his way, and he had shown himself capable of pointing a pistol at me.

I couldn't spot any wound or any blood, but he was

obviously in a bad way. His breathing was labored. His face, I saw, as I stretched him out on the floor on his back, looked near death, his skin pouring sweat and the color not good.

Stroud's eyes opened wildly as I bent over him to loosen his tie. I think he recognized me for a second and then said something I could barely make out.

"Hospital, old friend," he said, croaking out the words. I can't be sure but I thought he tried to smile. And then, by God, his eyes rolled up in his head. It was something I thought was only a phrase, until I saw it happen with Stroud.

I picked up the hotel telephone to call for help, believing with a sinking sensation that Stroud would be dead on my hotel-room floor long before any help could arrive.

12 On Getting No Sleep

The next hour or so was a nightmare, not because anything bad was going on especially but because everything seemed to take forever to get done and I myself had not much to do, just wanting to get the people out of my room so I could go back to bed.

Stroud fell into a terrible irregular breathing and twitched from side to side.

The hotel doctor came very quickly, a fat, balding man with his shirt tucked into his trousers all right but one of his shirt buttons unbuttoned. He looked sleepy too but was very polite.

"Why did he come to your door?" the doctor asked, when I explained what had happened.

I told him I could not imagine unless he had simply been walking in the corridor, probably on his way to his room, and had had an attack of some kind.

That seemed to satisfy the doctor and he confessed that he wasn't sure precisely what had stricken the man but it was certain that he could not be moved until the ambulance came to take him to the hospital.

The hotel clerk stayed with us for a few minutes and telephoned the ambulance from the room, on the doctor's instructions, as the doctor still knelt beside Stroud and prodded him this way and that and listened to his heartbeat with a stethoscope.

"I can't be sure what it is here," the doctor said. "He has to be in the hospital."

The hotel clerk was in and out of my room at least three times, urging us once not to make any noise, because it would be bad to disturb the other guests.

We weren't making any noise at all by this time, not even conversation. I had offered the doctor a drink and he had seemed tempted but had politely refused.

The hotel manager came, a tall, smooth, brown-haired, thin-faced man, who, unlike the doctor, had taken the time to put on a tie and wash the sleep out of his eyes.

"The ambulance will be here in only a moment," he said, gazing forlornly down at Stroud, as if seeing in him all the sudden middle-of-the-night crises created by the devil to plague conscientious hotel managers.

"He's an American, I'm sure. I saw him on the plane from Miami yesterday afternoon," I said, deciding that was a small piece of information I wanted to volunteer and get on the record early. Police tended not to like coincidences, and if Stroud died, I felt certain it would become a serious police matter.

The hotel manager stopped beside Stroud's body and began feeling his pockets gingerly, until he found a brown leather passport case in one of Stroud's inner coat pockets.

"Was he a guest in the hotel?" I asked.

"I don't know," the manager said. "I don't remember seeing him, but I will check his name." He took Stroud's American green-backed passport from the case and began examining it. "And then," he rambled on, "there may be relatives who should know if he is seriously ill."

The doctor obviously didn't like the sound of Stroud's breathing and paced to the window as if wondering where the blasted ambulance was. Then he pushed up one of Stroud's coat sleeves, unbuttoned and rolled up the shirt sleeve, and gave him a shot with a stubby hypodermic needle from his black bag.

The shot didn't seem to help Stroud's breathing any.

"I will take this and check downstairs," the manager said to me, holding up Stroud's passport. He left the brown passport case on the bureau.

I decided to fix myself the drink the doctor had turned down. The passing thought entered my mind to telephone Henry Winston, but there wasn't anything he could do, not at that hour. I probably subconsciously just wanted to wake him so he could share my wide-awake misery.

I strolled out on the small balcony, thinking that at this rate it wouldn't be long before the sun came up over the bay and the trim ships at anchor facing the hotel.

"Good God," I said, the words leaping out involuntarily. My room was 302, third floor, and near enough the main patio to look down on that long, wide, lighted swimming pool with the flowers floating on top of the water.

At the moment, there was a man floating in the pool, fully clothed, right in the middle of the flowers.

I wasn't the first person to see him, but I suppose I was close to the first. There were two men standing on the side of the pool watching as another man, also fully clothed, though he had taken off coat and shoes, lowered himself with apparent reluctance into the water and then swam a slow breast stroke out to reach the man.

The swimmer grabbed at the man's coat and began tugging him toward the side.

The drowned man, for he seemed that, was face down and gave no sign of life. But when the swimmer pulled at his coat, he started to turn slowly and grotesquely in the water. The swimmer didn't like the feeling of motion; I don't suppose I would have either under the circumstances and, as he neared the edge of the pool, he let go to shift position on the man's coat sleeve.

It had the effect of spinning the man slightly so that he rolled over, face up, and stared up at the hotel.

This was only the third floor, as I said, and I caught a good glimpse of the man's face. He looked very dead to me. He also looked very like the heavy-set Frenchman I'd met with Martel the night before, Roger, the one who didn't talk much at first and who worried about investing money. I had wished him pleasant dreams and a good night's sleep only hours before.

I noted that the hotel manager was one of the several people now standing at the edge of the pool. This just wasn't his night.

They had pulled the body of the man from the pool, and the doctor was already examining him. I looked over my shoulder and back into the room. The door to my room was open into the corridor. I hadn't paid attention but I suppose the doctor had looked out over the balcony too and then hurried down to see what he could do.

Stroud was still lying on the floor, breathing heavily, his eyes closed.

I had an impulse to go through his pockets and was just considering it but considered it a moment too long without doing anything. The hotel clerk came back into the room to say that the ambulance was downstairs and that the attendants were on their way up with a stretcher.

It took them a minute or so to get there and the fat doctor led them into the room and helped hold Stroud's head while they lifted him onto a stretcher.

"The man in the pool," I said to the doctor as he stood up sighing and watched the two ambulance attendants start out with Stroud. The doctor's shirt was still not buttoned but he didn't look sleepy any more, just 'fore God tired. "Was he drowned?" I asked.

"I don't know. It may be. He had hit his head severely, so it could be that. But he is certainly dead."

"The autopsy will show," said a new voice, "exactly what killed him. We should know very soon."

It was my night for late-night visitors. The man standing in the doorway was medium height, lean and wiry. He wore an open-necked sports shirt and was balding in the same way the Congressman was, hair receding right up the middle. His skin was a light West Indian brown and he smiled pleasantly, but his eyes were like the wrath of God, bloodshot and sleepy.

"You are Mr. Roundtree," he said, and I nodded. "I am Lieutenant Vitu. I don't want to keep you up. In fact"—he smiled wryly—"I don't want to be up myself. I unhappily live not very far from the hotel. The hospital lets someone on duty know when they are called. A man sick at the hotel"—Vitu shrugged—"that is not too unusual. But then to find a man dead in the hotel swimming pool by the time the ambulance gets here? The driver called the sergeant on duty, and he felt it necessary to wake me up."

Vitu talked in a soft, low voice, with his head tipped slightly to one side. He seemed good-humored and courteous and fatalistic all at once, and his moderately bloodshot eyes seemed shrewd and alert.

"There is probably no connection between the two things," said Vitu, "but I must ask you if you knew the man who collapsed in your room."

"Not really," I said. "I told the hotel manager that I think he was on the same plane I took from Miami to Martinique yesterday evening."

"Yes," said Vitu. He pointed at the balcony. "You saw the man found in the pool." I nodded.

"Did you know him?"

I shook my head. "I didn't get much of a look at him, but I'm pretty sure I did not."

This was probably a pointless lie for which I make no

excuses. I can only plead that I was exhausted, and it seemed to me that to admit that I had known the Frenchman, Roger whatever, and talked to him would only stretch out God knows how long the time before everybody would get the hell out of my room and leave me alone and let me get some rest.

Vitu nodded, seeming satisfied, and turned as if to go. "I am sorry to bother you this way," he said. The doctor was ahead of him and already out the door and starting for the elevator. "There's one more thing," he said, pausing. "You can't think of any reason why the man Stroud would have tried to get to your door, can you? Did he say anything before he fell over?"

I shook my head, giving way at the same time to a visible yawn. Vitu nodded politely, and was gone.

I had told the truth, really. Stroud had not been able to speak enough to offer any messages.

But there was one thing he had done that I had not told anyone. As he gasped out the words, "Hospital, old friend," and tried to smile, he had pressed his hand over mine and tried to give me a piece of paper. Actually, he had barely had strength simply to let it go, and it had fallen on the floor. I had picked it up and glanced at it a moment then, before calling the hotel desk for a doctor.

I pulled the note now out of my pajama top pocket, where I had stuffed it. It didn't help me much when I looked at it again. It was just a sheet of hotel stationery with three names written on it. The first two names meant nothing to me, though they both seemed to be French names. Then there was a line drawn underneath the two names, and a third name below. The third name was "Daniel Webster," which meant something to me all right but only as the name of a nineteenth-century American historical figure, one that Steven Vincent Benét had once chosen to write a fine short story about.

The Devil and Daniel Webster. I'd have to think about that, but it didn't seem to have much to do with whatever the devil was happening on Martinique.

13 A Little Civic Pride

I will not claim that I rolled out of bed bright and early after that kind of night, but I did sleep soundly when I finally got to bed and didn't feel too badly after I got up around 9:30, not at least after I shaved and had a hot shower.

I had ordered some breakfast before starting to shower, and I was just barely dressed when the bellhop's knock on the door came. I had him take the tray out on the balcony and put it on the little table there.

The water in the bay was blue and beautiful in the sunshine. I had ordered scrambled eggs and toast, and they were fine. I was well into a second cup of coffee when the phone rang.

It was the nice voice of a French-accented lady, telling me that the international edition of the Paris *Herald-Trib* had not come that day. Somebody was on strike, she said. I had asked for a newspaper, preferably the *Herald-Trib,* when I ordered breakfast. The lady said she had checked and the latest *Herald-Trib* they had in the hotel was Monday's. This was Thursday already, so I told her I would pass.

But I did ask her to ring Henry Winston's room. There was no answer, so I left word. He had probably gone down to the coffee shop or maybe to talk to Wexler the Senior.

There was no official anything on the little Troup-Kincaid agenda until 11:00 a.m. There was going to be a

little speechmaking and ceremony, I gathered, to welcome
the mighty Troup-Kincaid board of directors and friends
and associates. Then there was a small reception and lunch-
eon put on by Martinique's tourist people, all generally
along the line of how nice it was that T-K-I wanted to hold
a board meeting on the beautiful island. And, I suspected,
along the line maybe that it would certainly be nice if T-K-I
did indeed decide to build a thirty-million-dollar new hotel
there.

I decided to read through the memos about the board
meeting again once more, carefully. Maybe there was something on the general agenda that was important. Maybe it
wasn't the hotel project at all. But I made a point too of
reading the two short pages about the hotel venture.

The phone rang and I thought it was Henry but I was
wrong. It was Wexler Senior, whose gruff voice sounded
heavy.

"I just wanted to speak to you," he said, assuming I
would know who it was. "I just wanted to speak. I know you
talked to Henry last night, and I talked to him after you did,
but I just wanted to be sure. You haven't found out anything?"

His voice was not reproachful but wooden and with
maybe a slight hopeful hint that I might surprise him.

"Nothing about your son, Mr. Wexler, but there have
been some strange things."

I told him briefly about Stroud coming to my room and
about the man in the pool and that I was fairly sure he was
one of the two Frenchmen I had met with Martel. That
didn't seem to impress Wexler nearly as much as the idea
that the same man who had twisted my arm out on Long
Island and warned me about working for Troup-Kincaid
again had popped up on Martinique.

"He's got to be the key," Wexler said. "He's got to
know something. He may even know where Bill is. Why

can't you prefer charges against him for his attack on you?"

I allowed as how a man could always prefer charges but it would be my word against his and, in any case, the story would probably sound near incredible to the Martinique authorities. It might be better to find out what we could about Stroud while he was in the hospital.

"Let me work on that. I'll find out about that fellow," Wexler said, sounding happier at the prospect of having something specific to do. He hung up on me before I could say anything else.

It was just as well. I had been on the verge of asking him a question one ought not to ask a worried father, though maybe I needed the answer. What would happen to Bill Wexler's stock and interest in the company if he turned up dead? The money of it would presumably go to his wife, Helen, and their daughter, Susan. But how would that affect the company? Or would it affect anyone else in good or bad fashion?

Henry hadn't called, but I had told Wexler Senior as much as I knew about both Stroud and the man in the pool. I decided to wander on down to the hotel lobby. The welcoming ceremony in front of the hotel was supposed to begin at 11:00 a.m. and it was getting close to that time.

The lobby was a lot quieter without the steel band, and I was grateful for small favors. I left my key at the desk and walked to the front entrance of the hotel.

There was already a small crowd, fifty people or more, gathered in front of the hotel, ready for the speechmaking.

The front of the hotel faced out toward a road perhaps one hundred yards away. A long driveway wound its way between royal palm trees, curved into a covered drive directly in front of the hotel, then back around through a separate framed route through more palm trees and out again to the main thoroughfare.

The hotel was not too far from the main city, Fort-de-

France, but it stood quite alone on this part of the island. There was not another building in sight and across the paved road near the hotel stood lush green vegetation as far as the eye could see.

There was a microphone set up on the steps just in front of the hotel and people were gathering in the curved driveway, facing the microphone. There were no chairs. Everyone was standing up. I hoped they would hold the speechmaking to a minimum.

I ran into Henry Winston and discovered that he already knew about the man in the swimming pool but not about Stroud, and I filled him in.

Martel was there, in a white suit that looked expensive and matched his white hair. Jean, the lean one, was there with the same quick smile and wearing dark glasses against the bright morning sunshine. Martel said hello and we shook hands.

"Was the man in the pool . . . ?" I said, and he nodded somberly.

"A tragic accident," he said. "Roger apparently went for a walk quite late, before going to bed, and fell and hit his head in the swimming pool. I can never forgive myself. It was I who persuaded him to come here from Paris for this meeting." Martel shook his head sadly.

"He was in good spirits last night," Jean said. "There is that to remember. It is tragic but it is not your fault."

Martel just shook his head once more.

The crowd was getting bigger. Most of the Troup-Kincaid directors and staff people were there, but I didn't see Wexler Senior or Henry Winston. I counted five T-K-I directors scattered through the crowd, which made seven with Henry and Wexler. Our two missing board members were probably flying in that afternoon.

It was a mixed crowd. There were three or four young men in French military uniforms, military or police, I couldn't be sure. The bright sun was reflected from every sort of skin hue, from very dark brown to very light brown to the mostly Caucasian pink of the Americans and French. There were at least a dozen very well-dressed couples of varying shades of brown skin, and I presumed that they were distinguished citizens of Martinique invited to the welcome and to meet the Americans at the reception afterward.

The hotel manager, whom I'd met in the wee hours of the morning in something less than happy circumstances, came out the hotel front door and spoke to a dark-suited man standing there. The man walked over and tested the microphone and walked back to stand by the manager. The manager looked at his watch. I looked at mine and saw that it was a few minutes before eleven.

We all waited another ten minutes, I at least among those who didn't know who the hell we were waiting for, until at last a big black limousine drove up, right up under the covered part of the drive and almost to a point in front of the microphone.

The man who got out of the car was red-headed, or at least what was left of his hair around the fringes seemed red. He was stocky and dressed in a dark suit and the hotel manager and two or three other people made much of him, shaking his hand.

"That must be the prefect," the lady at my elbow said, and I turned and sure enough the lady was Helen Wexler. I had looked for her earlier in the crowd but hadn't seen her.

"It is nice that you are here," I said. "You look pretty."

She looked stunning is what she looked. She wore a sleeveless white blouse and a bright yellow skirt which did not cover overly much of her slim, tanned legs. There ought to be a law against a forty-two-year-old mother,

which Helen was, wearing skirts that short, unless of course
they had legs as good as Helen's.

She smiled and put her hand on my arm, a brief touch
that I did not dislike but rather feared I might like too
much.

"What is the prefect?" I asked Helen.

"He's like a regional administrator. You know, just
like in France. Martinique is a department of France. People
elect members of Parliament, everything."

Helen spoke and whispered, in French, to a brown-
skinned gentleman standing next to her. He nodded and
smiled.

"I told you. I knew he had to be the prefect."

Another man had gotten up to the microphone and
begun talking. First he spoke for a minute or so in French,
which I didn't understand, and then switched to English.

It was a welcoming speech, and the gentleman wanted
to tell us a little about Martinique. The island was big but
not too big, he said, nearly fifty miles long at one point and
close to twenty miles wide at the widest. It was beautiful and
warm and sunny all year round, sometimes rainy but rarely
too hot, usually like today, sunny and warm and very pleasant.

He knew we had a brief tour around the island and
then a visit to Fort-de-France planned that afternoon, he
said, and he knew we'd see our share of sugar-cane fields,
bananas, and pineapples. The pineapple was sometimes
called the "king of the fruit," he said proudly, and then
began speaking in French again for another few minutes.

He could tell us a lot more, he said (and I believed
him, hoping only that he wouldn't prove it), but in a moment we would hear from someone much smarter than he.
He only hoped, he said, that we observed what a beautiful
island it is, from the beaches and the vegetation to the
mountains in the north and center.

But that was enough for him to say, he said, though he knew we would like to see the remains of the town of Saint-Pierre, the first town founded by the French on the island back in 1635. It had been a wonderful and famous town, the man said, but suddenly on May 8, 1902, a sudden volcanic eruption from Mount Pelée had covered it, utterly destroying the town and its thirty thousand inhabitants.

There was one other thing, he went on, though he said he knew he had talked enough. Martinique was the birthplace of the Empress Josephine, the wife of Napoleon Bonaparte, and there was a Carrara white marble statue of Josephine in the center of Fort-de-France.

That was finally about all he wanted to tell us, though he broke into French for another brief comment, then turned and bowed to the prefect.

"Don't you speak French?" Helen asked me seriously.

"I'm just a country boy," I said. "Never had the advantages of your expensive Eastern girls' colleges."

Helen smiled and looked back toward the microphone and gave me a sharp kick on the ankle.

The prefect was stepping to the microphone, and he gave a small bowing nod of the head as he came forward.

"My friend told you of the terrible volcano, Mount Pelée, that destroyed Saint-Pierre so many years ago. It is certainly true, but I would want you to know it has given us no trouble recently. Our engineers say it is not likely to give us trouble." He smiled good-humoredly, as if to say this was all in fun but he wanted to be sure we knew Martinique wasn't covered with fearful volcanoes. "One thing he left out. There was one survivor of that tragedy of the volcano. One man was in the prison dungeon, and that saved him. Imagine! The man in deepest prison was the one man saved. God indeed works in marvelous ways," said the prefect. "As for the Empress Josephine, she is still sometimes called the first citizen of Martinique. Yet, for myself,

I would prefer we not look too much to the past. That is never good."

He grew more serious. He was pleased and delighted, he said, that a great American corporation such as Troup-Kincaid had chosen to hold its board of directors meeting on Martinique. It was a beautiful part of France, capable of preserving great beauty and yet showing new and important economic development.

Sugar cane was still the main industry, he said, covering something over twenty thousand acres, and producing both sugar and rum. This led him to an aside. "Fort-de-France is said to be famous for both Creole cooking and rum. I hope you have the chance to sample both while you are here."

He then went into French again for a few seconds, smiling, and I felt sure he was repeating that small observation for any of his constituents who did not understand English.

The prefect switched back to English.

Sugar, rum, bananas and pineapples were the main exports, he said, but that wasn't enough. Some years the value of things imported into Martinique ran, in U.S. dollars, to $100 million, while the value of things exported was far less.

"Martinique is a place where for centuries we, the government, have to do everything possible to develop the island. The main industry—sugar—has been in recession. It is better now, but that leaves many hands free, a lack of employment. Tourism needs services for those hands. If you build a modern oil refinery, as we have in Fort-de-France, only a few people are needed to run it. A big, handsome hotel, like this one"—the prefect gestured about him—"needs many people to serve it. It is good for you, good for the people who work, good for the tourists."

The prefect started up in French again, for no more

than a minute, then said in English: "You are most welcome." He had a deep baritone voice and a deliberate manner, but he was a good speaker, seemingly in French too, from the solid applause he got.

I applauded too.

"Let's go to the reception," Helen said, as the crowd in the bright sun started to break up. It was just before high noon by my watch.

"Let's move rapidly," I said, seeing Medlock pressing through the crowd in my direction with a deliberate, somewhat outraged expression on his face.

14 Mixing and Mingling

The champagne reception was upstairs, in a corner room on the mezzanine, looking out over the blue water and at the ships floating on the tide.

Helen and I avoided Medlock long enough to get through the short reception line, which included only the hotel manager, who was asking people's names and then introducing them to first the tourist office man and then to the prefect. We moved across the room, and I took two glasses of champagne from a tray in the hands of a smiling waiter and had just enough time to offer one to Helen when Medlock caught up.

"Roundtree, I need to talk to you," he said urgently, still smooth voiced with that polished baritone but seeming a bit haggard. "Hello, Helen," he said, taking me by the arm as if to pull me away for a private talk.

I set my heels in, and Medlock had to be satisfied with turning half away from Helen and speaking in a low, grumbling tone.

"Why didn't you call me about the man coming to your room? The same man who warned you against coming back to Troup-Kincaid. I thought you were going to keep me informed."

"There wasn't anything to tell you," I said. "Not that makes any sense. He just came to the door and passed out."

"He didn't tell you anything? If he was hurt, it seems damned funny that he'd turn up at your room for help. How do you explain that?"

"I don't explain it, Medlock. I don't have to." He glowered at me and I tried my next question in a politer tone, because I wanted an answer. "Tell me something else. Why are you against this big hotel project?"

He shrugged. "I'm not against it, exactly," he said. "It seems a bit high risk to me for that much money and with no immediate prospect of getting any of it back for a few years. You interested in it?"

"No, not really," I said.

"You let me know as soon as you can if anything else happens," he said. I promised I would.

Helen had wandered away in some other direction. I spoke to two or three of the board members, including one of the lawyers from the bank group. The Congressman and Henry Winston were standing with Wexler Senior in a small, separate group of their own. Even Wexler seemed good-humored but I had watched him sit poker-faced through enough tough sessions of one kind or another to discount his appearance as meaning too much.

As I watched, Martel moved over to join the other three men. He said something I couldn't hear, with that slight ironic smile, and the other men laughed.

"Mr. Roundtree?"

It was Lieutenant Vitu, from the night before, and he was still dressed in an open-necked shirt and his eyes looked more than ever as if he had not had enough sleep. I wondered if he'd gotten even the three or four hours sleep I had. But his round, light brown face seemed more good-humored now, even gay as he smiled.

"Are you here officially, Lieutenant?" I asked.

"No, no," he said. "I planned to come long ago. It is important, this company of yours, Troup-Kincaid. The officials hope very much that your company decides to build another hotel, a big luxury hotel, on Martinique."

"I didn't think policemen worried themselves about bringing in industry, or are you part of the tourist bureau too?"

My question was offensive, and I wasn't exactly trying to be insulting, but I couldn't quite make Vitu out. He refused to be insulted in any case, chuckling a little, and taking a sip from his glass of champagne.

"In my small way, I am part of the government too," he said.

"But suppose your investigation of a crime hurt the chance of some development on Martinique," I said, "what then?"

"Why, I would have to be a very subtle investigator then, wouldn't I?" he said. He was very polite, but I didn't get the impression that a thirty-million-dollar hotel project would weigh much with him if it interfered with an investigation.

"How is Mr. Stroud?" I asked.

"How did you know his name?" he said, very softly and politely.

"The hotel manager looked at his passport while he was in my room, trying to find out if the man were a guest in the hotel."

"He was a guest, registered under his own name," said Vitu.

Helen Wexler caught my eye from across the room. She was talking to a member of the board of directors, an elderly, somewhat cranky gentleman from Chicago. Not likely that he was being cranky with Helen, but she lifted her eyebrows slightly as I looked her way, as if to say come rescue me. At the moment, talking to Vitu seemed more important.

"What about the man in the swimming pool?" I asked. "I discovered I knew him slightly."

Vitu stared at me, still friendly, and said, "Perhaps you could tell me about him. I understand he was going to help finance the hotel your company is considering."

"I only met him once," I said, "yesterday, the same evening, at the party. To tell the truth, I don't even know exactly what his involvement with the hotel project was."

"That is curious," said Vitu. "Most curious. I thought you would be very much in touch with such things. I find it strange that you are not."

"Why so?"

"I spoke to Mr. Wexler. He is head of your corporation?" I nodded. "I told him that the man in the pool had died under suspicious circumstances, that there had to be an investigation. He agreed and told me you, Mr. Roundtree, would act as his personal representative. That is why I find it strange that you are not, apparently, involved in the project that brings your company's board of directors to Martinique."

"Well," I said, "you see, I used to work as a lawyer for Troup-Kincaid, and I left to go to a law firm in New York." This was a small lie, but I saw no reason to tell Vitu everything.

"I came down to this meeting to do some special legal work for Mr. Wexler. I suppose he meant it as a compliment by saying I would act as his personal representative."

"I suppose he did," said Vitu, flashing that quick, gay smile. "You will excuse me for a moment."

"Wait," I said, "I wanted to ask you. What was suspicious about the man in the swimming pool?"

"He didn't drown," said Vitu. "He had a terrible bruise on the side of his head. The autopsy says that was what all but killed him. There was a little water in his lungs, not much, and it may be that the water in the pool actually stopped his breathing, but he was already dying. The blow on the head would have killed him in any case."

"He could have gotten such a blow by falling into the pool," I said.

"Yes, he could have," Vitu nodded. "It is possible."

"Do you think someone killed him?"

Vitu stopped smiling, and his tired eyes suddenly seemed very serious. "I think there is murder here somewhere," he said.

15 A Few Simple Questions

The reception was going quite well. The prefect was holding forth with champagne glass in hand and several people gathered around, including the hotel manager and, I noted with interest, the fat doctor who had come to my room the night before. Helen Wexler was talking with three men and seemed content. I didn't see Martel anywhere, or the lean Frenchman Jean.

Wexler the Senior was alone now with Medlock, no one else talking with them, so I thought it was a good chance to get to him.

"Greetings, Mr. Chairman," I said.

Medlock looked unhappy at being interrupted. Wexler looked glum too. "I saw you talking with the detective, what's his name?"

"Vitu. Lieutenant Vitu."

"He tell you what I told him?"

"That you wanted me to represent good old Troup-Kincaid in helping him investigate the dead man and Stroud."

Wexler nodded. "I thought that was best. I didn't tell him anything about the things that have worried us, or that this Stroud had paid a call on you in New York. But I thought you could use your judgment along the way in telling Vitu anything you thought might be helpful."

"That could create a mess, a can of worms," said Medlock, making a face. "It might make the police imagine sinister things."

Wexler nodded. "Maybe Medlock is right. Use your judgment, but if you think you need to tell the police anything about our problems, try to talk to me about it first."

"I'll use my judgment," I said simply, a comment which made Medlock glare disapproval.

Someone touched me on the arm. It was the hotel manager. "Lieutenant Vitu asked that I request that you join him," the manager said.

I asked where, and he said back in his office, and led me from the corner room on the mezzanine past the elevators and around another corner. His office was spacious and square, and when we entered Vitu was sitting behind the broad desk that without doubt belonged to the hotel manager. There was a smaller desk at one side of the room, presumably for a secretary, and Jean was sitting there, with the chair turned away from the desk and facing Vitu.

Martel was in an easy chair directly opposite the manager's desk. I wondered if he had chosen that position or if Vitu had asked him to sit there.

Vitu stood up when I entered and waved me to another easy chair, somewhat to the side.

"I wanted to talk to you, Mr. Roundtree," said Vitu very formally, "because I am given to understand that you represent the Troup-Kincaid corporation and are willing to offer any help that your company can offer. I asked Mr. Martel and Mr. Clamence"—and he nodded at Jean, so that now at last I knew the lean one's last name—"to have conversation with me at the same time because they both knew the deceased, Mr. Roger Pirdeaux. I understand all three of you had some contact with Mr. Pirdeaux last night, and I would be grateful if you would tell me what you could."

Vitu spoke in perfect, unaccented English, if sometimes sounding a bit formal and stilted. He didn't dress very formally, however. I couldn't swear that he was wearing the same open-neck sports shirt at that moment that he had worn at five that morning, but the resemblance was close. It was a long-sleeved shirt but with the sleeves rolled up just above the elbow.

"I can tell you everything I know very quickly, Lieutenant," I said, and Vitu nodded.

"I flew in last night and got into Martinique about 11:00 p.m. and came straight to the hotel. There was a party, a big reception, as you no doubt know, and I was introduced by one of the T-K-I board members to Mr. Martel and Mr. Clamence and Mr. Pirdeaux. We all had some general conversation for a time and then drifted in different directions. I think the last time I saw Mr. Pirdeaux he was talking to some people at another table. I had been in my room a long time before the accident."

I used the word *accident* deliberately, to see if Vitu would take me up on it. He did not.

"But you saw Mr. Pirdeaux in the swimming pool?"

"Yes," I said, "the doctor was in my room, as I'm sure you know, and we both happened to glance down from my balcony at almost the same time. The doctor hurried down to see if he could do anything, but at that time some people were already pulling the man from the pool."

Vitu asked several other questions, such as whether the dead man had been known to any other Troup-Kincaid employees. I said no, I did not think so, that as I understood it the deceased had been associated with Mr. Martel and probably would have been associated with Troup-Kincaid if the planned joint hotel venture worked out, but that my impression was that only Mr. Martel had dealt with our people directly.

Vitu glanced at Martel for confirmation, and the Frenchman nodded.

"Roger was quite a successful businessman," he said.

"He had invested in my hotel in Paris, and in another hotel I own. He planned to invest in the hotel on Martinique, and I had assured Mr. Wexler, the president of the company, that I had put together the rather sizable amount of money that my share of the hotel would require and I was counting on Pirdeaux for part of that money." Martel shrugged. "He was my friend, and I mourn him, but I must say to you too that his death has created some immediate business problems for me. I must now find additional investment capital and at once."

"It is a tragedy," Vitu said, "from any point of view. Now I don't want to keep you, but I must ask, do any of you have any reason at all to believe this could be anything other than an accidental death?"

Martel's eyebrows rose as if to indicate how incredible such a question was, but he responded mildly. "I can't imagine why anyone would want to do Roger harm."

Vitu glanced at Jean, who said much the same thing, and at me, and I repeated that no one at Troup-Kincaid had ever really had any contact with Pirdeaux while he was alive, only indirectly in terms of the hotel financing, and that I could not imagine any reason why anyone would want him dead.

"Are you saying his death was murder?" asked Martel.

"No, no," said Vitu. "It is only that it is a difficult death. He is in the swimming pool but he did not drown, but rather died from hitting his head or being hit on the head. Perhaps he is out for a walk and he falls, eh?" asked Vitu. "But why should he go for a walk, fully dressed, all by himself, more than an hour after everyone else had gone to bed?"

"Yet that is what must have happened," Jean said.

Vitu smiled, that quick, gay smile that filled his face.

"Very likely that is the way it was," he said. Then, gesturing at all of us, "You have all been helpful. I probably will not need even to take any more of your time. Thank you."

We all stood up and started out the door. "Mr. Roundtree, if I may keep you just a moment, . . ." said Vitu.

Martel and Jean left the room, and I sat down again in my chair. Vitu sighed and lit a cigarette from the pack next to his hand on the desk and was about to speak when the telephone rang.

The phone call was for Vitu, and he listened a moment and then put a hand over the receiver. "It is official business," he said apologetically. "If you don't mind, I would appreciate your waiting outside for just a minute or two."

I nodded, thinking it likely that Vitu's phone call would be all in French, and if he but knew, that was a guarantee of secrecy as far as I was concerned, but then I suppose he couldn't know that for sure.

I walked outside the manager's office and, after waiting a moment, strolled down the hall for no reason especially. It makes me impatient just to stand around. I had walked forty or fifty feet, almost to the corner turn into the main mezzanine corridor, and was starting to turn back, when I heard (and overheard) a snatch of conversation.

The first voice, I was almost sure, belonged to Arthur Hinrichs, but he was speaking with a tough intensity that I didn't normally identify with his easygoing, storytelling jovial manner.

"You damned fool," he was saying, "I warned you before, this isn't Marseilles."

"I think you are very likely right, Congressman," the other voice answered, in light mockery, with a twist on the last word. "But it isn't New Jersey either. And I warn you about something. It is good to speak with courtesy to one's friends."

The second voice was low and fading as if the two men

were moving away from me. I hesitated and stepped out around the corner.

The Congressman and the lean Frenchman were walking together, their backs to me.

But a few feet beyond them, in front of the elevators, was Martel in his beautifully tailored white suit.

I hit it just right, or just wrong. Martel was turning his head to glance toward Jean and the Congressman just as I stepped around the corner. I had only stepped a foot or so out into the corridor, just far enough to be sure I recognized the Congressman's voice and to see who was with him, and I honestly couldn't be sure that Martel's glance had moved toward me enough to see me.

But I honestly had to assume that he *had* seen me.

16 Plumbers and Policemen

Vitu was still on the telephone when I opened the door to the office again, but he gestured to me to come on back inside, and he had finished his conversation within another thirty seconds.

"So," he said. "I asked you to stay for a moment, Mr. Roundtree, to ask you to consider one more question. Is there anything else, anything at all, that you can tell me that might help in this investigation?"

I told him briefly about having seen the dead man, Roger, in the lobby of the hotel and how we had a drink and he had said he had trouble sleeping but at that time was seemingly straight on his way to bed.

"Why didn't you say this a few minutes ago when I asked you about your contact with the deceased?"

"Oh, I intended to tell you, but I thought I would wait until I could talk to you privately."

He thought about that for a moment and didn't like it much. He asked me if I had any reason to be suspicious of Mr. Martel or Mr. Clamence, and I said no, but told him I was a lawyer by profession and suspicious by nature and that my only client, so to speak, was Troup-Kincaid, which did not include the two Frenchmen who might or might not be guilty of anything. I added, as an afterthought, that if Roger's death turned out to be murder that it was only

logical to consider first the people who actually knew him,
since it is infrequent for anyone to take the trouble to
murder a stranger, and as far as I knew Martel and Clamence were the only two people on Martinique who had
actually known Roger at all.

Vitu sighed deeply and shook his head, as if to hint that
amateur detectives were only one of the many burdens he
had to bear. He asked me again if there was anything else
I knew which might aid in the investigation of the *possibility*,
with heavy emphasis on the word, that the man's death had
been something other than an accident.

"I don't think so, Lieutenant," I said, rationalizing
that, well, there was no sure tie between anything that
concerned Troup-Kincaid and Pirdeaux's death, or even
between my having had former unhappy experience with
Stroud and whatever had happened to him on Martinique.

It is unhappily easy to rationalize telling policemen
something other than the whole truth, one reason no doubt
why they tend to be such a suspicious lot.

It was Thomas Wolfe, I think, who once wrote that
people in different countries were pretty much the same if
you treated them by profession. That is, a policeman in one
place tends to be very like a policeman in another place, a
soldier in one army very like a soldier in another army, and
so on. I always thought there was truth in that about nine
times out of ten, but that in about one out of ten cases it
broke down, and all bets were off.

I had begun to figure Vitu was that one in ten, and I
couldn't make out if he were the subtle investigator or a
great fool.

"I would not try for any frivolous reasons to create
difficulties for your Troup-Kincaid," Vitu said, after a
pause, "though I will say to you, Mr. Roundtree, that I am
not a great admirer of your hotel project."

"Why not?"

"You will think I sound very simple and old-fashioned," he said. "This is a beautiful island, Martinique. Oh, it has its bloody history, but not more bloody than other beautiful parts of the world. The Carib Indians were here long ago. They called it Madizina, the Island of Flowers."

"Were your Carib Indians the first inhabitants of Martinique?" I asked.

Vitu smiled ruefully. "You might say they were the first victors. Are you, by chance, a student of archaeology?" I shook my head. "Well," said Vitu, "there was another people on Martinique called the Arawaks. We don't know much about them except through archaeology, but they apparently lived here from about the first or second century A.D. They lived here for perhaps a thousand years, and they seemingly were a very peaceful and artistic people. The Caribs came over then from the South American mainland in about the eleventh or twelfth century. They weren't very peaceful or very artistic. One might say they were almost simple-minded. But they were good warriors and they wiped out the Arawaks, killed them all, every one."

"That's a lovely story."

"Oh, never worry, the French came along in a few centuries and treated the Caribs just as ruthlessly."

There were somewhat over 300,000 people on Martinique now, I had read, most of French and West Indian descent in various mixtures, some with Negro blood from the slaves that for decades were brought to Martinique from Africa. Almost everyone spoke and understood French, though the lower class, economically, tended to speak mostly in a Creole dialect.

"I don't understand why you object to a big new hotel," I said. "Wouldn't it be good for the people who live here? Wouldn't it make for a few jobs and for new money in the economy?"

"Perhaps I am selfish," said Vitu. "Oh, there are lux-

ury hotels here already, if not one so large as your corporation wants to build. The Hilton has one. There is the Lido,
the Diamond Roc. Oh, there are many, if few are as large
as your big Miami hotels. There is the Club Mediterranee
too, where many Americans vacation.

"I don't object to tourists coming, but I wonder if
there might not one day be too many. I am selfish, perhaps.
You know my favorite relaxation?"

I shook my head.

"There is a beach only a few miles from where I live.
You know, Martinique has many beautiful beaches, and
some are covered with white sand and some with black
sand. This beach I like is one with black sand, and it is a little
difficult to reach, so usually it is almost deserted. Sometimes, in the early morning or late afternoon, there is no
one there but me. I take a book along and put on my swim
suit and go out in the water just far enough so that the water
comes to my chest. The water is mostly very still there, not
any waves of any size. I can sit there and read quietly and
after a while the small, colorful tropical fish will swim up to
me in the shallow water and try to nibble at my toes or arms
or chest. They don't bite. It's as if they are trying to be
friendly. It is the most relaxing situation."

I didn't quite know what to say to all this. I was saved
from any comment when someone knocked on the door to
the office.

It was Helen, who pushed open the door a second after
she knocked.

"I was looking for you," she said to me, ignoring Vitu.
"If we are going to tour the island, we have to hurry. They
have two or three mini-buses, but the first one has already
left."

Vitu stood up and I stood up.

"Helen, did you meet Lieutenant Vitu? Lieutenant,
this is Mrs. Wexler. I believe you talked to her father-in-
law." Helen smiled and Vitu bowed.

"Hurry along, Jim," she said, "I want to talk to you."

I remained standing after Helen closed the door, hoping that Vitu was finished with me, yet a bit curious as to why he had talked so much and so long.

"Mrs. Wexler is a very pretty lady," Vitu said, after a moment.

"She is. I understand Martinique is famous for handsome and lovely women. I can only say I agree, from the few girls I have already seen."

This seemed to please Vitu, and he smiled that quick, gay smile.

"I have a friend," he said, "who once declared the girls of Martinique are always willing and often pretty."

I laughed with him.

"My wife, however," he added, his laugh dwindling to a chuckle, "objects to that phrasing. She says we should say, 'The girls of Martinique are always pretty and sometimes willing.' "

"Your wife is from Martinique?"

"Yes," said Vitu, sighing. "It is curious. My first wife was from Martinique also, but we moved to Paris and I had a job in the civil service. After a time she was very homesick and I made application for a civil-service job here, so that she could come home. After that, we were divorced. Now, I am married to another girl who also grew up here but who lived in Paris for two years and would like nothing better than to live there again. But I do not think we will move. A visit perhaps."

I was impatient to get away now, to join Helen, and said politely, "I should go, Lieutenant. Is there anything else I can do to help?"

"There probably is," he said. "I didn't tell you about your friend Stroud, did I? He had been drugged when he came to your room."

"Drugged?"

"It was heroin, a near overdose of heroin. He almost

died, but the hospital thinks now he may live. The most curious thing, the heroin injection had apparently been made in his foot. That, you may know, is not unknown or even unusual for heroin addicts."

Something Vitu had said a moment before finally registered, and I stopped him.

"Why did you call Stroud my friend?" I asked. "He's certainly not that."

"The man killed in the swimming pool, Pirdeaux," Vitu went on. "You asked me if it couldn't have been an accident. It could have been. That blow on the head was just of a kind he might have gotten if he had had too many drinks, and his blood check showed he had had several, and then had tripped and banged his head. If it weren't for Stroud, I think the man in the pool would have been considered an accident."

"What about Stroud?"

"I said a heroin addict sometimes uses his foot, as a new unscarred place for the needle, especially when he has almost ruined the veins of his arms and legs. But Stroud was not a heroin addict. There isn't another mark on his body to indicate that he was taking heroin. Someone tried to kill him with a heroin overdose, maybe even thinking it would seem like the death of an addict, the accidental death."

Vitu stopped talking, and neither of us said anything for a minute. He was smoking his cigarette and staring at me politely, as if waiting for my observations. "You're certainly free to go," he said. "Mrs. Wexler is waiting for you."

I nodded and started for the door, but I had to ask again.

"Why did you refer to Stroud as my friend?"

Maybe Vitu had been building me up to ask the question again, but he didn't give any sign of self-satisfaction if he had.

"Just before he came up to your room," Vitu said, "he stopped at the hotel desk. He was in bad shape then, of course, hardly able to talk, but it was late at night after a big hotel reception and the desk clerk just thought he had taken too much to drink. You know what he asked the clerk?"

I shook my head, but I had a sense of foreboding that I could make a good guess.

"He asked for your room number," Vitu said. "Said he had to talk to his old friend Jim Roundtree."

17 The Empress Josephine Got the Hell Out

There were still two mini-buses waiting in the curved, covered drive directly in front of the hotel when I got to the front door. I stepped up into the door of the first one, looking for Helen, and saw her about midway down on the left. She was leaning over the seat behind her, talking to someone, but the seat next to her was empty, and I was willing to cheerfully presume that she had saved it for me.

"Helen," I said, slipping into the seat.

She'd been talking to our board member from Chicago, the cranky one, who was also sitting alone, with his briefcase and a camera with leather strap attached on the empty seat beside him.

"Hello, Mr. Baldwin," I said. He spoke but he did not seem delighted especially to see me. I didn't blame him. My arrival made Helen turn away and sit in her seat and ended that conversation.

"I thought you needed rescuing a little while ago," she said, smiling. "I am glad you escaped from the clutches of the Martinique gendarmes."

Her short, bright yellow skirt rode well up above the knee, and I started to tell her that no forty-two-year-old mother of a grown-up daughter ought to have legs like that. But I refrained. I was inordinately fond of Helen Wexler, but God knows I didn't want to flirt with her just then.

"I escaped all right," I said, maybe more grimly than I intended. I was thinking of what Vitu had told me about the heroin overdose, or near overdose, and his suspicions that Stroud himself never touched the stuff, and wondering what kind of people would do that to someone, deliberately shoot him full of enough heroin to kill him.

"Was it bad?" Helen asked, frowning. She was as pretty frowning as when smiling, her wide, candid gaze from those lovely brown intelligent eyes just as striking. It didn't make for any new lines in her face when she frowned. When she smiled, on the other hand, it creased the little faint laugh lines at the corners of her eyes.

I thought again that Helen was a self-centered lady, probably as spoiled rotten silly as anyone I'd ever met, but she certainly was nice to be around, short yellow skirt and tanned, slim legs and sensitive brown eyes, and either a smile or a frown that could make you swallow, she seemed so lovely.

"No, not bad," I said. "Vitu thinks the man who drowned in the swimming pool may have been killed on purpose, murdered, and there's a vague connection with Troup-Kincaid because the man was one of the investors putting up part of the funds for the proposed hotel on Martinique, part of the part, that is, that won't come from T-K-I."

Helen nodded, seeming satisfied.

We were driving now along a beach road on the island, the blue water on one side of the bus and a sugar-cane field on the other.

"It is beautiful," she said.

"The lieutenant told me it was called the island of flowers."

The bus was air-conditioned and the tour was very pleasant. The driver had a small microphone and every now and then would point out something or tell us how many pineapples were exported every year, or coffee, or something of the sort.

There were probably twenty people on our bus, including the Congressman and his plump, placid brunette wife.

We stayed near the coast for a while, near the blue water, with the low, rugged mountains at the north end of the island giving the view a certain character. Mount Pelée, the highest peak, was 4,700 feet above sea level, the driver said. It appeared a friendly enough mountain, with white clouds against blue sky behind it, even if the volcano had wiped out the thirty thousand inhabitants of St. Pierre years before.

That was one of the places the bus took us to, a volcanic museum at the foot of Mt. Pelée.

We didn't stay long, but it was interesting. There were half-melted clocks, all stopped at the same hour, eight o'clock, when one fine day for about three minutes of hell the thirty thousand people in St. Pierre probably tried frantically to escape. At the end of about three minutes they were all dead, except for that one survivor in his prison cell. And there was what at first seemed a big curious rock, with crazed streaks and points jutting out of it. Look at it for a while and you could see that it had once been a pile of nails, now all melted and fused together.

Helen lingered to look at one of the museum exhibits, and I moved on toward the entrance. A little volcanic rock went a long way with me.

The Congressman caught up with me and took my arm, his bright dark eyes beaming at me from behind his glasses, the sun catching the glint from the top of his balding head. He wore a red-checked sports coat over light slacks and seemed to absolutely radiate good will.

"Can you imagine it?" he said. "All those people living calmly on the side of the mountain and all swept away by a volcano, too quickly for anybody even to run for cover. It's like Pompeii. You've been to Pompeii, haven't you, Jim?"

"Years ago," I said. "The summer when I was just out of college."

"I wanted to mention something to you, Jim," the Congressman said, his voice dropping confidentially. He had the public man's habit of using your name in almost every sentence, probably so that you would be sure he knew your name. "I'm afraid you overheard a rather embarrassing conversation back at the hotel, when I was standing with Jean Clamence and you were coming out of the hotel manager's office."

That answered one question. Martel indeed had glanced around in time to see me in the corridor.

"I was having to speak a little severely to Mr. Clamence," the Congressman went on. "He is a high-spirited young man, and of course he is French, but that is no excuse for being forward with a lady. No excuse."

The Congressman hesitated. "I am afraid Clamence is almost incorrigible. He said something suggestive to my wife and earlier I saw him talking with one of the pretty waitresses at the reception, and I don't know what he said but she moved away rather quickly. He was even talking to Mrs. Wexler, and while I pray God he said nothing offensive to her, I wouldn't be surprised at what he said. It was after he said something, well, *suggestive* to my wife that I felt I must speak to him. He simply must behave himself."

"Doesn't he work for Mr. Martel? Maybe you should tell Martel to put him on a leash."

"No, no, I hope that won't be necessary, I wouldn't want to hurt the young man's career," the Congressman said. "I feel a little responsible, you know. I was in Paris last year when Medlock first talked to Martel about the hotel project. He asked me to sit in, and I've known both Martel and Jean since then."

This was something I had not known, and I wondered how it fitted in.

The bus driver was taking a small poll of the passengers when we boarded the bus again. We could visit a sugar-cane plantation a few miles further on, and cut back through a coffee-growing area on the slopes of another mountain, Le Vauclin, and then go in to Fort-de-France.

Or, he said, we could go directly into Fort-de-France right away.

Normally, the driver said, he would urge us to first visit the sugar-cane plantation and be shown around, but he understood we had to be back at the hotel by five o'clock, and that limited the time somewhat. He asked the question, he said, thinking some of the ladies especially might prefer to have more time to go shopping in Fort-de-France. And, I thought, the driver might have more time for a few quick beers.

"I've seen enough sugar cane," Helen said, and it seemed the other ladies did indeed prefer to have more time for shopping.

"The French perfume is supposed to be a good buy. It's duty free," said someone at the rear of the bus.

The driver wheeled the bus around and we started back down the road toward Fort-de-France.

I couldn't resist.

"I was speaking to the Congressman," I said. Helen cut those quick brown eyes at me and raised her eyebrows slightly.

"He was worried about one of the Frenchmen, the lean one, Jean. He said he saw him talking to you at the reception and he was afraid he might have said something . . ." I couldn't think of any other word for the moment, so I used a word the Congressman had used, ". . . well, *suggestive.*"

Helen smiled and didn't say anything.

"Did he?" I persisted.

"He said I was a very lovely woman," she said, still smiling.

"That's all?"

"And that I must be a demon in bed."

I decided I would have been just as happy if I hadn't asked the question, not only because what Helen said sort of confirmed what the Congressman had told me but because I admit I did not like the thought of lean Jean talking that way to this lady in the short yellow skirt with the tanned nice legs.

But she was still smiling about it.

"Was he rude?"

"No," she said. Helen frowned a bit. "Is it important for some reason?"

I shook my head. "Have you had any word from Bill at all?"

She shook her head now, frowning more than ever, and looking more serious than she had before. She had been flirting a little a moment before. Now she was serious in an anything but happy way.

"I tried to call him from Miami yesterday and I tried to call him from Martinique this morning."

"Where did you call him?"

"I called everywhere, home in Connecticut, his office in New York, his club, the San Francisco office. I called Susan's apartment in New York, and I didn't get Susan but I got her roommate, Kathleen, who was pretty sure that Susan hadn't heard from her father. But I left a call for Susan anyway."

"How is your darling daughter?"

Helen smiled again gently. "She is entirely too pretty, thank you, and looking too grown up. It is all very well to pretend I am her sister, but no grown woman really believes anybody believes very much of that. It would be much more conforting if Susan were still around ten or eleven."

"You wouldn't trade her, though."

"I guess not." Helen's smile drifted and she seemed troubled. I thought she was about to say something, but the bus hit a good bump about then and blasted us both half out of our seats.

"I'm worried about Bill, Jim," she said, after we had settled back again. "It isn't like him to be so completely out of touch."

I was worried too, but it wasn't my place to share what really worried me. *Where have you been, Billy Boy, Billy Boy, where have you been, Charming Billy?*

Wexler Senior thought maybe his son had been kidnapped. If necessary he'd cash in all his stock, fifty million worth, to bail Charming Billy out. But what worried me more was that a kidnapper out for money usually doesn't waste any time getting in touch. And it had now been a full three days since anyone, Wexler Senior or Helen or anyone else far as I knew, had been able to reach Bill Wexler. And nobody had yet gotten in touch about money.

Being kidnapped is serious and dangerous enough no doubt, but it is not quite as final as being dead.

We were coming into Fort-de-France, a bustling harbor town of maybe 100,000 population. Our bus driver had told us that until 1902 and the volcano eruption Fort-de-France had been the seat of government on the island but Saint Pierre had been where the wealthy planters and the social elite made their homes. After the volcano had turned Saint Pierre into a New World Pompeii, almost everything began to be centered in Fort-de-France.

There were narrow streets on the way in. The driver cut away from the direct road to the center of the city so that, he said, he could drive us through some of the old parts of the town where the houses looked as if they came from some small French village and had been plucked up and moved thousands of miles.

The buildings and houses, many of them, were three and four stories high and had iron balcony railings and heavy shutters.

"It reminds me a little of New Orleans," Helen said. "Don't you think?"

"I have a confession," I said. "I have never gotten to New Orleans."

Helen seemed shocked in a good-humored way.

We were winding our way through the close streets toward the center of the city. Here and there the driver pointed out streets and even particular shops which, he said, were modern on the inside no matter how they looked on the outside. There were nice things there, he said—French crystal and perfumes and some often fascinating local art and handicraft created on the island.

He brought us finally to a green park near the waterfront and pointed out the solid marble statue of the Empress Josephine.

Earlier, the bus had taken us by the remains of the house where Marie Josephine Rose Tascher de La Pagerie, fated to become Napoleon Bonaparte's first wife, was born. There wasn't much left of the house. It had been destroyed, we were told, by a hurricane in 1766. One small stone building, once used as a separate kitchen, survived, and it had been made into a little museum which contained among other things Josephine's wedding certificate (and also her divorce papers).

I wondered if it was any friendlier getting a divorce if you happened to be the emperor. It was probably a damned sight easier, even if more visible.

"I don't know why they make so much of Josephine," Helen whispered to me. "She was never able to give Napoleon a child, and as far as being an illustrious great citizen of Martinique . . . why, honey"—and Helen's voice fell into a syrupy imitation Southern drawl—"as soon as that child saw her chance, the Empress Josephine got the hell out of Martinique.''

The bus driver parked the mini-bus near the park. It was only a few minutes back to the hotel, he said, and he would plan to leave to take us back at just ten minutes before the hour, before five, so that would give us ample time to walk about and shop.

"Let's walk about and shop," I said to Helen. "It's our duty to support the island's economy."

The Congressman and his wife bustled off the bus ahead of us, Mr. Baldwin and his camera, and the others all scattering quickly into the narrow streets off the park.

We walked for a few minutes near the harbor. There was a pick-up volleyball game nearby, not over one hundred feet from the waterfront, and the young men batted the ball back and forth with considerable enthusiasm and occasional accuracy. There was a huge war memorial, solid and maybe twenty feet high, dedicated to those Martinique sons of France who died in World War One and World War Two.

Further away from the harbor, still in the wide green park, was a sandlot soccer game on the grass.

The sun was bright and warm but not too hot, not over eighty degrees and the blue water and the frequent shouts of the teen-age soccer players combined in a relaxing fashion. It was as if that soccer game was probably the most important thing happening anywhere at that moment. I began to suspect that it might be very, very pleasant to live on that island.

"Come on, you're daydreaming," Helen said.

She wanted to shop, at least a little, and we turned up one of the little streets away from the park.

Helen said she wanted to shop but her heart didn't really seem in it. We plunged into and out of four small shops in a matter of minutes. She would surge in, smile at the shopgirl or clerk and look all around and smile again, and want to leave. The only time she even hesitated was in one small, quite modern little shop where they sold only perfume. "The prices really are good," she said, looking at two or three different perfumes. But she didn't buy anything.

"You move too fast for me," I said, after we reeled out of the perfume shop. "Let's find a place to sit down where I can buy you a drink."

We walked another two or three blocks and found a small café with three tables outside on the sidewalk. It was not a very expensive place, the men inside at the bar were in their shirt sleeves and looked a bit rough and ready. But it was delightful, nonetheless, a place where we could sit and watch people go by.

The heavy-set moustached waiter looked admiringly at Helen's legs when he came to take our order.

I ordered a cold beer, Heineken's, and Helen considered her choice carefully. "Beer goes right to my hips," she said, and ordered a cup of black coffee instead.

"They are very nice hips."

"That's what the Frenchman said. Do you think I would be a demon in bed?"

I sighed, remembering that company reception when for no good reason Helen and I left together. My wife and I were already separated then, but Bill Wexler had been at the reception, big as life.

"I suspect there are some people who believe I already know the answer to that."

"You had your chance," Helen said good-humoredly. She suddenly put her hand out and covered mine. "I suppose you thought then you and your wife would get back together, didn't you? Do you ever see the girls?"

"I write them a letter every Friday afternoon, and I telephone at least once a week. Once a month, I go pick them up on the weekend and take them around for a day."

"How old are they now?"

"The oldest is eight. The baby is five."

"Do they understand about the divorce?"

I shrugged and sipped my beer. "We don't fight, their mother and I, not at least in front of them. Children get used to things. I'm not sure the youngest even remembers clearly that I used to live in the same house."

Helen nodded. She seemed preoccupied and somber.

18 Susan's Song

"What are you worried about?"

Helen took a long drink from her glass, then put the glass down and nibbled at the knuckle on her right thumb, as if debating earnestly with herself.

"It's Susan, my clever daughter," she said abruptly. "I'm afraid she has gotten herself into terrible trouble."

I made appropriate encouraging sounds as Helen started to tell me about it.

Susan was twenty-two years old now, close to twenty-three, so she was considered of adult age and responsible, and after some friends had helped her get out of jail on bond the police had felt no obligation to call her parents. After all, she did not live with her parents and had not lived with them for more than a year since she finished college.

Helen and Bill found out that Susan was in trouble only when a college friend of their daughter's had telephoned one night. The friend, a girl who had known Susan rather well at Smith College, suspected the exact truth, that Susan had not let her parents know anything about what had happened. "She will hate me if you tell her I called," said the friend, a bouncy girl named Cheryl, "but this is serious. She could really go to jail. She should have called you herself but I was afraid she had not. She needs the best lawyer anybody can find."

What in the world had Susan done?

Helen was edging up to that part but it came hard for her.

Susan had gotten a research job for a small magazine the summer after she got out of college. She didn't like that much and after a while, only a few months, she had quit to work as a receptionist for an insurance company. In fact, Helen said, Susan didn't really need to work very much at all. Her grandmother had left her a fair amount of money, more than one hundred thousand dollars, and while Susan couldn't use the principal until she was twenty-five she could and did draw the interest on the money. And her father persisted in sending her an allowance, even though Helen had tried to persuade him to let Susan earn her own money.

Anyway, Helen went on, Susan had tired of the job at the insurance company too and had quit that after six months and decided just not to work for a while. Her parents weren't too upset, according to Helen, because Susan had always been a level-headed girl and they thought it was just a matter of time before she would be bored without a job of some kind. Helen half-hoped that Susan might decide to go to graduate school, something she had once talked about doing.

Now was the hard part, the telling me just exactly what kind of trouble Susan was in, and Helen bit at her knuckle again. She asked me if she could have another drink and I said of course and ordered her another rum and another beer for myself.

The only way to tell it is to tell it, I prodded gently. I know, I know, Helen said, and when she started telling me the story it seemed to me that it was not embarrassment that made her hesitate but just still near disbelief that her daughter, her only chick, her level-headed Susan, could have gotten into such an insane damned mess.

Susan had been sharing an apartment with a girl she had met while working on the magazine, Helen said, and their friends, the ones Helen had met, had seemed pleasant and normal enough. Oh, the young men had hair down to their shoulders sometimes, but that had become so commonplace these days that it didn't really mean anything.

It seemed however that one of those nice young men, one that dated Susan's roommate steadily, had some sinister connections, namely to people dealing in narcotics on a big scale. The young man told them one evening that he needed money, as they all probably did, and he knew of a simple way that they could earn several thousand dollars without much work and without any risk.

It was one of those absolutely crazy things, Helen said, that people later say somehow seemed like a good idea at the time.

The plan was simple. All three of them, Susan and roommate and young man, would fly down to South America to Bogotá, Colombia, as if for a vacation. They would have reservations in a splendid hotel and would spend several days doing all the things tourists do. While they were there, someone would bring a suitcase by the room. It was an ordinary standard suitcase, very like the one that Susan had, but with a false bottom and just enough space for a few extra pounds.

"That is crazy," I muttered to Helen, but she was hardly listening. She wanted to tell me the whole story as quickly as the words would come.

It had all seemed simple and foolproof, at least the way the young man told it to Susan and the other girl. The three of them would be paid ten thousand. Susan would get five thousand, because she would actually carry the suitcase through customs, and the other two would share the other five thousand, and they would also be paid their expenses for flying to Bogotá and staying at the hotel there.

"Why was Susan the one to carry the suitcase?" I asked.

"She had been to Europe with us, and she was the only one of the three whose passport showed she had traveled to other countries. They thought that made her more believable as an American tourist, somebody who traveled a lot, and that might get her through customs quicker than the others. At least that's what they told her."

"And of course they caught her at customs."

Helen nodded angrily. "Of course. It sounded so well organized, the flying to Bogotá and all that, and the special suitcase. Except it just didn't work. Susan told me that when they opened up the suitcase they didn't even have to find the secret compartment. They knew at once. One customs official called another one over, and they both stood over the suitcase and started sniffing the air. 'Cocaine,' one of them said, and they took the suitcase apart until they found the false bottom."

Helen's little horror story didn't shock me. I'd heard others like it. Young Susan was lucky in one thing, that she had been caught coming into the United States, rather than in another country. What were the figures he'd seen recently? That there were more than nine hundred American citizens now serving time in foreign jails on drug charges of some kind, most of them probably near Susan's age.

"How much cocaine was involved?"

"I can't remember how many pounds. It was pure cocaine. There was enough so that *The New York Times* carried a brief story. The police said by the time it was diluted and sold on the street it would bring more than one million dollars.

"Good God," I said, thinking that Susan had found herself some wonderful friends in New York.

Helen told me the next part of the story a little defiantly, as if she were sensitive about it. Susan had been scared, not certain what to do after being arrested, but the federal agents and police had urged her to cooperate. They had treated her very politely, in fact, Helen said, and they warned her repeatedly what serious trouble she was in but they also noted that she had never been arrested before, and they said to her quite candidly that since she was young and attractive and had no previous record any judge would probably tend to go easy on her *if,* they said, it was clear that she had cooperated with the authorities after being arrested.

So, Susan had led the police to her roommate and the young man and told them what she remembered of the names he had mentioned in talking about making the Bogotá arrangement.

"She was right to cooperate. If I had been her lawyer, I would have told her to do exactly that."

Helen looked at me doubtfully. "You don't think it was wrong of her to bring her friends into it after she was caught?"

I shook my head. "They're the ones who brought her into it in the first place," I said. "They didn't prove to be such outstanding friends, in my judgment."

Helen agreed, but she said that part of it had worried Susan, that she was betraying other people to partially save her own neck. For she was far from out of the woods yet, Helen said. The authorities were pleased that she had cooperated and would say so in court. But Susan still faced trial, and their attorney had told them frankly that the general public concern about cracking down on narcotics and the undeniable fact that more than one million in cocaine was involved made this a much more visible case than, say, a group of college students arrested for possession of marihuana, or even someone arrested in precisely the same kind of situation as Susan but without that dramatic one-million figure involved.

"The case won't come up for several more weeks, but it will be a miracle if Susan doesn't go to jail, at least for a time."

Helen's voice trailed off. She was upset and I couldn't think of much to say in a comforting fashion. I tried to remember exactly what young Susan looked like. I'd met her two or three times, and she was slim and pretty like her mother but with light brown hair instead of Helen's glossy black. I could remember her face and smile and, I thought, a certain restless quality. Or was that sense of restlessness only something that occurred to me now? After I knew that Susan had acted the young adventuress and used bad judgment and might even go to jail?

Helen seemed to run out of conversation after she told me about her daughter. We finished our drinks and I got the check, thinking that we needed to begin walking back to the bus if we weren't to be left behind in Fort-de-France. Not that it really made much difference. There were taxis lined up at one side of the green park, and the hotel was only a short ride away.

"Helen, I know you must have already gotten good attorneys," I said, leaving unspoken the thought that she and Bill could afford the best lawyers around, "but you know I'll be glad to help if you need me, any way I can."

"I'll need you in less than an hour," she said, as we started to stroll back toward the bus. She suddenly seemed perky again, cheerful. She put her hand on my arm and gave me that perfect, dazzling smile. "Bill and I are officially hosting a cocktail party in just over an hour. God only knows when he'll get in. You can help me play hostess if Bill isn't at the hotel when we get back."

"Sure," I said. But now there was something else troubling me. I decided to take a shot. Why not? Helen had been frank about Susan's trouble.

"You know where Bill is, don't you Helen?"

She stopped walking and turned and stared at me. For an instant I thought there was a touch of panic in her eyes but she smiled again slightly, perfectly in control, and asked quietly, "Why in the world do you say that?"

"You aren't worried enough. Wexler the Senior, your father-in-law, is scared to death. You had to feel it yesterday in Miami, when he was pressing you to try on the phone to reach Bill. This is a full day later, and Wexler the older still hasn't been able to find his son. He's more worried than ever. But you aren't. You're worried about your daughter, but you aren't really worried about Bill, so that makes me think you know where he is."

Helen thought about what I had said for a moment or two. We started walking again but she did not put her hand again on my arm.

"You're right in a way," she said carefully. "I think I know where Bill is, and I don't think there is any reason to worry about him. I'm sure he's fine."

I sighed, since Helen had confirmed my guess, but what she told me didn't really help anything. All right, so Bill was maybe off on some kind of mission or trip or whatever, and Helen knew enough about it not to be worried, and the most likely explanation was that it was something personal and private or that it was simply something he didn't want his father to know about, and that's why he was hard to reach.

All this added up to not very much, since I had been operating on the theory that Wexler the Senior was at least semi-right, that even if Bill Wexler hadn't been actually kidnapped, at least on any basis, his absence had something to do with the strange things that had been happening that involved Troup-Kincaid. I suddenly thought, almost wistfully, of Lieutenant Vitu, who, damn it, after all hired out for a living to investigate things, and I wondered what he would make of the dead ducks sent to members of the board

or the garbage and dog shit on the uncluttered desks or a
man named Cornelius Martin who may—or may not—have
been deliberately killed in a car crash in California.

Vitu's deep brown face, the shrewd tired eyes, and the
light, gay smile that sometimes flared unexpectedly when
you talked to the man all came to me in the mind's eye. I
had told Wexler the Senior and Medlock both that I would
use my judgment in talking to Vitu. My judgment, I decided, was that I wanted to talk to him in frankness soon.

I had another thought.

"Helen, wait a minute." She stopped. I had stopped a
split second before, and when she turned that bright yellow
skirt whipped around with her. Those tanned legs would
drive me wild yet.

"I was just thinking of something I wanted to tell you,"
she said.

"Can it wait a moment or two?" She nodded and I took
her arm and guided her into the small shop we were just
passing. It was a tobacco shop but it also had a public
telephone sign outside. There was a pretty West Indian girl
behind the counter, leaning over it with her perfect face
resting on her two folded hands as she propped up on her
elbows. There were three young men, teen-agers really
. . . the girl herself looked no more than sixteen or seven-
teen . . . all standing in the small shop talking to her. I didn't
blame them.

It was a small, cramped little shop, and Helen stood
just outside the doorway, looking puzzled.

"I want half a dozen cigars, long thin ones," I said to
Helen. "Why don't you negotiate for my cigars while I
make a telephone call?"

I asked the girl if I could use the telephone and she
nodded.

It took a minute or two to get an operator who spoke

English. The first one did but with a French accent I had trouble understanding, but in a moment or three she got me an overseas operator.

I didn't really think it could be so quick. I thought you had to reserve a circuit or something, as you do sometimes in making a call from New York to London or Paris or Tel Aviv, or wherever overseas, place the call, and then wait until the operator could call you back with the happy news that you had gotten through, often at a prearranged time.

My hasty thought really had been to put in a call to Hank and tell the overseas operator that I would be back at the hotel within half an hour and to let the call be completed to my room there. But no, the operator assured me, it was not necessary to wait, not always at least, she added quickly. If I wanted to hold on, she could try the circuits to New York at once and if a circuit was free it would be possible to complete the call right away.

I said that was wonderful, though I was doubtful about it all. I said in that case I would have to make the call collect but could she please try?

It was amazing. There was a circuit, and the operator got through to the law firm and Hank was actually there, available and ready to talk to me.

"Good to hear from you," he said. "I was going to call you."

"Let me talk first," I said. I fished out the piece of paper and gave him the names and told him what I needed and that it had to be sooner than soon, and he promised. I told him too what I had begun to suspect and in passing exactly what had happened on Martinique already, specifically with Stroud and with the late lamented Frenchman, Roger.

"Be careful for God's sake," Hank said grimly. I allowed as how I thought that was a fine idea. "There's one thing I have to tell you," he went on. "You won't like it much."

I waited, and it took Hank a minute or two to explain what he had done in checking out Stroud, using just the name and the rental-car record. It was routine, in a way, but he had hit something and then checked further and he knew that what he had found was not something I would want to hear.

"That can't be right," I said, a little desperately, when he finally got it out. Hank didn't say anything. He knew that I knew he wouldn't tell me such a thing unless he had checked it and rechecked it.

"Be careful," he repeated, and promised to call as soon as he could dig up the other information I wanted.

Helen had negotiated a handsome half dozen cigars for me by the time I got off the telephone, and I paid the young lady behind the counter mechanically, my mind unable to focus on anything except what Hank had told me.

"You know what I think?" Helen asked as we neared the bus that would take us back to the hotel. "You know what I think is really important, what people really remember and care about?"

"Old dogs, and children, and watermelon wine," I said.

Helen looked at me blankly. She was as beautiful as a goddess, but a goddess can have limitations, such as not listening to Tom T. Hall songs.

"It's a line from a song," I said.

She shook her head politely. "I was thinking while you were on the telephone that there are only two things important really to anybody in the long run."

"In the long run we're all dead," I said.

Helen paid no attention. "Making love and children," she said. "Those are the two things." She had taken my arm again as we almost reached the bus and she looked at me and smiled. "Don't you think?"

"You mean," I said, playing along, "that you would dismiss all art and politics and science and philosophy and history in favor of screwing and youngsters."

"Most days," Helen said, grinning like . . . what? . . . that proverbial Cheshire cat. "Wouldn't you?"

I had no ready answer but I had to grin back.

19 How the Money Talks

"You are a traitor, a back-stabber," roared Medlock, almost as soon as he saw me.

It was a subdued roar but subdued only because there were other people in the room, certainly not from any sense of courtesy to me. Medlock was dressed in what I would call one of his more modish creations, a white . . . how to describe it . . . kind of White Hunter's outfit. You know, the kind people probably really wear on safaris but which have been taken over as style by designers who charge people like Medlock a solid chunk of cash for an expensive modified version to wear in unlikely places, such as to a board meeting of Troup-Kincaid directors on Martinique.

In addition to the white White Hunter garb, Medlock had a bright red ascot around his neck, seeking a touch of color, no doubt.

He had descended on me as soon as I walked into the room.

"Traitor," he hissed a second time, when I hesitated.

"What in hell are you talking about?" I demanded.

His lowered voice was presumably because most of the members of the board, including Wexler the Senior, were in the large conference room. I have no doubt he would have yelled at the top of his voice had they not been nearby.

What he was talking about, Medlock explained, in

terse outraged tones, every word vibrating, was that I had
promised to keep him informed of whatever was going on
that he needed to know, and I was a hypocrite and a de-
ceiver because I was not doing so. First, I had failed to let
him know at once about Stroud and the Frenchman who
drowned or was hit over the head or whatever the police
might finally decide.

"Didn't want to wake you up that time of night," I
interrupted mildly.

Second, he persisted, he had just learned that I had
actually talked to the Frenchman in the hotel lobby when
he was on his way to his room, that I had told as much to
the police lieutenant—what was his name? Vidal—and that
I might even have been the last person, last *known* person
at least, to have seen the man alive.

"His name is Vitu," I said.

And I had told Medlock none of this, he plunged on,
and what kind of game did I think I was playing?

I sighed and looked Medlock in the eye. I was a little
taller, so it was with pleasure that I could look slightly down
at him. "Fuck you, Harrison Medlock, oh high corporate
executive," I said to him with feeling and sincerity.

His face got incredibly red in an instant, and I thought
he might roar some more, this time without bothering to
subdue his outrage and irritation at all. But no, after a short
bout of heavy breathing and a fierce stare he turned
abruptly and walked away from me. Hank might make fun
of my handball and weight lifting but it had the small advantage sometimes of giving a man pause before he decided to
try to punch you smack in the nose.

The meeting of the board of directors was getting
underway.

Wexler the Senior was down at one end of the table.
Medlock took a seat away from the table, on a chair against
one wall. All the directors were gathered around the long

table itself, and there was room for Medlock but he was probably still too mad even to want to sit at the table. Pettigrew was in the room, and there were half a dozen other T-K-I staff members from one department or the other there.

Henry Winston was sitting at the table, just to Wexler's left. He caught my eye and nodded. I nodded back, trying to guess what Henry Winston was really like.

The only surprise was that Martel was in the room too, big as life, sitting to Wexler's right.

Wexler had his black cigar case on the table before him, and a cigar in his right hand, though it was not lit. He looked serious, even glum, but it was hard to tell with him. He had as good a poker face as I'd ever seen on a man and seemed now only intent, patiently, on watching everybody get settled around the table.

"As is our custom, this is only a preliminary session," Wexler the Senior began. "I think you all have copies of the general agenda." He held up a copy, which looked from a distance like the memo Henry Winston had given me. "There are several additional reports, all stacked over here." Wexler gestured at a long, narrow table against one wall. There were four high stacks of papers.

"This is our initial session and, as you know, it usually lasts only long enough to hand out the reports," Wexler went on, "but today I have taken the liberty to ask Mr. Martel to sit in with us. You have a memo already about the hotel we may build on Martinique, in cooperation and partnership with Mr. Martel and his associates. My son Bill had planned . . ." Here Wexler broke off and started to cough, and I thought for a second that his emotions had gotten away with him. But no, he continued blandly when the coughing subsided.

"Bill, incidentally, was delayed a little and was not able to get here for this initial meeting, but he will of course be

at the more comprehensive board meeting in the morning."
I would have wagered money on that note that the old
pirate was bluffing, that he still had no idea where Bill was,
but it was a fine performance. "In any case, Bill had planned
to introduce Mr. Martel to you. I know some of you have
already met him but perhaps everyone has not yet had the
opportunity . . . and in light of our hotel project here I am
sure you will all want to get to know him well."

Martel, looking splendid in a white suit, probably a
different one than he'd worn the evening before, sat next
to Wexler with a long, yellow legal pad in front of him. He
nodded appreciatively at the good chairman's introduction
and started to speak.

"It ought to be noted, I think," interrupted a voice,
"that this hotel proposal would commit the corporation to
an investment of more than twenty million, at a time when
there seems the chance of a new credit crunch, and I think
it is certainly a commitment this board of directors will want
to consider carefully. I don't think it should be implied that
such a commitment has already been made."

It was Medlock talking, in that smooth baritone voice,
and I had to admire the son-of-a-bitch. He was angry,
maybe still at me for all I know, but he was tough and
perfectly willing to take on the chairman of the board if
need be. I had always suspected that was what Wexler the
older liked about him.

Wexler the Senior flushed a trifle and started to answer
and was interrupted in his turn, this time by Martel.

"That is certainly true, and it is important to say," said
Martel, turning half around in his chair to smile that gentle
ironic smile at Medlock. "It is the reason, I think, that my
friend Bill Wexler wanted me to be with you even at this
preliminary board meeting. For me, this hotel project is
probably in a relative sense bigger than for you, though my
friends and I will finance only about one-third of the thirty
million in cost. Yet, there is an advantage for you in that.

It means that my associates and I will work very hard at making the hotel succeed in every way."

Martel paused, and one of the board members, one of the two representing our banking friends, leaned forward. "You do understand, Mr. Martel," he said, "that the possible credit crunch mentioned by Mr. Medlock is an important concern for us. There are companies, and I think every member of this board could name a couple, which seemed to be doing very well financially several years ago and found themselves in great difficulties when interest rates went up and credit became more difficult to obtain. Troup-Kincaid is a large corporation but it is possible for anyone to become overcommitted. Frankly, the initial research report that indicates this proposed hotel might not really generate any income for the first five years concerns me."

Martel nodded briskly. "It concerns me too," he said. "I do not agree with your research report."

Both Medlock and the board member started to make some comment. Martel silenced them both with a friendly wave of the hand and a continuing flow of words. "No, no, it concerns me too," he said. "My associates and I have talked about it, and we wanted to suggest two things to you. First, we are willing to up our investment to an even fifty percent, so that we will put up roughly fifteen million, rather than ten million. Second, we are confident that the hotel will begin showing a substantial profit by the end of the three years."

"That's not what the projections say." This from Medlock.

"We are so confident, indeed," Martel went on, "that we have a new proposal. If at the end of three years, the hotel is not already making enough money to cover all expenses and also service the debt still outstanding, at least the interest on the debt, then we on our side will shoulder your share of the interest payments. Is that not fair?"

Martel smiled that gentle, ironic smile and the proposal seemed generous enough so that even Medlock had nothing to say.

"We'll talk about it all at length in the morning," said Wexler the older. He stood up and pointed at the table where the reports were stacked. "Everybody help themselves. I'd suggest dropping them by your room before the reception starts." He glanced at his watch. "You've got just about time."

Martel looked around the table, good-humored and friendly, as if hoping for someone to ask a question. No one did and he stood up too and everyone began milling around, most waiting their turn to get a chance to gather up copies of the research reports on the long table.

"Gentlemen, I must apologize for coming so late. I was afraid for a time that I might miss my own reception."

It was Bill Wexler, standing suddenly in the door of the conference room, wearing a summer light suit, his sandy hair burned lighter than usual with tennis and golf and swimming in the summer sun, a cigarette at one corner of his mouth in typical fashion. The younger Wexler was taller and blonder and thinner than his father, but the heavy jaw was there and the set of the eyes, and his voice sounded just a little, in rhythm and tone, like that of Wexler Senior, who now incidentally came abruptly to life.

"Where the hell have you been?" he demanded.

Martel turned and took one step toward Bill. "My old friend," he said. "We were talking about you a second ago."

"Where am I usually?" Bill asked his father, ignoring Martel. "Where but about my father's business?" He looked around the conference room, taking it all in. His eyes didn't pause when they met mine but I had the feeling that he was taking due note of everyone there.

"This is a thirsty crowd. I can tell by the whites of your eyes," he said.

Most of the members of the board spoke to Bill casually, in between picking up copies of the reports. After all, they came from Chicago and Houston and Detroit and other cities and as far as they were concerned it was routine for Bill Wexler to be there, not unusual even for him to be a little late. But there were three of us watching Bill closely, listening to his every word with care. Wexler the Senior was not one of the three. After his initial reaction he seemed to relax and lit a cigar and had gotten into conversation down at his end of the table with Pettigrew and a board member.

Henry Winston still sat next to Wexler the older but his pale eyes and thin, angular face focused with immense concentration on Bill, as if the answer to a puzzle were somewhere about and the right clue might turn up at any second. I watched Bill with probably the same kind of stare. So did Martel.

"Bill, my good friend, it is good that you are here," said Martel, moving in closer. It occurred to me that good friends don't keep saying, in those words, what good friends they are. Yet Bill nodded at him, cool and courteous, but then that was his normal style, and they shook hands.

"Let's have a drink, Jim. I want to talk to you," said Henry Winston. I looked at Henry, that graying white hair and thin patrician face, clear eyes. He looked like a U.S. Senator ought to look, one who had earned a bedrock reputation for integrity over decades. I had thought of him that way until that afternoon when I talked to Hank on the little phone in the Fort-de-France tobacco shop. Hank was right, I didn't much like what he had told me, and standing talking to Henry Winston was painful. I smiled and pretended we were the same, friends despite the difference in ages, but if Henry wasn't the man I thought him . . . why, then he was someone else, a stranger.

It was painful, as if I had lost someone by death, a

friend maybe that I'd seen only the day before and expected to meet that weekend for a tennis game and then learned that he was dead and there would never be any more tennis games. Henry Winston, the stranger, smiled at me.

"Let's get a drink, Colonel," I said, patting him on the shoulder in friendly fashion.

20 A Friendly Little Gathering

Gambling is perfectly legal on Martinique, if you have the proper licenses and permissions, and the hotel had built its casino in the basement floor level beneath the lobby. It was lavish and plush enough, in a modest way, running to the color of good wood in the panels around the room, rich red carpet, and a long, comfortable bar at one side of the room.

Bill Wexler had apparently made arrangements to take the casino over during the cocktail hour that day. There was a gentleman dressed in a tuxedo just outside the casino entrance asking people politely if they were there for the Troup-Kincaid private party. If this produced a blank expression, he turned people away. I heard him say to one couple, probably Americans, that the casino would be open again as usual at ten o'clock that night. One rather stooped, elderly gentleman made inquiry and was told presumably the same thing in another language, in German, and he frowned a lot as he turned and retreated back toward the elevator. Maybe ten o'clock was past his bedtime.

I had dutifully gone by my room, as the worthy chairman of the board suggested, to drop off my copies of reports. The one about the hotel was thirty-three pages long, I noted, glancing at the back page.

I did another thing since I was in the room, called the operator and explained that I would be at the Troup-

Kincaid reception and that I would like to be contacted there if I had an overseas call. I didn't really expect Hank to call me back as swiftly as that but it did no harm to make sure that he could get to me if he did, just in case.

Bill and Helen Wexler were already playing host and hostess, standing just inside the door, not exactly in a receiving line but close enough to greet every newcomer. Helen had changed clothes and was wearing a light summer cocktail dress, one that showed off her round, perfect tanned shoulders and which was cut low enough not really to be daring but to hint at white perfect breasts, not often touched by the sun.

The two of them, Bill and Helen, looked like rich summer people in an F. Scott Fitzgerald short story.

I saw Henry Winston bearing down on me and moved closer to speak to Helen.

"You said he'd show up," I said, "even if his father had me worried."

"Hello, Jim," Helen said. Bill gave me a neutral smile and we shook hands. I remembered the night when I had walked out of another reception with his wife, Helen, at my side. It occurred to me that this was the first time I had seen Bill since then, not because of avoiding each other but because I had had my fight with Medlock and cleaned out my desk at Troup-Kincaid the very next day, and I suppose it had not been likely in any case under the circumstances that either Bill or I would pick up the phone and call the other for a friendly chat.

"I understand dad was worried," he said, smiling thinly. "I only got a chance to talk with him for a minute after the board meeting just now, but he mentioned you and seemed to be saying you were intended to be part of the rescue squad."

Henry Winston had joined our little circle. "You don't look like you need much rescuing to me," he said. Bill gave him a careful, neutral smile too. "No, I'm fine," Bill said, "but excuse me a minute. I've got to talk to two people, and I see them standing together right now. Two birds with one stone. Excuse me."

Bill moved away from us, and I kept my eye on him while pretending not to, as I think both Henry and Helen did, while he walked over to where Harrison Medlock and Wexler the Senior were talking earnestly just beyond the first roulette table.

When I turned, I discovered I had almost lost Winston and Helen. They had moved half a step away and were carrying on their own low-voiced earnest conversation. Henry in his aging years seems as tall and thin as a knife blade and was bending down to whisper something to Helen, his face serious.

"It hardly matters now," she said in a louder tone, shaking her head.

"Oh, it matters very much," Henry said. "Everything matters, Helen." Of the two, he seemed much more relaxed, but those keen eyes were intent on her face. I knew Henry well enough, though I now believed him a near stranger, to know when something concerned him. His eyes were trying to read Helen's face in the way I had seen him once or twice in court, when a witness whose testimony might decide the case in either direction first took the stand.

"Come, Jim," Henry said. "I've hardly seen you. Walk over to the bar with me. Helen, I'll get you a drink," he said.

She shook her head. "I think I'll speak to Mr. Martel," she said. "You know, a hostess's work is never done."

She offered that dazzling smile in parting, with I thought special affection toward Henry. Or was it special malice? He did not respond, peering after her gravely as she walked away.

"I wish she wouldn't do that," he said, almost muttering to himself.

"Do what?"

"Talk to Martel." Henry came to himself. "Oh, you

know Helen, Jim. Martel is rich and a handsome Frenchman. She'll flirt with him enough to leave at least half the wives of our board members with something to think about, and don't think some of them won't mention it to their husbands, who will then mention it to me. Let's get that drink."

The bar on one side of the game room was doing good business. So were the two roulette tables and the dice and blackjack games. The manager of the casino was a striking figure, a great big heavy man who resembled Sidney Greenstreet, except for possessing a bushy gray moustache. He was outgoing and full of humor and, at some point a little earlier, he had gotten everyone's attention long enough to explain that the regular casino cashier would issue one thousand dollars' worth of chips to every guest of Mr. and Mrs. Wexler. Oh, it wouldn't be treated as real money, he said, but there was a chance for one person to win a lot of money. Everyone could play roulette wheels or whatever with their chips and in exactly one hour everyone would be asked to turn in their chips. The big winner at the end of the hour, whoever it was, could keep his or her winning pile of chips and either cash them in or use them for gambling later. Somehow, this chance to win maybe thousands of dollars at no risk excited the ladies much more than the men. Most of the women present were making bets and giving an occasional squeal when fortune smiled. Most of the men stood against the long bar, several holding their handful of unused gambling chips.

Neither Henry nor I had yet bothered to pick up our chips, and at the moment I much preferred the drink and straight talk from Henry Winston.

"Henry, you haven't been telling me the truth," I started, in not very subtle fashion. There wasn't any way to be subtle with the fact that Henry had lied to me about something critical, and I had given it some thought and decided that I really didn't have enough pieces of information that fitted together, in the right holes and squares, to waste time trying to cross-examine Winston in casual fashion. Aside from which, I suspected that at his advanced age he was still too canny a lawyer to let me slip up on his blind side about much of anything.

He didn't seem surprised at what I said. "What particular truth is it that you think I've not shared with you?" he asked.

"This man Stroud, the alleged insurance investigator who came calling on me. He's an old friend of yours, isn't he?" Henry smiled blandly, warily.

"That doesn't seem likely, does it?"

I shook my head. "No, it doesn't." Then I went on and related to him exactly what I felt sure I knew to be true, what Hank had told me on the telephone. Hank has a very thorough mind, and though I am sure he assumed what I assumed, that a man coming to my home and pushing me around and threatening me probably wouldn't use his right name, he decided to be sure. Stroud had said he was an insurance investigator. All right, Hank had gotten a friend at the State Insurance Commissioner's office to check lists of claims adjustors and to make a couple of telephone calls to get some other people to check some other lists.

Sure enough, he found a man named Stroud. He then found that he couldn't reach the man by telephone, that the man had also worked as a detective, a private investigator, and that his general height and weight and physical appearance matched the description I had given Hank.

What else?

Well, at this point, Hank had gotten someone to read him Stroud's license application when he sought a private investigator's license. It listed Stroud's background, including eight years as a police detective and two years as an investigator for a congressional committee.

"Your lawyer friend must have a very good eye," Henry said, as if admiring in an academic way.

Hank was sharp, I acknowledged, and when he saw the

congressional committee stint listed in Stroud's background it rang a small, slight bell, not much of one, and he puzzled over it at first, but Hank's memory was phenomenal. He recalled my talking to him about Henry Winston's service in Washington once, really probably in the context of repeating to Hank one of Winston's funny stories about the remarkable twists and turns of Washington nonsense.

One I had always liked was about a most distinguished U.S. Senator given to sipping a little bourbon with the then-majority leader late in the afternoon who, once while driving home, drove his car somehow up on the median of a street with a median just about the width of the bottom of his car. He got his car hung up on it somehow and was driving slowly down the median when the police stopped him. "Officer," he declared, "holding out his car keys. I am a drunk United States Senator. But if you will just get me home, I promise you I will never drive a car again." The officer took the Senator home and, sure enough, from that day on, even though his bourbon consumption lessened in his later years, the Senator had a staff member pick him up in the morning and drive him home in the evening.

There was probably no connection, Hank thought, but he would check it, and guess what? Turned out, Henry Winston had been chief counsel for the very congressional committee for which Stroud had worked as an investigator.

"Do you deny you know him?" I asked Winston.

"No, no, of course not," he said, leaning one finger along the bridge of his nose. Winston peered at me and considered, seeming . . . what? not worried but uncertain. That made him seem more of a stranger to me than ever.

When he didn't say anything else after another moment, I turned away. "Ah, Henry, Henry," I said.

He reached and held me by the shoulder. "Jim, I never meant to keep any truth from you. Sometimes there are hard choices."

I pulled away without replying. Winston was trying to

be reassuring and evasive at the same time. What was clear to me was that he'd been less than honest with me, when he was probably the one person with Troup-Kincaid that I would have trusted regardless.

It was a good party, I suppose. Too many people were smoking for my taste, myself included, with one of the thin cigars I had bought in Fort-de-France, but the air-conditioning was good and kept the air in the room reasonably clear.

I got another drink, half guessing that Henry might follow me with some effort at explanation. But he left me alone.

I felt very alone. I had glimpsed Helen Wexler talking with Martel but he was talking to someone else now, and she was standing with her husband and several other people. They all seemed cheerful.

There were some more announcements, also from the casino manager, the Sidney Greenstreet with a moustache. There were only twenty minutes to go for people to place their bets and try to win. Bill Wexler had an announcement. After the cocktail hour, there would be dinner in the main dining room. Afterward, there was a cock fight and taxis would be available from 9:00 P.M. on to take people there and later back to the hotel.

Wexler the Senior was talking with some people, but he broke away as I watched, chuckling about something, and started toward the bar with his empty glass. I intercepted him.

"What do you think?" I said, planting myself directly in front of him.

He frowned at me. "About what, son?" he said. He was in control and didn't even slur his words, but I think he was a little drunk.

"Your son Bill," I said. "He wasn't kidnapped, apparently. It won't take any fifty million to get him back."

He frowned some more. "You're right." He looked at me hard. "Don't you think tomorrow might be a better time to have this conversation?" He shrugged and glanced around us. "More privacy?"

I started to say something else, then shrugged myself. It was so obvious Wexler the Older didn't want to talk to me at all. His vague expression almost indicated that he couldn't quite remember who I was, though I was damn sure he did.

Wexler left me, and having nothing else to do I walked over to the cashier and asked for my one thousand dollars of phony money chips. He stared at me politely, making sure in his own mind that I hadn't already picked up such chips, then pushed them over and glanced at his wristwatch. "There isn't much time," he said, "no more than fifteen minutes."

"That's time enough to lose," I told him.

I put one hundred dollars on the red and won, by God, and someone tapped me on the shoulder. It was a bellhop, who gestured back over his shoulder in an indefinite direction. "They said you are Mr. Roundtree?"

I admitted it, and he told me that I was wanted on the telephone and that, if I wanted, I could take the call on the house telephone at the far corner of the room. I said I wanted, my heart literally starting to beat faster. It had to be from Hank, and I hurried to pick up the house telephone and identified myself to the operator and told her to put my call on that line.

"Mr. Roundtree, I need to ask you a question," the voice said.

It was Vitu, the police lieutenant, who I had learned after talking to him worked with the sturdy gendarmes of Schoelcher town, which I knew because I asked the hotel manager to explain to me how law enforcement worked on Martinique and how, say, a murder at the hotel might be investigated. That question had gotten his attention. The gendarmes of Schoelcher town would deal with any immediate law-and-order crises, he told me, meanwhile alerting the district attorney, who on the spot would deliver what he called a "rogatory commission" to the chief of the Judicial Police Officials, who would start the investigation.

"You notice that the district attorney belongs to the Ministry of Justice, that this is to say of the French government," the hotel man told me, as if that explained everything, and I had decided at that point, despite my own lawyerlike interest, I would simply assume that Lieutenant Vitu had the appropriate authority to do whatever he needed to do. If anybody tried to put me, me personally, in jail I might have to research the process of law enforcement on Martinique more thoroughly.

"Ask any question you want, Lieutenant Vitu," I said on the telephone.

He was glad I felt that way, the lieutenant said, because it seemed now that the man Stroud might not die after all, despite the near overdose of heroin, and it was likely that he would be able to talk with the police, namely with Vitu, the next morning. And, he said, frankly, the one thing nagged at him, that Stroud had asked for my room number at the hotel desk before staggering upstairs to knock on my door. I had told him how we had been on the same plane flying into Martinique, Vitu added delicately, and that probably was the explanation, that somehow Stroud had seen my name while we were both on the plane, and that when stricken by whatever or whomever had stricken him he had remembered me, a fellow American, and had in the last stages of consciousness tried to get to someone he knew, if only by name, to seek help.

But, Vitu concluded, since he might be able to interview Stroud at the hospital in the morning, he thought he would call me and ask again if I could remember anything else that might be helpful.

All of which, translated, meant that Vitu didn't believe a word I'd said about having no other contact with Stroud than seeing him vaguely on the airplane and he was trying to give me one more chance to come clean. Vitu was good, I decided. That is, nothing he said even hinted that I had not told him the truth, or that he would make any attempt to pressure me. Of course, a lawyer's mind is a cynical one sometimes, and I thought that just maybe if I wasn't part of a company thinking about building a new luxury hotel on Martinique, one the prefect of the island had praised highly the day before, just maybe Vitu might not have been quite so delicate.

I sighed. I had told Wexler Senior and Medlock that I would use my judgment about confiding in Vitu. I used it at that moment and started to talk. I didn't go into all the details but I told Vitu something of my background with Troup-Kincaid and how I had been hired again on short notice and how Stroud had come calling on me in New York and seemed somehow clearly involved in whatever might be going on.

"I am glad you are frank," Vitu said, apparently without irony, evidencing no surprise at all. He asked me a question or two and said that what I had told him made him think more than ever that Stroud had something to do with the death of the Frenchman in the swimming pool. It was coincidence enough that the two things happened the same night, both unusual, but both men obviously had ties to Troup-Kincaid, though it was not yet clear what Stroud's ties meant.

Vitu asked me a favor. What if I made a point of telling several people at the reception that Stroud was alive and would be questioned by police in the morning? Maybe it would make someone nervous.

I told him I would. He gave me two telephone numbers and asked me to call him later that evening if I heard or saw anything that seemed significant.

21 Spreading the Good Word

The Congressman Arthur Hinrichs was standing by one roulette table, seeming sunk into intense thought and concentration.

He brightened when I walked over to him.

"Jim, see what you think of this," he said. His plump wife was beside him, wagering a ten-dollar chip on either red or black with each twirl of the roulette wheel. Judging from the size of her little pile of chips, she was holding her own fairly well but not winning much.

The Congressman had taken his chips in one hundred-dollar tokens as I had, I noted. Why not be a big plunger when it's all on the house?

"I've been trying to figure the odds," he whispered to me. "My wife"—and he gestured with a slight nod of his head—"is doing what most people are doing, trying carefully to build up winnings. But let me tell you my plan."

The Congressman's theory was, he told me, that he would pick one number on the roulette table and then wager two hundred dollars per shot on the same number five times. He could lose everything, of course, but if he hit on any of the five tries he'd win at thirty-six to one odds and end up with seventy-two hundred dollars in chips. That might be more than anybody else would end up with, barring some real plunger putting five hundred or the whole

thousand dollars on a number and then being struck blind
with luck.

"I've almost a one in seven chance of hitting," he said.
"What do you think?"

The Congressman had gotten a little sun that afternoon
and his already tanned balding head looked healthy. His
quick, alert eyes behind those glasses seemed so intent,
pleading for my opinion of his little Mickey Mouse gambling scheme, that it almost made me smile at him.

Lord knows Hinrichs already had plenty of money.
Even if he hit the number and then got to keep seven
thousand dollars in real cash the money couldn't mean that
much to him. He was just calculating the odds, trying to
think of a way to beat the system of the little parlor game
someone had devised for our cocktail-hour amusement.
After all, as the world wags, at that moment it was the only
game in town.

"What do you think?" he persisted.

I told him it sounded brilliant and watched as he se-
lected number nineteen and it failed to come up five times
in a row. On a hunch, I put my one thousand dollars in chips
plus the single one-hundred-dollar chip I had won on red,
all of it on nineteen. It didn't come up that time either.

"That's what happens sometimes," sighed the Congressman, looking longingly at his wife's sturdy pile of
ten-dollar chips. "You figure the odds the best you can, and
then nothing works out."

I agreed with him and told him about Stroud, that the
police hoped to question Stroud the next morning and that
they thought somehow the shooting him full of heroin to
kill him was connected with Troup-Kincaid, probably in
some way tied to the Frenchman who had died in the swimming pool.

All this made the Congressman's face very serious, but
he didn't really say anything out of character. I moved on.

Martel was standing over in a corner, drink in one hand and his unused casino chips in the other.

The thin Frenchman Jean was next to him, smiling that white-toothed, clean smile and seeming very content. He had his arm around the lady next to him, a cute dark-haired girl, the same girl that I had seen once earlier come to the table where Martel was sitting to call him away for a telephone call. I presumed she might be a secretary. Martel seemed the kind of man who might well carry a secretary, solely for secretarial duties, halfway around the world with him. From the possessive way Jean's arm encircled her it didn't seem likely that she meant anything else to Martel.

Medlock was standing there too, still in that bloody damned White Hunter's outfit and red ascot I had seen him in earlier. He gave me a cold glare when I joined the group, and I smiled at him with my warm, friendly I-didn't-mean-to-say-it-smile. He didn't seem impressed.

"My dear Yvonne, my dear girl, it will be a striking room, beautiful."

It was Martel talking, his broad, blunt face animated and cheerful. He was really not a handsome man, the features a bit craggy and rough in a way that somehow didn't quite come together in the way of some strong faces. His nose was too wide and his chin tapered down to too much of an angular, well, not to a point but close enough. Even with well-tailored white suits, the good tan, and the full, prematurely white hair, he wasn't really a very attractive man when his face was in repose, as I'd observed it, watching him from a distance several times.

But when he smiled, that gentle, ironic, slightly twisted smile gave his face a humorous, sophisticated look. It was the same now, when he talked with outgoing lively ease, smiling some, reaching to touch the girl's hand with his hand occasionally, but only for an instant's touch to emphasize a point.

He was talking about the plans for the hotel. The main lounge, just off the casino, would be spectacular, he insisted. The hotel naturally would be near the ocean and this lounge would be long and with broad glass windows looking over the blue water.

It would be called the Gauguin Room, after the French painter, Paul Gauguin, said Martel.

"He lived here, he lived on Martinique," crooned Martel, his deep voice full of a low-keyed excitment. "Did you know that, Mr. Roundtree?" he said, turning to me. I shook my head.

"I have a quite good . . . well, it is small, but what is considered a rather good collection of nineteenth-century French paintings," said Martel. "Some are in my home outside Paris, some are in the hotel in Paris. But I have two Gauguin paintings, and I would donate both"—he smiled that ironic smile—"at least put them on loan, for this hotel. Paintings are expensive today, but there is no reason we could not buy other examples of his work. It thrills me, I confess. I only discovered this morning that Gauguin once lived on Martinique. Think of it! He was here, in 1887. That was four years before he moved more or less permanently to Tahiti. I never realized he was here, not even"— he nodded now to Medlock—"when we first talked of this hotel on Martinique that time in Paris last year."

Medlock did not seem overly excited at the prospect of a Gauguin Room, and sipped his drink noncommittally, maybe for all I know pondering what he might say to the board of directors in the morning in an effort to block the hotel project altogether, at least as far as Troup-Kincaid was concerned.

"It's in a place called Turin Cove, the spot where Gauguin lived when he was here. I went there this afternoon. He lived in what was not much of a little house for four months in 1887, quite near an old viaduct. I find it fascinating."

Martel's enthusiasm was compelling. He seemed to be talking mostly to me and to the young girl, Yvonne. But I suspected that he was waxing so enthusiastic on behalf of Medlock, who for his part wasn't saying much.

I was tired of the Gauguin talk, and I had a few rounds to make. I considered telling Martel and Medlock both at the same time about Stroud's recovery and the likelihood that the police would interview him in the morning. I almost did it, feeling no love for Medlock. He was a prick, a conclusion I had reached while at T-K-I, and had seen no evidence yet warranting even tentative second thought. I decided against it though, because it would piss Medlock off so highly, he of the view that he had offered me a perfectly reasonable bribe (call that consultant's fee before the grand jury) to keep him better informed than anybody else and I wasn't keeping my end of the bargain. Ah well, we all have these little disappointments. Yet I didn't want to irritate Medlock overly much at that instant because I wanted to ask him one question and preferred having him in reasonably cooperative spirits.

But there wasn't so much time. The Sidney Greenstreet of casino managers had already called time on the hour people had been given to gamble, and they were adding up the chips to see who had ended up the big winner entitled to keep them for real. The cocktail hour wouldn't last much longer, and I had rounds to make. How get the word to both Martel and Medlock without telling them together?

Medlock solved my problem at just that point by saying he wanted another drink and starting for the bar.

I went into my song and dance and told Martel and Jean and the girl about Stroud and the police suspicion that somehow he might be involved in the death of their friend, Roger Pirdeaux, and that the police would talk to Stroud in the morning.

The young girl, Yvonne, looked sad, and Martel and

Jean both looked concerned but not in any way I could read as out of the ordinary.

"Why is your Mr. Medlock so opposed to the hotel project?" asked Martel after a decent interval of silence.

"I don't know. You heard him at the board meeting. He's paid to worry about the bad possibilities, like getting overcommitted to any venture that might not offer a satisfactory return on corporation money."

Martel pursed his lips and looked grim. "I wish it not so. I have the feeling his view is respected by the members of the board." This was true enough, and I nodded.

What about their friend Roger? I asked, a bit taken aback that there had been so little reaction to my story of Stroud. It was a tragic accident, of course, but did not their friend leave a family behind?

Jean and Martel glanced at each other.

"There was his mother," Jean said.

"She was quite old, but he looked after her," said Martel. He shrugged. "He was married twice and divorced twice. I don't think either of his wives will mourn him."

Children? I asked. No, none, said Martel. There had been a little girl in Roger's first marriage, he thought, but the girl died very young. I wondered what had happened to that fine young son and daughter good old Roger had told me about in the lobby, the ones he told me he brought that time to Martinique for a vacation, all of them together, but this didn't seem to be the time—or the people—to ask.

This was confusing me, and I didn't think it was yielding any new information.

I moved on, excusing myself to get a drink, and sought out Medlock, who had presumably already gotten his fresh drink, but it was hard to tell because his glass was near empty again. I buttered him up a little, told him I had heard from the police and wanted to tell him what I had not yet even told Wexler Senior. He liked that part and urged me to contact Lieutenant Vitu again in the morning so I could let Medlock know what I could learn.

I tried to make the one question casual.

"Why were you in Paris last year? I mean, the Congressman, Hinrichs, told me he happened to be there when you first talked to Martel about the Martinique hotel."

Hmmmm, he grunted. Be more accurate to turn that around he said. He had been there on business for three days and had run into Hinrichs and his fat, dumb wife, who insisted he come to their hotel for drinks. It turned out that it was Martel's hotel, the same hotel where Hinrichs and his dumb wife stayed two weeks each summer, and Hinrichs and Martel had already been talking about the French West Indies and hotels, and the first thing Medlock knew, it had escalated out of just talk to a serious proposal.

Not that it was a bad proposal, he added. He really rather liked the idea if money were a little less tight. But he remembered all too clearly what had happened to some of the conglomerate companies when the last ball-busting credit crunch came, and he just wasn't convinced this was a time to tie up millions of dollars in anything that wouldn't yield a profit for a while. The way the goddamned interest rates were going, and with the mounting evidence that those American gnomes at the Federal Reserve shop had lost their fucking minds, it was almost better for anybody to put extra cash into anything solid with high interest, government bonds, whatever.

Medlock was a little drunk, but I decided I liked him better that way. He seemed more good-natured, even as he raged about this and that. I told him I would by all means check with the police in the morning, first thing, and let him know if anything else had developed.

Henry Winston was standing with another member of our board, talking quietly, when I started his way. He saw me coming and separated himself.

"I've news of Mr. Stroud," I told him. "He may live. The police think they'll be able to question him in the morning."

Henry knew I didn't know quite what to think of him at the moment, and I stared at him, waiting for reaction. He smiled without much humor and then frowned. "Jim, I honestly don't know exactly who sent those damned notes to us, or even frankly what Bill Wexler Junior is up to. I wish I understood more. I can tell you this, for what it's worth?" It sounded like a question, the way it came out. And he smiled faintly. "If the man Stroud you asked me about, the one you say the police are going to question in the morning, is the same Stroud I knew in Washington, then I can offer you one free prediction." He smiled some more, bleakly. "He won't tell the police much, or anybody much, unless he wants to."

Henry Winston ended our conversation with a wave of his hand and that bleak smile. He nodded at me and turned and not only walked away but out of the casino.

"Take me out of this place."

It was Helen Wexler, eyes vivid and wide and angry. "I saw you talking to Martel." This was like an accusation. "Take me out of here right now."

"Helen, you are lovely, and I will do anything for you," I lied, "but the last time we walked out of a reception, also one with your husband present, it made a lot of trouble. At least for me . . ."

"That son-of-a-bitch won't listen to anything I tell him." I presumed she meant her husband, but just maybe she meant Martel, and though the information as to which son-of-a-bitch might be helpful, at the moment, with Helen looking ready to stamp her foot, eyes flashing, I didn't want to ask. I began looking, not frantically but with interest, for her husband.

She read my mind, as angry women will do when you

least want them to. "Bill is behind you, talking with his
father and another son-of-a-bitch." I held in, and refrained
from either whirling toward Bill and yelling for help, or
even glancing over my shoulder to see who was where.

I sighed. Suddenly I didn't care much. Helen made as
much sense as anybody else I knew on Martinique and she
had those wide, deep, candid dark eyes, and those slim
tanned legs, and an absolute electricity about her when she
was angry.

"What do you want me to do, Helen?" I asked.

"Walk me out of this room, right this minute," she
snarled at me, not sure if I were still humoring her or if I
really were willing to be putty in her hands.

I was perfectly willing to be putty, though it seemed
like a bad idea even at the time.

Sometimes you can't even tell yourself that it's the only
game in town.

22 But, Darling, That's Murder

Helen and I walked out of the casino together, nobody paying much attention, as far as I could tell. I was just as glad that Bill Wexler the Junior was standing a good distance from the door and facing the other way.

"Helen, this is not only not a good idea, it has the potential for stirring people up. Before too long, everybody is going to break up and go to dinner, and then maybe to that cockfight thing, and even if nobody else notices, your husband will notice you are nowhere to be seen. Then he is likely to observe that I too am nowhere to be seen."

I was prepared to go on developing this grim scenario but Helen was unimpressed. We got in the elevator and I tried a different tack.

"Why don't we go for a walk out by the swimming pool?"

Helen shook her head. "Let's go to your room." I had been afraid she would say that, and I sighed, but I did not think it would make any difference if I offered other suggestions. Not that, under different circumstances, it wouldn't have been a sensational suggestion.

My room was still on the third floor, just where I had left it, and there were still the bottles of Scotch and bourbon and rum on the small table. Helen suggested it would be nice if I fixed her a small drink. I made it as small as I dared,

Scotch, and mixed myself a somewhat heftier one of bourbon.

I opened the window out onto the little balcony and we stood there sipping drinks and peering out over the bay.

"That's the son-of-a-bitch's boat," Helen said, pointing down to the craft belonging to Martel. Oh, Helen was in a rare mood. Best I could make out, her current SOB list included her husband and Martel and Lord knows who else.

"What is it, Helen?"

I put my drink down and put my arms on her shoulders. She paid no attention for a moment, standing stiff and staring out at the Martel boat. Then she took a long, shuddering breath and hugged herself, wrapped her own arms around until her hands touched mine on her shoulders.

She turned around in my arms, a move I helped along, and I held her with both arms. It wasn't a romantic embrace, more of an awkward, friendly try at easing someone's pain. But it changed while I held her and she relaxed a little. I kissed her eyes, half thinking from the sound of that long breath and sigh a moment before that she would have tears in her eyes. Not so. And when I kissed her eyes it seemed more natural than not to kiss her on the cheek and then on the lips.

She pulled away after a long minute that left my heart beating at a rapid clip.

"I liked that," she said, smiling at me and seeming all pulled together again. "Let's sit down out here on the balcony. Freshen our drinks first."

I had liked kissing Helen too and didn't especially like liking it, if that makes sense. The party was probably breaking up downstairs and Bill Wexler just might be beginning to wonder where in hell his wife was.

It popped into my head, the Bruce Catton Civil War book. I had told Hank I was like General Pemberton of the Army of the Mississippi, as Catton described him a man dedicated but wholly without good luck. And he had re-searched it, and by the next day insisted to me that I was more like General Van Dorn, who I later discovered had perished at the hands of an outraged Tennessee husband. The thought struck me that I might manage to combine the two: prove dedicated and without good luck and perish at the hands of Helen's husband.

"Bill is likely to come looking for you," I tried.

"No, he's not," she said cheerfully. "I told him where I would be."

That gave me considerable pause, whether it was true or not.

"Wonderful."

"He's got other things on his mind. He's going to dinner to try to influence two members of the board of directors on something, and then they're all going to that cockfight somewhere after. I told him I didn't want to go."

Helen paused and stared at me. She put one hand to her mouth and nibbled a little on a knuckle.

"You like me, don't you, Jim?"

"I like you a lot."

"Would you kill a man if I asked you to and told you why?"

It was probably something in the Martinique air, or that last drink, but I could have sworn Helen had asked me to kill somebody.

"Would you?" she persisted.

I sighed and worked hard on my drink. "Helen, tell me what in the world you are talking about."

"It is Martel," she said. "He is a monster and he ought to be killed." I stared down at the Frenchman's boat, shift-ing a little in the water of the bay.

Helen didn't seem angry or upset or emotional any more. She started talking, telling me the story.

It got back to her daughter, Susan, and part of it somehow was Susan's being arrested for smuggling cocaine and facing maybe a serious jail term. She had wanted to tell me all of it that afternoon in Fort-de-France, she said, but then she had held back, expecting really to find Bill back at the hotel, or at least to have a message from him at the hotel. He had taken Susan up to Canada, Helen said, to an out-of-the-way place where an old friend owned a vacation home. They planned to stay there for two days, then he intended driving Susan on to Montreal where he would leave her in a small, expensive hotel, and then Bill planned to fly back to New York and on to Martinique.

It was a stupid plan, I thought, if the point was to protect Susan. It was like the American draft dodgers during the Vietnam war. A lot of them went to Canada, some with a sense of great idealism, but most didn't want to cut themselves off forever from their own, their native land, and many drifted back maybe wishing not that they had accepted a draft call but at least that their protest had taken another form, even facing the possible jail sentence for draft evasion. No matter how serious the cocaine-smuggling charge was, it still didn't seem likely to me that Susan could actually get more than a relatively brief jail sentence, with every prospect of getting out, even at the worst, in a year or two.

"But it didn't work," Helen was saying. "They found them in less than two days."

"The police?"

She looked at me, puzzled. "No, no, not the police. Oh, you thought . . .?" She chuckled. "No, no, that's the kind of thing I'm capable of. Bill is too law abiding for that, I'm afraid." She frowned. "Or he was."

No, no, it wasn't the police that found them. Bill and Susan never saw anyone in fact. But on the second morning they had found an envelope on the front doorstep, propped against the door. It had a colorful tourist brochure of Martinique and a short note attached. *Don't forget the board meeting,* it said.

Bill had brought Susan back to New York with him and left her there.

"Who do you mean found them?"

It had to be Martel, Helen said, and that was why the man needed to be killed. He was very evil.

Oh, she couldn't prove any connection with Martel, she admitted, which was why it was so diabolical.

The first telephone call had come no more than a week after Bill had made a decision against letting Troup-Kincaid cooperate in a joint venture to build a new hotel on Martinique. Both Medlock and Arthur Hinrichs had talked to Bill about it, after both had earlier met and talked to Martel. Bill was mildly interested and for several months there had been some correspondence, some preliminary studies. But then he had made a decision, that it wasn't particularly the kind of new venture that suited the needs of the corporation at just that time, and he told Medlock as much.

Medlock later cooled, but at that initial stage he liked the idea of a hotel project in the French West Indies, and he argued that they ought to postpone the decision for a time. Bill agreed.

The first telephone call came to their home which, Helen said, had an unlisted number. The caller was polite but wouldn't give his name, just suggested there was reason for Bill Wexler to reconsider his Martinique decision. Bill had gotten a little impatient when the man refused to give his name, Helen said, but it didn't even seem a frightening call. Not threatening in any way.

The second call came after the letter to Wexler about the insiders' selling stock, though Bill at the time didn't even know that his father had gotten that first letter. Then there was a call after the board had gotten the dead ducks in the mail. Bill knew about *that* all right. The exact sequence got mixed up in her mind, Helen said, but there was a call when all the garbage was piled up on everyone's desk, all the uncluttered ones, that is (Bill's among them, like his father's), and then the worst call came the day before Cornelius Martin was killed out in California.

"It seemed so terrible later," Helen said, "to think that whoever called Bill on the phone was part of killing that man, and he was putting us on notice that it would happen."

"What did he say?"

"Well," Helen said, "of course the message wasn't clear until after Martin was dead. It was the same message on the note that went to Bill's father."

I could quote it by heart. *If God had Intended Man to go to the Moon, he'd have laid a ROAD. Bye, Bye, Martin.*

They'd gotten that call and not understood it exactly and then within a day or so they had come to know that the "Bye Bye, Martin" had to mean Cornelius Martin, who was running a plant that had just started planning for carrying out a just-signed contract, one relating to the space program.

And then came Susan in Bogotá and the arrest at customs.

"I told you one lie this afternoon," Helen said. "I told you that Susan's friend, Cheryl, had called us about Susan and about how much she needed a good lawyer. That part was true, but the lie was that we didn't already know. Bill heard on the telephone three days after Susan was arrested."

After that, the calls came once every two or three days, always almost the same, just to suggest that the hotel on Martinique was very important, that Bill ought certainly to use his influence to make sure it was built, that there should be no mistake, and that a young girl . . . how old was Susan, the caller asked once . . . that a young girl, age twenty-two, in a woman's prison could be forced to endure sometimes crude and horrible treatment. Certainly, the caller said, that is something everyone would hope to avoid.

At some stage, the caller managed to suggest, without precisely saying it in those words, that there were people in the world who had more influence with judges and police and prison officials than Bill Wexler could possibly imagine. If the hotel project worked out, the strong hint went, it might well be possible for Susan to receive a suspended sentence or at maximum a period in jail of one year or less, a time that would not be so unpleasant because there would be people with instructions to protect her and care for her as a man might personally care for his own daughter. Ah, but sadly, there was the other side. If the project fell through, then Susan would most certainly go to jail, even possibly for twenty years, which would mean seven or so years probably before the chance of parole, and there would be those who would see to it that she would not have a good record in the prison.

"It drove Bill up the wall," Helen said, "but he came to believe the man on the telephone knew what he was saying and was telling the truth. He contacted Martel twice about the calls, and of course that evil bastard denied any awareness of what might be happening. Can you believe? Who else could have that much interest in making sure the hotel was built?"

I shook my head. I didn't know the answer, but there were loose ends that worried me. I was very suspicious of Martel, but after all it was his friend, his fellow investor, who had been killed, maybe by drowning and maybe by that blow on the head. That didn't fit in with an all-knowing bad-guy theory. And there was Stroud, the wild card in the deck, the old acquaintance of Henry Winston. He didn't fit in anywhere, far as I could make out. Except that the thought still made my shoulder twinge where he had twisted it.

Helen stopped talking, and I could figure out the rest, I thought, but I started putting a question or two to her to be certain. Bill had, I presumed, taken Susan to Canada to hide her out, to somewhere he thought she would be safe and out of the reach of the mysterious caller. And with Susan safe, he hoped then to smoke out Martel or whomever and block the hotel deal and in general raise hell. But the plans changed topsy-turvy when he found that he and Susan had, with ease, been followed or traced to the borrowed home in Canada. So now what?

Helen thought killing Martel would be a solution, and her husband had refused to talk seriously to her about it, which was why she had been so angry a bit earlier. So now, Bill Wexler would move to make sure the hotel venture would be approved, and that was why he was wooing and influencing a couple of board members who might be swing voters.

The Congressman was for the hotel. Wexler Senior would go along with his son, Bill, as would the older Wexler's old Texas friend. So, normally, would Henry Winston, but Henry seemed to be playing funny games. That meant Bill Wexler needed at least two other sure votes to be sure, only one if he could be sure of Henry.

"Hell, the last thing you want to do is kill Martel," I told her, when I had gotten this far in my musing-along reasoning. Why, she wanted to know. Well, I argued, because the only threats made against Susan, the only pressure put on Bill was solely on the basis of getting the hotel project approved. Suppose you shot Martel down or cut his throat, and it turned out that he actually wasn't the villain? Then, with the hotel project shot down, Susan might be in real and terrible immediate danger. Or even if it was Martel and friends at the root of the pressure, still, all that had ever been asked was that the hotel proposal be approved.

The best thing for Susan, for her safety, if that was the principal consideration, was for the T-K-I board of directors to approve the Martinique hotel the next morning.

"That's what Bill says," Helen declared accusingly. We were out on the balcony, our glasses empty, both feeling a bit drained with the intensity of our talk, and we could both see Martel's ship floating at high tide now on the bay. "I can't fight both of you," Helen added dreamily. She didn't sound now as if she wanted to kill anyone.

"I'm going to throw you out of here in a minute," I said, picking up both our empty glasses, "but I'll offer you a nightcap."

"Please," Helen said, tossing her dark hair a little, frowning out at the bay but not especially at Martel's boat.

She wasn't frowning when I came back. "Let's go inside," she said. "It's almost too warm, there's not enough breeze." She stood up and stretched like a cat, old cliché that that is, but there are ladies who stretch wonderfully and sometimes even purr.

I closed the windows to the balcony and turned on the air-conditioning, and we sat in the room, she on the corner of the double bed and I in a wide, comfortable chair. I got up once and went to the bathroom and when I came back Helen had taken off her cocktail dress and draped it carefully over the other chair and was sitting in the middle of the bed in bra and panties. She took a long sip of her drink when I came back in the room and I stopped and stared, admittedly a trifle dumbfounded.

"Do you think I'm shameless?" Helen demanded.

No, no, I shook my head silently, certainly not that.

As I stood there a little foolishly Helen unsnapped her bra and put it aside, freeing those lovely white, untanned breasts which offered a marvelous contrast to her deep tan. She smiled, not that dazzling public smile but just a small, good-humored, friendly smile.

I turned out the light.

I'd offered to throw her out, hadn't I?

23 Our Last Board Meeting Altogether

I didn't mean to go to sleep but these things do happen. Helen woke me up with a lazy shifting of her hip, and I came very awake, glancing quickly toward the window and praising God that it wasn't dawn or bright daylight.

We both woke up then, and making love this time was slower and more gentle. Helen might be a demon in bed, but she could be a tender, loving demon.

Later, though it was already in my mind, she was the one who whispered that she had better go, even though a look at my travel clock indicated it wasn't nearly as late as I had first feared.

I went to sleep again, and this time when I woke up there really was sunshine outside my window. It was still early and I lay there staring out the window for a while.

I believed Helen's story about the phone calls, the threats, all focusing on getting the hotel for Martinique approved. It made sense in a bizarre way, even if it didn't make clear why anyone would go to such ruthless lengths. I had some notions about that, but I didn't know quite how to explore them. The one thing Helen had asked me in fact, and I had promised her, was that I would do nothing before that morning's board meeting to call the hotel project in question, no matter what I now believed or suspected about Martel. Helen was sure that Bill would have persuaded enough members of the board to get it approved, and she had now come around to Bill's argument and to what I had said, though my argument had been less from conviction than from a desire to get her away from the idea that killing Martel might solve everything.

Susan would be all right, Helen now thought, simply if the hotel project were approved, and since it was the very argument I had used I found myself reluctantly promising her that I would make no waves before the board meeting.

It wasn't necessary. The waves were already there, great shattering whitecaps.

I was shaving when the phone rang.

It was Vitu and his voice was low and hoarse and angry. "Why didn't you telephone me last night?" he said.

"Why should I call you?" I said stupidly, only vaguely making sense out of his question. But then I remembered the two phone numbers he had given me. "I don't think I said I would call regardless," I said. "Just if I ran into anything or anybody, any information that would help you. I told people what you asked me to tell them, that you planned to question Stroud this morning. Nobody seemed frightened or even much interested."

"All right," Vitu said, now sounding just weary rather than angry. "It would be good if you could sit down and try to make a list of exactly the people you told and what you said. I will be at the hotel some time this morning."

I didn't really want to ask, but Vitu paused without volunteering anything else.

"All right," I said, in turn, "I'll make the list. Tell me what has happened."

Stroud was dead, said Vitu, killed around 3:00 A.M. by a twenty-year-old West Indian, a native of Martinique, who broke into his hospital room and stabbed him several times with a knife. There had been a police guard outside the room and one inside the room too, hidden in the closet, but the killer had come in through the window and had broken it so expertly and quietly that the officer in the closet didn't hear him until he jumped softly on his bare feet, landing next to Stroud's bed and beginning to stab with a long knife at the instant the policeman burst out of the closet, pistol in hand.

The policeman had shot the man in the shoulder, just as he lifted the knife to stab Stroud yet another time. But Stroud was dead.

"Who was the man?"

Vitu said he was from Martinique, not a very well-educated or very bright young man, one who had been in trouble several times before, but never in anything approaching this. He was in jail being questioned but so far he refused to answer any questions.

"Could it have been robbery?"

It could have been anything, Vitu said, but Stroud was in a hospital bed. Why not just look around the room quietly for valuables? Why start stabbing at the man at once? No, it was murder, Vitu said, deliberate murder. His guess would be that someone had hired the murderer, and since Stroud had been in Martinique for less than two days, why it was certain that the real killer, the employer of murderers, had done his work and hired the assassin in that period of time.

"There is something else," Vitu went on. "I am sorry to tell you this, since you knew the man. Mr. Medlock also died last night, in an automobile accident, in a taxi coming back from Fort-de-France. The taxi driver was killed too. They ran completely off the road and crashed over a small cliff. The drop was not far, really, but the car landed on its front end and the automobile caught fire."

Good God, I thought, there was no end to it. Cornelius Martin in California, the Frenchman in the swimming pool, and now Stroud and Medlock and some taxi driver I would never know but yet a man who had died because he was unfortunate enough to be chauffeuring Harrison Medlock, well-known corporate executive who had, in the eyes of some, doubtful views on certain hotel projects.

There was madness and evil in the world, and I had known that for a long time, but it seemed very close that morning, and what seemed worse was that I felt there was some dreadful logic to it all, more than somehow I could quite get a handle on.

"You're sure Medlock's car accident was an accident?" I asked Vitu.

"Officially, there is no evidence that it is anything but an accident," said Vitu. "Unofficially, you can guess what I think. I am beginning to despise the day that your Troup-Kincaid barbarians ever came to Martinique."

The lieutenant hung up, reminding me that he would want to talk to me when he got to the hotel later that morning. Barbarians, huh? Maybe Vitu was right.

It was still fairly early, not quite nine in the morning, and I telephoned Johnathan Pettigrew in his hotel room. He was there and sounded sleepy. I told him I had things to do and needed his help, and he came awake and made cooperative sounds. I asked him to telephone Wexler the Senior and then Wexler the Junior, telling them both about Medlock's accident and asking them both who else, if anybody, should be told before the 10:00 A.M. board meeting. I said I presumed the authorities were taking care of notifying Medlock's family, but that he ought to call Miss Gerlock, Wexler the Senior's secretary, and have her discreetly find out, first, for sure that the family knew and then, second, if there was anything she could do to help. Mrs. Medlock might want to fly down to Martinique to bring her husband's body back.

Pettigrew said he would do those things, and I went down to breakfast. I felt mildly guilty putting those housekeeping errands on his shoulders. The main reason I did so was not that I had other chores but that I didn't relish the idea of telephoning William Wexler the Younger's room and talking to Bill or Helen, either one of them.

Breakfast was uneventful. I didn't see any familiar faces and judged that most of our people had stayed up late at night and would get downstairs just in time for coffee and the board meeting.

Stroud and Medlock, both of them killed the night before. It kept pulsing away in my mind, just the two names, *Stroud and Medlock.* I still couldn't make much sense out of Stroud's involvement even yet. Or of Henry Winston's. But Medlock? I remembered standing with Martel and Jean and the young girl the evening before and Martel suggesting, worriedly, that he was sorry Medlock opposed the hotel because Medlock was no doubt influential with the board of directors, and I stood there agreeing, nodding my head. Did that amount to signing a death warrant for a man?

I was absorbed in such sorry thought, drinking a second cup of coffee, when someone stopped by the table.

"They're paging you, Jim." It was Henry Winston, looking somberly down at me, those sharp eyes seeking a sign. "I think they have a telephone call for you."

"You heard about Medlock?" I asked. He nodded. "That ought to get the hotel venture off to an easy start, at least in the board meeting."

Henry started to say something else, but my facial expression must have discouraged him. I'd give him a sign if he wanted it.

"Excuse me," I said, standing up from my breakfast table.

The desk clerk asked me to wait a moment while he checked about the telephone call. It was long distance, from New York, he said. I could go up to my room to take it or I could take it at a pay phone in the lobby. The lobby would be quicker, I said, and he pointed out the phone on which the call would come through.

It was Hank. "Our overseas telephone bill is going to be more than our office rent this month," he started cheerfully. He didn't know yet about Medlock or Stroud. He had been on the telephone to Paris three times since I had talked to him the afternoon before, checking the two French names on the sheet of paper Stroud had pressed into my hand. I had even asked that Hank throw the Daniel Webster at them, maybe as a nickname, a name used by some known criminal. That had not gotten anywhere, but there was information on both the Frenchmen. They were both very successful in their line of work, or reputed to be, at least, since the police had never been able to pin their activities down with precision.

I told Hank I had to go to the board meeting and asked him to stand by in case I needed to call him later, and he said he would wait in the office until he heard from me.

I had not thought to check things like agendas that morning before I left my room, and I had to ask at the desk about the place of the scheduled session. I suppose I could have guessed, it was in the same good-sized conference room as before.

It was the morning after what might be called the Company Picnic, if you could define a board-of-directors' meeting in the French West Indies, with a reception and blue water and sunshine and a town with a statue of Empress Josephine facing the harbor and, yes, that goddamned cockfight that took people off late at night and provided that easy opportunity for a taxicab to be nudged off the high road.

I had not liked Medlock, but there came to my mind the vision of bouncing along in the back seat of a large black tourist car, when someone in another car started systematically to batter the other car into your rear end, and you think first that it's an accident, and then you think the man behind you is drunk and can't control his driving, and then long about the third bump you start to understand that the car behind you is doing it on purpose, and on the fourth bump, as the quick sheer drop is coming up, you and the taxi driver both understand it too late and you yell and he screams too as your taxi gets battered right off the road and you know at that instant that you are probably about to die, barring miracles.

And it turns out that there just aren't any miracles, not on that road that night outside Fort-de-France.

All this passed through my head, not happily, in the corridor outside the conference room. Inside, there was a big silver urn of coffee, just to the left of the door, in tribute to those who, unlike Medlock, had lived through the night and yet who needed a revival of spirit.

I was not late, exactly, but it was all about to begin. Wexler the Senior was at one end of the table, as if he would preside, but Henry Winston was at his right, as he usually was during these formal item-by-item meetings, and would read off the agenda items one by one. Usually Wexler the older had an initial word to say but today he did not, only first tapping on the table to get everyone's attention and then nodding grimly at Winston to begin.

The beginning was about Medlock, of course.

It was easy to judge by the faces and lack of surprise that most of the members of the board had already gotten the word, though there were a couple of startled expressions and one of the bankers muttered something not quite audible and leaned over to whisper to the man on his left, Baldwin from Chicago.

Winston coughed and cleared his throat and said, almost apologetically, that the death of Harrison Medlock, a man we had all come to know well and whose great ability had meant a great deal to Troup-Kincaid . . . well, of course his unexpected death in a car accident was tragic and wasteful. It was a great shock to everyone, he felt sure, said Winston. Yet, he said, the business of a big corporation had to go on in some fashion, and callous though it might seem, Medlock himself would be the first to understand that.

There was a general nodding of heads around the table. Everything possible was being done in relation to Medlock's family and the immediate arrangements regarding the accident with Martinique authorities would be taken care of immediately, Winston said. Whatever needed to be done would be done.

Meanwhile, he continued, it would be an appropriate thing for the board to pass a resolution expressing its high regard for Medlock and his work and the collective sorrow at what had happened.

I wondered about Medlock in those last seconds when his taxi was plunging off the road, sudden sweat on his face as he realized the full danger and cold, leaping fear somewhere inside . . . would it have cheered him any to think that T-K-I's board of directors would speak of him in such high praise during, so to speak, the period of their collective sorrow?

I couldn't take much of it seriously. Winston began to go down the official agenda list, most items there as a matter of information, some requiring a board vote, but only the one of the hotel project likely to provoke any discussion.

The hotel project was last, for that very reason I suppose, and Martel would not sit in on this session, as he had at the preliminary one to take part in discussion.

I waited for the fireworks.

There were none.

Winston read the agenda item, peered up and down the table, holding up a copy of the research report on Martinique and the financing and the hotel project, part of which I remembered explained what an excellent hotel man

Martel was. The president of the corporation, Bill Wexler, had taken a special interest in this project and was perhaps more interested in it than anyone, Winston said, without even a hint of irony, and perhaps Bill would say a word.

Bill's word was brief. He had never quite been a good speaker, not in the sense of the gruff authority of Wexler Senior or, say, with the cool, convincing reasonable persuasion Henry Winston could muster. He was better with just two or three people, especially when something did interest him and the enthusiasm made his face light up. Bill spoke with authority however, even as now, when he sounded almost noncommittal in saying briefly that he thought the hotel project was a sound one, particularly since Martel's group had agreed to up their share of financing from one-third to one-half, and he thought the board ought to approve.

The Congressman said a good word for the hotel, and one of the bankers asked a question about the interest rates and interest costs, and said of course he would expect that Martel's suggestion that his group pay the entire interest on the debt if the cash flow didn't cover it in three years would be part of the written agreement. Of course it would, Bill said.

That was when I broke my promise to Helen, the one about doing nothing to block the hotel proposal.

"Mr. Chairman," I interrupted, and Wexler Senior and Bill and several others looked at me in surprise. Even when I was general counsel for Troup-Kincaid I had not been expected to take part in board meetings unless someone asked me for an opinion or comment.

The Congressman in particular didn't like it, as his glare indicated.

"I know that the board is about ready to vote on the plans for a hotel on Martinique, and it suddenly struck me that there is one consideration that ought to be mentioned

before the vote." I had their attention but they weren't
going to like the next part. "Frankly, it is a consideration
of such a delicate nature that I would prefer to talk to you
about it privately, Mr. Chairman, and trust your judgment
about bringing it to the full board."

Wexler the Senior didn't like it much himself, but it
was Bill Wexler who replied crisply.

"We don't have that kind of secret here, Mr. Roundtree, corporate secret I mean," he said. "If you are aware
of any consideration that would affect the proper action of
this board on anything important, there is no reason for you
not to tell everyone sitting at this table."

"There's only one reason," I said stubbornly. "I'm not
willing to do that, and if the chairman will let me talk to him
for only two or three minutes . . ."

"This is frivolous," said one of the bankers. "I suggest
we go ahead and take a vote. I'm ready to vote."

The Congressman expressed his agreement and Bill
Wexler was nodding his head. Wexler was frowning and
chewing on one of his cigars and he looked, for literally
almost the first time I had ever seen him, genuinely in doubt
about what he wanted to do. He glanced at Henry Winston.

Well, to hell with them, I had tried.

"Perhaps we should have a short coffee break," murmured Winston all of a sudden. "We have plenty of time,
and this is the last item on the prepared agenda."

I didn't give anybody a chance to object but simply
stood up and pushed my chair back and started from the
conference room. "I'll be in the hall, Mr. Chairman, if you
can give me only a minute or so."

I got through the door before voices burst out, two or
three at once, but they subsided when Wexler shrugged and
got up and followed me out, closing the door behind him.

"What is all this?" he demanded cautiously, as we
walked down the hall a few steps away from the conference
room.

"It's amazing," I said. "You look just like this corporate tycoon type I saw the other day in Miami, a man who went to some trouble to practically shanghai me down there and then to Martinique, all so I could nose around and try to find out why anybody would dump dog shit on his desk and send dead ducks to members of the board and, this man suspected, have a good and competent man killed in California for no known reason except to brag about it. The man I talked to then acted interested in finding out about all those things. Whatever happened to him?"

"What makes you think I'm not interested?" Winston asked gently, more relaxed than I would have expected.

He let me rant and rave on for another minute or so, about the things that had happened on Martinique, Stroud and Medlock and the Frenchman, three men dead in as many days and given the background only an idiot could believe that two of the three were accidental deaths, the way the police now had those deaths listed. Four deaths, I thought suddenly, if you counted the innocent taxi driver with Medlock. "Are you scared?" I finished. "Are you afraid that those toughs who pushed you around in Las Vegas will show up again? Or don't you give a damn about any of it any more?"

He finally flushed angrily, which is what I wanted, but he still responded in a low key. "I'm not scared, not at least in the way you mean." He started to add something, then shook his head, more to himself than to me. "This won't get us anywhere," he said. "You'll understand better later. I appreciate what you have tried to do." He put his hand on my arm as if to walk me, both of us, back to the conference room.

I pulled away, abruptly seeing a way it could make sense. Sure, he had been concerned in Miami because his son, Bill, was missing, and that concern was over. I had been about to tell him what Hank had learned, how I thought the two names on the piece of paper from Stroud tied in, but I suddenly knew that wouldn't make any difference. Sure, he had been concerned about Bill in Miami but also about the strange things happening in relation to Troup-Kincaid. Now he didn't want to think about them or talk about them. There was only one way it made sense.

"Bill told you about the threats, about Susan, and you told him you'd make sure the hotel project passed the board. That's crazy."

Winston narrowed his eyes at me and tightened his grip on my arm. "So you know about that," he said after a moment. He would probably guess later, if not right away, that Helen must have told me about it.

"Son, there's not much you can do about it," he said, after another pause. And then Winston explained that he'd given it some thought, that even assuming that the pattern all fitted the way I read it, that the people wanting to get that hotel project approved, presumably Martel and friends, were ruthless enough to kill people, shrewd enough to play little games with Troup-Kincaid, even far-reaching enough to arrange for Wexler Senior to be sought out with ease and shoved around in Las Vegas, able to trace Bill and his granddaughter, Susan, when they went up to Canada, this was the pattern and that all those things pointed to big stakes, big illegal stakes, and whatever it was had to involve the proposed hotel. Assume all these things, stipulate it even, said Wexler the Elder.

"I don't give a damn if what's planned involves stealing teen-aged girls to sell to Arab kings, or smuggling and narcotics, or taking over this island politically, or making that hotel the biggest, crookedest gambling center in the world, with dwarf screwing on the side. I don't care," he said.

Whatever it might involve, he said, that could be dealt with later. Right now, the only thing in the world he cared about was that his granddaughter, Susan, was up in federal court in a few weeks on serious charges, charges that could put her away in jail for a long, terrible time, a thing that could wreck her life, and that as an immediate tactical move, despite hell or high water or anything on God's green earth that I could say to him, he was going to have that board of directors approve the hotel project. His son, Bill, had only told him about the blasted telephone calls and Susan's trouble early that morning, and if there were more time maybe he would agree that something else could be done, but right now he was clear on his own intentions.

There wasn't much to say after that, though I suggested to Wexler Senior that maybe he believed this was just a tactical move, but it might be a hard thing to undo once done. He snorted at that and pushed his way back into the conference room ahead of me.

He suggested that the board vote on the hotel, without any comment at all on what that "consideration" was which I had suggested might be relevant. No one asked any questions, though two or three board members gave me a curious look.

24 And a Last Boat Ride

There's the old saw about how the lawyer trying to represent himself has a fool for a client.

There's something in that but there's another level of foolishness and frustration quite akin to an attorney discovering that he's been representing himself, a fool; and that is to find that he's been fool enough to represent a client who refuses finally to be represented and takes over the case himself at the critical stage and says, yes, thank you very much but I'll handle it from here now that the thing has gotten to the important part.

It was in that cheerful frame of mind that I ran directly into Vitu in the lobby. He was sitting on a small couch talking with the hotel manager. I presume that he was aware of our board meeting and waiting for it to break up, and he came to his feet when he saw me.

"I must talk to Mr. Wexler, rather to both Mr. Wexlers," Vitu said, "but I want to talk to you too. Can we speak together in a few minutes?"

"I'm just here to help," I said. Vitu nodded curtly. He seemed a good deal less pleasant than the last time I'd seen him. I couldn't blame him. He must have decided by now that Troup-Kincaid's invasion of Martinique was the worst natural disaster on the island since the 1902 volcano eruption.

"I'll be out by the swimming pool," I told Vitu.

It was my day for running into people, everybody in sight.

Martel was out on that wide sunstruck patio area behind the hotel, staring out over the blue water of the bay, probably at whatever he could see or maybe even not at anything especially, just reflecting on the things he chose to worry about, like the board meeting I had just attended. But it seemed to me that he was looking down toward his own boat, that beautiful, trim three-masted beauty, tossing a little now with wind and wave but not much, anchored a bit closer than when I had seen it last, close enough to the long wooden dock for people to get to it via a short rowboat ride. Pettigrew had explained it to me, somewhere between Scotches, the other evening. The plan for development at this hotel was to scoop out the bay right up against the short rocky cliff next to the water, but it hadn't been done yet and that meant that any vessel of size had to take care near the shallow water.

Martel was wearing a white suit again but in more casual fashion today; he had on an open-necked pink sports shirt and he had his coat off, folded over one arm.

I walked up next to him and he turned and smiled. "You got your hotel," I said.

"It is good of you to let me know," he said, smiling that gently ironic smile. He chuckled. "I will make you a promise. You heard me holding forth about Paul Gauguin, the Gauguin Room, last night. I talk sometimes much too much." He shrugged deprecatingly, a likable, charming, beautiful man, premature white hair that went with the tan, a bit too narrow in the chin but with a rugged, broad face and clearly, with his coat off, strong shoulders and back and arms. "When it opens, the Gauguin Room, you will fly down from New York as my guest, my personal guest, and we will drink to the foibles of the world." He chuckled again, as if to suggest that he himself was prey to most of the weaknesses of the flesh.

"You make it sound attractive," I said.

"It will be a magnificent hotel," he said simply. He looked at me. "I must go. There is the afternoon and things to make ready. You are coming on my boat? We will have lunch on the beach on the other side of the bay."

"Wouldn't miss it," I said.

Martel smiled at me some more and put on his coat and turned and walked away. I liked him, I decided, realizing for maybe the third or fourth time in my life that liking someone had no necessary connection to your considered judgment about that person's merits or demerits.

I told you it was my day. I was hanging around that open patio area partly, admittedly, to think my own thoughts, but I could do that in my own room, where the air-conditioning worked. Mostly I was there because Vitu said he wanted to talk. But the next person I saw was Helen Wexler.

She looked a dream, just as if she had had a restful night's sleep. "I've been shopping," she said, walking up and touching my arm.

I had the great impulse to touch her several places all at once, but it didn't seem an appropriate whatever. She smiled, the dazzling one, just as if she had read my mind, and leaned over to kiss me on the cheek. Given the public setting I didn't think that was very appropriate either but I liked it.

"I bought a headdress," she declared, raising a paper bag up high as if it were a banner.

She showed it to me and framed it on one hand. It was shaped like a pretty cap. I'd seen picture postcards in the lobby with West Indian girls in colorful Creole costumes wearing such headdresses.

"The girls put points at the corners," said Helen, "and it advertises their romantic status."

She showed me what she meant. One such point would be worn by an unattached single girl who wanted you to know her heart was free. Two points meant she was single but her heart was more or less taken, yet you could certainly talk to her if you wanted and try your luck. Three points meant forget it, that the girl was either married or had utterly given her heart away. Four points had a somewhat naughty meaning, Helen said, that the girl was married or committed, but well, she just might be available if she liked you.

"They told you all that in the shop?"

Helen nodded. "Think how much time it would save if American girls wore these."

"They usually get the message across somehow," I said.

Helen seemed happy and completely relaxed. She had convinced herself, I suppose, that the board approval of the hotel solved all problems, that now Susan would be all right. Maybe that was true. Anyway, I didn't have the heart to inflict my own gloomy feelings on her. I asked if she wanted something cool to drink and she said no, that she had to change clothes and get ready for the board trip across the bay.

Helen left me, and I beckoned to one of the hotel stewards out in the patio area and asked for a cold beer. I had the makings of a theory, ever since Hank had given me the information about the two names after his telephone calls to Paris. Trouble was, I didn't see how to prove it or disprove it, and with Wexler Senior and Junior in their frames of mind I didn't even see how to pursue it any further.

It was close to twelve noon, almost the time when Martel's boat was supposed to load up and take people

across the bay for an elaborate picnic. I could see no reason
for me to go at all.

The path down to the water slanted off to the right at
a far corner of the patio, then curved back in a horseshoe
curve to the water. I could watch as the first Troup-Kincaid
people began drifting down. Martel's ship was anchored
out sixty or seventy feet, and there was a good-sized small
boat in use ferrying people from the dock at the end of the
path out to the larger vessel.

You absorb things, almost by osmosis, at a big hotel.
I had noted without thinking about it much that there were
two general groups of people at the hotel mostly, other than
the T-K-I bunch, I mean. The first was a fairly sizable group
of travel agents, down to Martinique on some joint program, a group that on the whole seemed attractive even if
they tended to wear those infernal paste-on name tags most
of the time. The second group was less organized but iden-
tifiable, family tourist groups, mostly American, like the
family sitting at the table next to me. Mother, father, two
young children, a girl no more than seven or eight and a
boy perhaps nine or ten.

The little boy wore short pants, cut-off-dungaree style
and a red short-sleeved shirt and red baseball cap. He and
his family were eating an early lunch but he was quite
finished and had a tennis ball that he was rolling around,
seeing if there wasn't a way he could find to get in trouble
with it.

The ball squirted loose after a minute and skidded and
rolled over to my table. I leaned over and rolled it back.

The little boy after that began edging over toward my
table, not giving me a glance but playing with the tennis ball
and maneuvering nearer to me.

"Hello, son. What's your name?" I said finally, when
he had gotten no more than four or five feet away.

"Billy. What's yours?"

I glanced over at his parents and shrugged my shoulders. "Don't let him bother you," the lady said brightly. The father stared at me for a moment warily and then went back to his lunch, either deciding that I didn't look like a bad influence or more likely just that it was easy enough to keep an eye on his son on a sunny, open patio where the tables were no more than ten feet apart.

"My name's Jim," I told the boy. "Are you having fun down here, Billy?"

He nodded his head vigorously, giving up the rolling of the tennis ball for a minute. He was leaning back on slender, tanned arms, his baseball cap pulled rakishly to one side.

"I'm on vacation with my parents. Why are you down here?"

Young Billy didn't know what a good question I thought that was. "Oh, I'm just on a business trip with my company," I said.

That didn't interest Billy much. "Did you know there was a volcano on this island?"

"Yeah, but I bet you don't know when it last erupted."

Billy's open young face took on a look of sudden cunning.

"Will you give me a quarter if I know?"

"No deal," I said firmly, not because I begrudged him the quarter but because I was enjoying the talk and I rather feared that my handing over a quarter to their son would be a signal to Billy's mother and father that this conversation between their lad and a stranger had gone quite far enough.

"It was 1902 and it covered the town," he said in a low voice while he concentrated on the tennis ball.

"You're a pretty smart kid. I didn't think you'd know that."

Billy sighed, deciding to forgive me the lost quarter.

"Well, I studied about it in school." I doubted that, suspecting that he had heard the date on a guided tour as I had, but anything was possible.

"What grade are you in?"

"Fifth, but I'll be in the sixth pretty soon."

"You like football?"

Billy considered, giving his cap a tug. "Well, I can take it or leave it, but I love baseball."

"You like Hank Aaron? I saw him hit home run number seven hundred." That struck a few sparks, and young Billy seemed impressed.

"What do you like?" he offered.

"Personally I like golf and tennis and football, but baseball's okay."

"Yeah," he said, "they're all okay."

Billy's mother and father were gathering things together and getting up from the table, little girl in tow. "Come along, son," his father said, nodding at me in a friendly way.

"See you," Billy said, friendly too but without regret. At that age, on a sunny day, there are too many other new adventures maybe just around the corner even to regret the end of one brief small one.

I ordered another cold beer, and the steward had just brought it to me when Henry Winston appeared coming from the rear of the hotel, dressed in light slacks and sports shirt and a blue sports coat with brass buttons and a yachting cap yet. His lean figure and craggy face and white hair made him seem as distinguished in those clothes, say an admiral on a busman's holiday, as he had looked a while earlier in his dark business suit at the board meeting.

"You look absolutely spiffy, Colonel. That is the only word to describe." I didn't mean it especially to sound sarcastic but it did.

"I tried to give you your chance with Wexler," he said,

unsmiling, somewhat grimly. I couldn't make out if he were angry with me or just in general.

"I thank you for that help, Henry," I said. "It was my last service for good old Troup-Kincaid."

Henry stared at me, lean and erect and getting old, my sometime friend and mentor, with his blue jacket and brass buttons and yachting cap, the very picture of a fine old gentleman out for a holiday on the water. I liked him yet. It was a shame I had found I couldn't trust him.

"I just talked to Lieutenant Vitu," said Winston. "I think he's suspicious of all of us." Winston chuckled without much humor. "If he had the slightest evidence of anything, I think he'd lock up enough Troup-Kincaid people so that we could have the next board meeting in jail."

"Might be a good thing," I said.

Winston did not even smile at that. He asked if he would see me on the boat cruise across the bay, and I said maybe, maybe not. And he told me that Lieutenant Vitu had said he wanted to talk to me too, and I said that gave me something to look forward to.

Vitu was along in another five minutes, pulling out a chair without invitation and joining me at my table.

"I don't like anything about any of it," he began.

"It would be a nice day, I have no doubt, to find a beautiful beach and sit in the water and let the little fish nibble gently without meaning any harm."

Vitu nodded. The steward came over and he ordered a cold beer like mine. He wanted to know when I had last seen Medlock, and I told him. And he wanted to know exactly, in the very words, if possible, what I had said to people about Stroud's upcoming interrogation, and I told him that. There were no other clues, and the man who had killed Stroud was still in custody and still refusing to answer any questions . . . oh, except to say that he had believed Stroud had money in his hospital room and that burglary was his motive, and Vitu didn't believe that. The death of Medlock and of the unfortunate taxi driver were labeled accidental, officially, and Vitu didn't believe that either.

I considered. I had told Vitu about Stroud coming to see me in New York. That was one of the reasons why he was so suspicious, so sure that all the deaths were connected and not accidental. The only thing I knew of real consequence that I had not told him was about the blackmailing telephone calls to Bill Wexler, the implied threats to his daughter unless he helped win approval for the hotel project. Well, there was one other thing, the two names . . . three names counting Daniel Webster . . . on the piece of paper Stroud had passed on to me.

I considered and concluded that all of it would serve to make Vitu three times as suspicious as he already was, but I did not see what it all proved. But just suppose Vitu's further investigation threw the hotel project into doubt, wouldn't that possibly put the Wexler girl, Susan, into danger without solving anything?

"I want you to help me again," Vitu said.

"I didn't know I had been any help," I said.

"The man Stroud died because of my incompetence," Vitu said flatly. "I asked you to help me bait a trap by telling people that he would be questioned this morning. Then I handled the security part of that trap in such bungling fashion that Stroud was killed, murdered with no cause other than that I bungled."

Vitu's round, alert face seemed flat and hard as he recited all this. It wasn't in the way of a man feeling sorry for himself or crushed with his own sense of mistake. It was said in a rather angry tone, low key but angry and bitter and determined. It gave me suddenly a new degree of hope that maybe the game wasn't over yet.

"What can I do?"

Vitu pointed out from where we sat at the table to

Martel's handsome ship, still anchored not far off the end of the hotel dock, while a half-dozen guests waited for the small boat to ferry them across.

"When that vessel gets across the bay, and it'll be a leisurely trip, probably forty-five minutes or an hour, the boat will dock again or rather drop anchor. There's no real dock on the other side. Some of the people, those with bathing suits, will probably swim ashore. Others will ride in on another little boat. Martel lives on that ship of his part of the time. He lived there more than a week before moving into the hotel here. There's a lot of space below the main deck. He has one large room, a combination library and study. He has a large desk in that room. There are probably papers and records there somewhere."

"You've been on Martel's ship?"

"No," Vitu shook his head, "but I've talked to someone who has been there. When the people go ashore, you could try to stay behind, try to get into Martel's study and see what you can find."

"What if I'm caught?"

"I wouldn't think you would be in any danger," said Vitu. "What can they do, even if you're caught? You'll be less than one hundred feet from the beach and dozens of people."

I remembered Stroud at my door, breathing hard and sweating and passing out in a near coma, shot full of heroin. It occurred to me that if any of my suspicions were correct, and Martel's band caught me prowling through his desk, there were probably quite a number of unpleasant things they could do.

"You don't carry a weapon, do you?" Vitu asked. I shook my head. "This could be useful," he said, taking a small cigarette case from his pocket. It was one of those inexpensive ones designed really only to permit a pack of cigarettes to slip inside, so that you could open the top of the case and shake a cigarette from the opened pack.

"What is it?"

Vitu showed me a little lever at the top, quite visible, one that looked as if it might be part of the catch of the case. He showed me how to shift it to one side, quite easily.

"It's tear gas," said Vitu. "If you shift that little lever and then drop the cigarette case, not even throwing it, just dropping it on the floor, it will release enough tear gas to amply fill even a good-sized room." He shifted the little lever back and forth once more, as I watched, and then left it in safety position and handed me the case.

"I don't like these things," said Vitu. "They have a James Bond flavor, but this one has quite a simple mechanism and might help you if you are caught and want to get out of a tight place."

I thanked him for his concern and told him I would think about it, since I really hadn't decided if I would go to the picnic on Martel's ship or not. Vitu didn't much like that answer but when he got up to leave a minute later he left the cigarette case on my table.

There were still guests waiting on the dock to be taken out to Martel's ship, and I could hear music already coming from the ship, seemingly from the same trio I had heard in the hotel lobby that earlier evening, a time which now seemed a long time ago.

I had finished my beer and stood and walked over to the edge of the patio, looking down at that beautiful bay, Martel's ship stirring on the water as if it were a conscious part of the scene.

"You forgot your cigarettes," the steward said, catching up with me and handing me the case, the gift of Vitu.

Oh, I don't suppose there was ever any doubt about my trying to help Vitu, no, not help Vitu but simply persist in trying to find out the truth for my own reasons too. I had a stubborn feeling about it, the not letting go of a situation, even if Wexler Senior's refusal to go on pressing had left me without . . . how to put it? . . . any real standing in the case.

Yet I must be candid. The idea of getting on Martel's ship and trying then to pry into his private papers, dig out his secrets in a stray minute when no one would notice, frightened me more than I could remember anything ever had. If my own theory proved out at all, it would mean not only that Martel and his group had killed others but that they would not hesitate to kill me. I did not share Vitu's conviction that the fact of dozens of people on the beach one hundred feet away would do much to guarantee the safety of anyone prowling for secrets below decks.

Wexler Senior was a tough old bird, I told myself. Maybe he was quietly going along with the hotel, the behind-the-scene scare pressures on his son, but that was only for now until he had time to figure out a way to be sure his granddaughter came to no harm. All that had happened had served to alert him. He'd be determined, as soon as he felt his granddaughter was clear of the action, determined to get to the bottom of all skulduggery.

I think I could have convinced myself of that, and convincing myself would have been a perfectly sound reason not to get on Martel's damned ship. But I kept thinking about the children. The story is in one of the Kennedy books, perhaps even Robert's book about the serious days of the Cuban missile crisis. I'm not sure now which book, but in one someone describes President John Kennedy's agonizing over that terrible chance of nuclear war and destruction of much of the world which perhaps a miscalculation by Russia or the United States in that tense few days might bring. *I keep thinking of the children,* he told someone, explaining that he himself had lived a full life and that all adults had at least had the chance to grow up and begin living an adult life. But the children, all of them, still had so much unfulfilled possibility for life and fullness and joy ahead of them.

I was thinking of the children then on the patio, not, please understand, in any sense of comparing myself with Presidents but just . . . well, thinking of the children, all the children, my own two girls and . . . this thought made me smile . . . of one youngster in a red baseball cap who would wager you a quarter and probably take your money too if you gave him half a chance.

"You better hurry, Jim. They're about ready to leave."

It was Johnathan Pettigrew who had walked partway back up the long, sloping path down to the water to call to me. "All right, I'm coming," I said. I put the cigarette case in my pocket.

The small boat ferrying guests from the dock out to Martel's ship was crowded, close to a dozen people. I nodded at a few faces I recognized, most, like Pettigrew, younger T-K-I staff people. The rear echelon bringing up the rear.

Martel himself was greeting people as they pulled up to the ship and climbed aboard. He was in his element, expansive, smiling, reaching down to offer a hand to the ladies as they stepped up. He wore sandals and a white bathing suit and an open-necked white terry-cloth pullover. He had a yachting cap too, though it looked a little more battered than the spanking new one I'd seen on Henry Winston's head.

I'm sure Martel didn't know everyone by name, but he acted as if he did, speaking a word of greeting to each newcomer. My name he knew. "Jim, Jim, Jim, I am glad you came." He reached and grabbed my arm above the wrist, so that I was gripping his forearm too, and helped lift me aboard. Martel was a powerful man.

After the last of our little group had gotten aboard, Martel turned to the young man in charge of the smaller boat and spoke to him quickly in French. The young man, a muscular, deeply tanned one with sandy hair, nodded and pushed away from the larger vessel.

The canvas sails were folded on deck. Martel's ship would use its engines for the short cruise across the bay.

I could see Bill and Helen Wexler at one end of the ship. She had changed to slacks and blouse and had her dark hair pulled behind her head in a ponytail. They stood, interestingly I thought, with the Congressman and the thin, younger Frenchman, Jean. Helen was talking on animatedly and the others were listening with seeming enjoyment, except for Bill, who seemed preoccupied.

There were two small makeshift bars, one at each end of the ship, and I headed for the one away from Helen and Bill.

Unfortunately, that was also the bar nearest the music, which as I had direly suspected was being hammered out by the same trio from my first evening on Martinique. They were still loud, but the open air dissipated the effect a good deal.

There were three or four young men visible on Martel's ship, apparently crewmen, and I observed them carefully. They all resembled the first young man in the boat, in being young and tanned and muscular. They all wore sarongs, for God's sake. Don't misunderstand, my own initial reaction to the word sarong is to think of Dorothy Lamour and other pretty ladies who have worn them in a host of South Sea island movies. But on a solid, muscular man, even though the long piece of cloth is still wrapped around the lower body and fastened, almost like a skirt, it can look anything but effeminate. Martel's young crewmen were all bare from the waist up, and the sarongs seemed comfortable and colorful.

Wexler Senior and one of the banker board members were in conversation, and Henry Winston was talking to the Congressman's wife.

Everyone seemed to be having a fine time. Two of the young crewmen were tending the two bars, and one was moving around the decks with a good-sized tray of rum drinks. He had plenty of takers.

I went below decks once, ostensibly to go to the bathroom. Someone else on the same mission was coming out at that moment, but in another instant I found myself alone in the corridor and moved quickly to open doors. The second door revealed a large, comfortable room, big enough for one of our board meetings, with a wide mahogany desk in one corner. It had to be the room Vitu told me about.

I closed the door swiftly and started out again. No one had seen me.

The timing would be the thing. There were two possibilities. One was to try to snake down to the room again, while we were still crossing over to the other side of the bay, and see what I could find in a quick, furious search. If I were lucky, I might find something sufficient and be able to get back on deck in time to join the other guests on their way in to the beach and the picnic.

The other chance would be to wait until we had anchored near the opposite beach and people started going ashore. Certainly Martel and at least one or two of the crewmen would go ashore. No one would miss me, surely, if I ducked below deck and into the room at just that time.

If Martel went ashore, I could see no reason why any of the crewmen would find it necessary to look into the study. The picnic would surely go on two hours or more, and there would be time to search more carefully.

I tended to favor the second approach. But there was also a safety factor. Suppose I were caught. I didn't relish being surprised by one of the crewmen in Martel's study, caught maybe in the act of going through one of his desk drawers, after everyone else had gone ashore.

We were not quite but almost halfway across to the beach. There was probably another thirty minutes left in the short cruise. I wanted in the worst way to try my luck right then. Surely it would take only minutes to break into the desk, even if it were locked, and then to search swiftly through whatever papers I could find.

The warm sun was beautiful, glinting on the water as the ship moved leisurely across the bay. I had drifted by this time to the small bar at the point furthest away from the music, and I liked it better there. There was a slight breeze and I got a gin and tonic with a lot of ice, and the cold feel of the glass in my hand was good.

I didn't like where my thinking led me. This was probably the only one chance anyone might have to search through Martel's desk. I felt sure that if Vitu could think of a way he could do it as a police matter, that he would have done it already.

Therefore, I concluded, I had better wait until the end of the little cruise and try for the study then in the hopes of having the longer time, two hours perhaps, to search the room.

There was no reason the chance for being caught was really any greater, I told myself, resolutely refusing to dwell any more on the safety factor, the relative safety, that is, of being caught while there were sixty or seventy relatively ordinary people on the deck of the ship as opposed to being caught when no one was left aboard except me and Martel's crewmen.

I avoided the Wexlers and Henry Winston and the Troup-Kincaid people.

There was a scattering of other people from the hotel, people, I suppose, that Martel or somebody had invited to come along.

I found myself talking with a tall, dark-haired man with a moustache from New York, in his late fifties maybe, deeply tanned and looking healthy but putting on a little weight. He was with one of the big travel agencies and specialized in booking cruise ships for month-long holiday cruises.

He was about to retire, he told me and didn't like the idea much, but the company had already asked him to serve sometimes as a tour director aboard the cruise ships now and again after he retired, which meant he would more or less take charge of a group for a month at a time. He liked this idea but his wife did not and said she had been on enough damned cruises and he could go off for a month at a time after he retired if he wanted to but she wasn't going with him.

Women make life very complicated, the man told me morosely, and I agreed with him and got another cold gin and tonic and the two of us then got into conversation with a young blonde girl from Nashville, Tennessee, who had saved her money and quit her job and for the last two months had been traveling from one island to another.

She said she was twenty-four. That was a nice age for retirement. I liked the girl, probably mostly because she was pleasant and pretty and wearing skimpy shorts and halter.

My New York friend seemed to worry about her. Wasn't it dangerous to travel alone that way? Well, she hadn't been alone completely, she said, there had been a girlfriend with her until a week ago but her friend was running low on money and had a boyfriend she wanted to see and so had gone home. She didn't want to go home yet, our blonde acquaintance said. In fact, she had met a Danish couple on Martinique who owned their own sailboat and they had invited her to travel with them through the islands for a time and she was thinking she might do that.

This stunned my New York friend anew but he muttered politely that sounded very nice.

"What do you think?" the girl asked me.

"Oh, I think you or anybody ought to try to do what you honestly want to do, as best you responsibly can."

That was me, the old philosopher, riding a gin-and-tonic wave and getting that word *responsibly* in there rather cleverly, I thought.

We were almost at the beach on the other side of the bay. There was a low building, not building so much as just a roof perched on lean poles, shading the tables underneath. There was, dear God, a new batch of musicians, and from what I could already hear they were loud enough to drown out our trio without a trace.

It took only another minute or two before we dropped anchor, and some of the guests, those in swimsuits, started to dive off the sides of the ship to swim the short distance into the beach.

I got another drink, just tonic water this time, thank you, and placed myself near the below-deck entrance. I waited until the first boatload of people on the small boat had been taken in and the boat was almost back to the ship. Half the people aboard had chosen to swim in, the rest were grouped ready to be ferried in when their turn came.

Martel was one of those swimming in, and I watched him in the water, moving powerfully with long over-arm strokes.

25 The Devil and Daniel Webster

When the second boatload started toward the shore, one gentleman slipped and almost fell over the side and there was much laughter and a few good-natured catcalls from the people still on deck. I looked around as carefully as I could and could see no one looking at me. There was one crewman in sight but he was at the far side of the boat and his back was turned.

I moved swiftly down below deck and directly to the study door. I had already planned all that, a bold move into the study, and if anyone happened to be there I could say at once that I was looking for the bathroom and back out of there at a high rate of speed.

The room was empty.

I turned and examined the door as soon as I had it safely shut. It was a heavy, big wooden door, not the kind of door you would expect to find on a ship, but it went with the room, dark, heavy hard wood. There wasn't a key on the inside but I could lock it by turning the knob, a double lock, and that, hopefully, meant that only Martel had the key to unlock the door from the outside.

I gave a huge sigh, breathing deeply. So far, so good.

I started in on the big desk first, checking the cubbyholes and surfaces easy to explore. I found a ledger that seemed a ship's log, but the only things recorded in it seemed to be the daily entry about the weather. There were a few bills, a letter from Paris with a short note, and a handful of newspaper clippings, all of them, at a glance, seeming because of the photographs to be about horse racing, and another small ledger which excited me at first because it listed names and amounts of money, but then at closer scrutiny this turned out to be the same list of seven names on each page with usually the same amount of money listed by each name, not very much money for the most part, not at least any large sums, and I figured out that it probably represented the payroll for Martel's ship. Even my French is enough to understand that a capital letter "F" must mean Francs.

There was one locked drawer in the desk, the middle drawer of three, and I resisted the impulse to try to pry it open at once in favor of a quick check through the rest of the room. After all, whatever I was looking for, if it were there, might just as well be concealed in some other fashion as in the one locked desk drawer.

There was a large couch at one side of the room, and a combination phonograph-radio next to it. There were two comfortable easy chairs at the other side, with a small table with a built-in table lamp and ashtrays between them. There was a round table in the middle of the room with six straight-backed chairs around it. I checked under and over and around every piece of furniture in sight, even peering under the edges of the rug, without spotting anything.

That left me two more places to look. One was the two rows of books in the small built-in bookshelf, the other was that single locked desk drawer.

The books were easy and quick. Nothing hidden in any book crammed between the pages, as I ascertained by pulling each one out quickly and fluttering the pages and then replacing it on the shelf.

The books were a hodgepodge mixture, everything from a French-English dictionary to one of De Gaulle's books of memoirs, several books about hotels, assorted novels of one kind or another, both in French and English.

One book that caught my eye was *The French Connection,* for obvious reasons, I guess, if you know the book. It was a realistic and factual account, though told almost in a fictional style, of how New York police in the early 1960s ran down and seized the biggest single batch of narcotics ever confiscated by American law-enforcement officials up to that time, enough pure heroin to bring eventually probably twenty-five or thirty million dollars when cut and sold on the street, small bag by small bag.

The book, a paperback, looked well worn and I thumbed through it excitedly, noting that some passages were marked and two or three corners turned down. It took me a moment to settle down and realize that the markings didn't mean anything, certainly didn't prove anything.

There was one other book that I found fascinating, at least fascinating to find it on that shelf. It was a report really, in brochure form, forty or fifty pages long. "Calendar Year Report," it said on the cover, with a round seal in the upper left-hand corner identifying the government agency: U.S. Department of Justice, Bureau of Narcotics & Dangerous Drugs.

I flipped through the first few pages. It had been pretty well marked up, too. There were circles, carefully drawn in ink, around two paragraphs in the director's summary at the beginning of the report. One was about expanded intelligence in Europe and information that "led to the arrest of two persons as they arrived in a cab at the Miami International Airport." Agents found two hundred thirty-eight pounds of heroin in their suitcases, the report said. That amounted to close to twice as much as had been involved in seizure of pure heroin by New York police and federal agents in the real-life story recounted in the book and movie *The French Connection.*

There was one other paragraph circled. It was a summary, mostly figures. Federal narcotics agents that year had removed from the illicit market in one way or the other 178,785 pounds of drugs with a street value of 1.7 billion. That included 7,079 pounds of heroin.

There was a sound behind me and I stopped breathing, almost, turning slowly to face the door. Someone was turning the doorknob and trying to open the door, but of course I had locked it by turning the double lock from the inside. There was then a knock on the door. I didn't answer, needless to say, and then someone turned the knob again, rattling it pretty thoroughly this time.

It was a crewman, I assumed, who for some reason wanted to get into the study and couldn't figure out why the door would be locked. The man apparently didn't have a key, however, and there was no way for him to be sure Martel had not locked the door before swimming in to the picnic.

After another moment, I heard someone moving away from the door and I felt I could breathe freely again.

There was only one chance left in the time I had, though that was probably the best chance, since people don't usually lock desk drawers unless there is a reason, and I hoped in this case I knew what the reason was.

The heavy letter opener on the desk served well as a means of picking the lock and, while I claim only amateur status in such matters, I worked at the bloody lock for a good twenty minutes, once letting the opener slip and cutting a sharp gash in the dark mahogany of the desk. Also a nick in my finger.

Finally, I had it open.

There were mostly papers inside, many of them in French, and I began pawing through them frantically in search of something of value (forgive me, Robert Ruark).

When I found it, I almost didn't recognize it for what it was. It was a set of plans, drawings, four narrow sheets of schematic drawings. I almost put it aside but the drawings struck a familiar chord, and I looked closer and I suddenly recognized and then I knew that's what it had to be. There were some names and addresses on the back of the first drawing, the name of a company and then names and addresses of two men.

I pushed the drawer shut and looked around, wondering if it were worthwhile trying to make everything look normal. I did my hasty best, fearful that the scratch on the desk and the smaller but visible scratches on the lock were enough to give it away. But I didn't care if Martel or anyone else knew someone had been there. I just wanted to get off the ship.

One porthole in that study, one of the few shiplike things in the room, faced at a slight angle toward the beach, and I could see some of the Troup-Kincaid people swimming. I didn't want to swim, but with any luck I'd be having a drink on that beach in five minutes.

I took off my shirt and shoes and left them beside the study door. I was wearing tennis shorts, if not a bathing suit, and I stuffed the drawings in an envelope from the desk and into one pocket. They'd get a little wet but I wouldn't be in the water long enough to matter. I planned to move out the door of the study, up the short stairway to the deck, and dive off whatever side of the ship didn't have a crewman between me and him.

They could hardly shoot me in the water within fifty feet of the beach with dozens of people watching. Could they? Anyway, it was the only plan I had.

The first part of my plan went splendidly. I opened the door quietly and moved swiftly out into the hallway and started for the stairs up to the deck.

That was where my plan bogged down.

One of Martel's crewmen was sitting on the top stair facing down toward me. He stood up when I came bounding out of the study, looking startled.

"Where the hell is Martel?" I shouted, leaping up the stairs three at a time. "I've got to talk to him."

"You'll have to . . .," the young man said, then adding something like " . . . ooooofffff" when I hit him in the stomach. I was jumping up the stairs at the time and I wouldn't claim it was my best punch, not like that time I hit Stroud, the late and by me unlamented Stroud, after he had twisted my arm.

But it was enough to pretty well knock the breath out of a man, and as I got on the same level, almost, with the other fellow and started to wrestle him a little, it was easy to feel that he had, for the moment, little strength in his arms. All I needed to do was push him aside and jump for the water and the beach.

I never even saw the man who hit me, hardly felt it, just WHAM and I was no longer with those present.

I felt it though later as someone slapped my face gently back and forth. The face slapping really was gentle, relatively speaking, especially compared to the feeling along the back of my head above the right ear, where it was very tender and very painful.

"He's awake," someone said.

It may have been the voice of the same young man I had last seen standing at the top of the stairs, just before someone tried to cave in my head. At least he was sitting next to me, at the table in the study, and he was the one slapping my face, no doubt a happy volunteer, in return for that punch in the stomach.

"You wanted to see Mr. Martel," he said without smiling. "I brought him for you."

The room was a bit blurry but it was getting better. I was sitting at the round table, next to the crewman. Martel was sitting relaxed in one of the two large easychairs, his leg stretched over the arm. The thin Frenchman Jean was at another of the chairs at the round table. A second crewman stood with his back to the door, arms folded in front of him.

I tried, but anyway I could figure it the odds were about four to one.

"I hope you are feeling better, Mr. Roundtree." It was Martel, swinging one leg lazily as he stared at me, that slow, ironic smile still making him seem handsome. But I could remember when he called me Jim. How soon they forget!

"You said you wanted to see me?" asked Martel.

I shook my head gently. The cobwebs were fading from behind my eyes but it took a little time.

"I'm afraid I hit my head," I said, risking a touch with one hand, There was the beginning of a bump but it didn't seem serious. It was a guess, but from the early feel of the swelling I judged I hadn't been unconscious long, probably the five or ten minutes it took for one of the crewmen to go ashore and in a deliberately casual fashion pull Martel away from the picnic and then for Martel to get back to the ship. They probably started slapping me awake as soon as he got there.

"I must have stumbled and hit my head," I said. I made a great pretense of coming to myself. "Well, I'm embarrassed," I said to Martel.

"There's no reason for embarrassment," he said. The young crewman who had just been enjoying slapping me looked sad. He wanted me to be embarrassed.

"I had too much to drink, I'm afraid," I said. "I guess I came down this way looking for the men's room and when I opened the door to this room, well"—and here I gestured toward the couch—"it just seemed too appealing. I turned the lock on the door and stretched out. I thought I would just close my eyes for ten minutes and would be back on deck before anybody noticed but I fell into a good sleep." I shrugged and looked around humbly at the other four men in the room, two of whom counted at the decision level, Martel and Jean. "I'm sorry."

"I'm sorry your head hurts," Martel said kindly. He turned to Jean and frowned. "It's not bad, really, considering."

"No," said Jean. "Not true either, considering."

Martel nodded and sighed, as if to say, yes, he understood that it wasn't true and he was very sorry because it made it necessary for him to do terrible and cruel things. Or, at least, I managed to read all that into his nod and sigh.

"You were going through my desk," he said. "Why would you do that?"

I suddenly thought of the envelope and the drawings, the envelope I had stuffed into one pocket. It wasn't there any more, though my cigarette case was. I realized with a new, sinking feeling that what looked to me very like that same envelope was now lying casually next to the lamp near Martel.

He read my mind, or more likely I let my slight flicker of gaze betray my interest in the envelope.

"Oh, yes," he said, "I know you took some papers from my desk. But I can't make out why you would want them?"

Jean said something to Martel in rapid French and whatever it was I didn't like it. For one reason it made my friendly crewman, the one who had been slapping me, smile good-humoredly.

"Oh, no, no," Martel said, smiling too but at me reassuringly. "There's plenty of time."

My fingers had started to itch a little, thinking of the cigarette case Vitu had given me and the tiny trick lever. Don't even throw it, he said, just drop it on the floor and it might help, anywhere, that is, where you think a room full of tear gas might help.

I thought just then that a room full of tear gas might help a lot.

All right, then, the conviction was growing on me ever

since I saw my friendly crewman smile after Jean's burst of rapid French that these people weren't going to let me out of this room, not alive anyway. Maybe Jean had just said, well, now, Martel, no harm's been done and let's all go back to the picnic. But I didn't think so. I had once had a chance to take college French. How did I know it was the one course I might really need one day?

"Why would you go through my desk?" Martel asked, still gently, smiling that smile that turned his triangular, tapering face into a friendly mask.

I figured the tear gas would give me a second of surprise, and all I really needed was to use that second to kick the crewman standing at the door in a vital spot and get past him out the door. If I could get through that door I'd take my chances on getting off the ship and swimming to shore in one piece.

But, I thought, if I were going to have to do that anyway there was no reason not to try to find out anything I could first.

I reached, slowly enough so as not to get anyone upset, for the envelope on the table next to Martel. Jean frowned. Martel raised his eyebrows a trifle but he nodded benignly as I picked it up and began taking out the drawings.

"I went through your desk, sir, because I admired your planning," I said to Martel, ignoring the other three men, Jean and the two crewmen.

I spread the drawings out on the round table, carefully and slowly. That damned Jean was wearing slacks and a light sports jacket and he kept his right hand in the coat pocket. I wasn't sure what was in that pocket but I didn't want to make any nasty discoveries before I even got a chance to play James Bond with my cigarette case full of tear gas.

"It made sense as soon as I checked the two names," I said, and then I offered my best try at the two names. "My pronounciation isn't good," I apologized. The names didn't mean anything to the two crewmen but they did to both Martel and Jean, the two French names I had asked Hank to check in Paris after Stroud had pressed his small message on me, the last real message he offered to anyone, I suppose.

"I told you," Jean insisted, speaking to Martel. "This one and the man Stroud. There was no other reason for Stroud to be found in this one's room."

I didn't much care for being called *this one* a lot but it didn't seem a good time to object.

I pointed to the drawings on the table. "These were what I didn't understand at first, I mean how a hotel on Martinique fitted into a scheme with two men in Paris who are understood, let us say, to be very prominent in large-scale narcotics dealings."

"Oh, very prominent," Martel said dreamily. I couldn't make him out but for the moment it suited me fine that he was willing to let me talk.

"The two names in Paris meant narcotics, and then when Stroud got shot full of heroin . . . well, that was unusual enough to be a tipoff, especially after the doctor said there were no other marks on Stroud, nothing to indicate that he was an addict." I shook my head. "That was clumsy."

"I quite agree with that," Martel said, frowning. "It was clumsy and simple-minded. But sometimes decisions have to be made on the spot."

Jean flushed at this, and it was not hard to guess who had been on hand when a certain clumsy decision was made.

"I just didn't see quite how it all fitted together, though, until I found these." I gestured at the drawings.

"You recognize them?" Jean asked.

I pulled out my cigarette case slowly, casually, and

opened it for a cigarette. My thumb fondled the little lever for a second. It was almost time.

"Certainly I recognize them. I've been in the plane a dozen times." I put the cigarette case back in my pocket and lit my cigarette.

The professional schematic drawings were of a large jet, same type as the main Troup-Kincaid company plane. Well, actually, there were two such planes, but in truth Wexler the older considered one of them his personal vehicle and the other was used as needed by other company officials. The drawings were of different parts of the plane, different angles, showing parts removed and cross sections and much detail.

The last page was of what at first seemed another complicated cutaway of some kind, but then you looked closely and it was an ordinary passenger seat, one just like the . . . oh, thirty or so, I suppose, in the T-K-I jet. It was drawn from several angles. From one, looking from underneath it seemed as if the seat was hollow . . . as, of course, it would be for Martel's purposes. The other drawings included a good many measurements, figures scrawled next to them.

"You must have figured it," I said. "How many pounds of pure heroin in plastic bags could you cram in one of those hollowed-out seats?"

Jean looked pained at this. Martel didn't say anything but I had the sense that he was losing interest in our conversation. I put out my cigarette in an ashtray on the table and reached for the cigarette case again.

Just then there was a brisk knock on the door and without any pause the door to the study swung open.

It was Arthur Hinrichs, the Congressman, prancing in where angels might fear to tread, his tanned, balding head looking as if he had just come out of the sun and his quick, alert eyes seeming to take in the room at a glance. I could have hugged him and started up out of my chair.

"No, no, Jim, keep your seat," he said, waving a hand at me, letting the door close behind him.

I almost put the tear gas gimmick into operation, thinking now was the time. Martel's next words cut me to the bone, as I realized, of course, what I probably should have realized earlier.

"You didn't have to show yourself," he said to the Congressman mildly.

"Can't make any difference now, can it?" said the Congressman, beaming at me. "Jim, I want to say"—and he looked somber for a moment and reached, I swear to God, out to clap a hand on my shoulder in almost fatherly fashion —"I am very sorry you got mixed up in this. I really am. I have always liked you."

Of course, then it made sense, the nickname.

"You're Daniel Webster, aren't you?" I said.

The Congressman beamed at me some more, just as if I were a bright pupil.

"It's vanity, I know," he said. "I used to read a lot of American history when I was in Congress those two terms. Always admired Webster. He really should have been President."

"How in God's name could you get mixed up with these people?" I asked him.

Martel and Jean both thought this was funny. Martel smiled with more good humor than I had seen in him since they caught me. Jean laughed aloud.

"You don't understand at all. He's the expert," Jean said. This provoked a chuckle from Martel and a frown from the Congressman.

"That's enough talk," the Congressman said.

I was beginning to think both the devil and Daniel Webster were on hand, maybe both incarnate in one person. The Congressman had a practical side, and he wanted to know now exactly how Martel planned to deal with me.

"There have been enough bodies," he said, and though that
line had an ugly side to it, it gave me cheer since it sounded
as if the Congressman were suggesting it wouldn't be good
to kill anybody else.

But, no, that wasn't exactly the gist of the conversation
that followed.

I would rest in a canvas bag in the engine room during
the short cruise back to the other side of the bay. It wasn't
clear to me if that meant bound and gagged or already
drawn and quartered, since I wasn't being consulted about
the arrangements, but it had a very permanent sound to it.

They knew my hotel-room number, and one of the
crewmen would go ahead on the small boat in order to have
time to get into the room and find my passport and pack all
my belongings.

There was an afternoon shuttle flight to Guadeloupe,
the next island, less than an hour away. Jean would substitute his passport picture for mine in my passport in flying
first to Guadeloupe, spending the night in a lovely hotel
there, right on the most beautiful white beach, the Congressman said, and then he would catch the early-morning
plane back to Miami, still using my passport.

While on Guadeloupe, that night at the hotel, Jean was
to place several calls to New York. They would be mildly
abusive calls, Martel said, because this part of it was his idea,
directed to Troup-Kincaid people who did not know Jim
Roundtree well. He hoped, said Martel, that the Congressman might offer some names, people who would know
Roundtree enough to know who he was but not well
enough to really know his voice on the telephone.

The Congressman thought about it and suggested
three names, the son-of-a-bitch, and I confess grudgingly
that they were just right: a secretary who had worked for
Henry Winston but not for me, an attorney who had joined
T-K-I only two months before I left, and last, Medlock's

wife, a lady I barely knew. The Congressman said he knew that she was not flying down to take Medlock's body back, that she was at her parents' home in Connecticut, and he said he even had that telephone number. It was unlikely that Jean could actually get Mrs. Medlock on the telephone, the Congressman said, but he could easily get one of her parents, and he should make a point of saying that Medlock was a self-centered bastard and had fired me and ruined my career and I was damned glad when he was killed.

Should he hint that I had anything to do with Medlock's car accident? Jean said.

No, no, Martel interjected, that would stir the waters unnecessarily.

Jean would land in Miami, carrying my passport, and then go back to being himself. It would be necessary to make some special arrangements, Martel said, to get Jean back to Martinique without going through any passport control but that could be done. The main thing was to leave a clear path showing that Jim Roundtree, disgruntled Jim Roundtree, had thrown up his hands after Wexler Senior refused to heed his advise against the hotel project and gone to Guadeloupe for one night and then back to Miami. In a few days or weeks, someone would worry about him enough to report him missing, but there would be no trail leading anywhere.

I listened to all this, probably in something like shock, but without feeling any sensation much except an amazement that it was happening.

"Can I ask a question?" I tried, after the general conversation about me on canvas bags and phone calls from Guadeloupe bogged down a little.

Martel smiled that gentle, ironic smile, the one that made his face handsome, and the Congressman beamed at me, his quick, sharp dark eyes gripping mine from behind his glasses, as if to encourage. *Certainly, my son, ask any question you want, for in a few minutes you will certainly die.*

"All this is about smuggling heroin," I said, "and there is no doubt a lot of money in it. But why would bright men like you"—and I nodded to both Martel and the Congressman—"go on in such roundabout fashion? Why in the world would you have to build an entire luxury-hotel complex in the French West Indies, and"—this with a nod to just the Congressman—"try to terrorize the top executives of a huge goddamned corporation just to smuggle narcotics?"

I was flattering them both a little, and I did not in these circumstances believe that flattery would get me much of anywhere. But I did think that it might help them both talk a little, and I had taken out my cigarette case again, thinking the time really had come to make my move, and when I made the move I'd either be dead or up and out and clear of these evil bastards, a thought that made me not want to rush into it exactly, but at the same time also made me want to try to find out whatever I could.

"He doesn't understand much, really." This from Jean, who said it with pleasure, and I gave him a dirty look.

"Jimmy, my young friend"—this from the Congressman—"it would give me pleasure really to help you understand." I believed that, for just the small moment's interest it was worth. Henry Winston sometimes took on with the same pedantic tone.

"You are right," said the Congressman, "it does seem like a lot of trouble, building a hotel on Martinique in order to smuggle narcotics into the United States, but no one has ever made such an arrangement on such a scale before. We may only do it once. That Troup-Kincaid plane will be flying down here at least once each month while the hotel plans are being completed over the next year and then while the construction is underway. We may substitute the hollow seats, probably that?"—he looked at Jean, who nodded—"but there are other possibilities."

How much heroin, I asked, in this one big smuggling effort?

"We think more than three thousand pounds in pure heroin," Martel said.

I started trying to figure that in my head. It might translate, at the small-bag, street-price, into narcotics selling for . . . well, the figures boggled my mind, something like more than seven hundred million dollars.

"This is a business," said the Congressman, frowning at me, as if I ought to be able to see at least *that.* "Nobody's ever managed anything on this scale before for two reasons. The wholesale price of heroin is, of course, much less than the street price, but we may have to invest as much as twenty million in cash front money to accumulate the heroin."

"More than that, probably," Martel said softly.

The second reason that no one had successfully operated with this large a single shipment of heroin, said the Congressman, was that no one had ever before devised such a foolproof scheme. The Troup-Kincaid airplane might not be Air Force One and it might not get the preferential treatment of a plane with the President of the United States on it, but nonetheless it would get quite courteous treatment. There was literally no chance whatsoever, the Congressman said, that any cursory customs inspection could discover the heroin that would be hidden in bulk on the airplane.

You know, it was at this point that I started almost to believe that what the Congressman and Martel were doing made sense, at least made sense in that it might work. I had my cigarette case ready, and it is the only time in my life that I had the feeling that it didn't make any difference if I personally lived or died. Somehow, with the help of Vitu's tear gas, I had to get out of that room and try to keep what they wanted to do from happening.

I had one more question.

"Don't you people care about what narcotics can do to people?" I tried.

The music from the beach was loud and clear, even in the room, but we all heard some kind of banging sound up on deck. Martel glanced up. "Go and see what it is," he said to one of the crewmen. "Some of the people may be ready to come back to the boat. Fix them drinks, and say that we leave for the hotel in about another thirty minutes."

That was a break. One of the crewmen slipped out of the room and closed the door. It helped the odds a little, if not much; there were still Martel and Jean and the Congressman and the crewman sitting next to me at the table. But there was no one now, except for the Congressman partway, standing directly between me and the door out of the room.

I didn't think anyone was going to answer my question. What was there to say? They were all part of a thing that made it clear on the face of it that they didn't give a damn. But then Martel spoke again.

"What do you think heroin does to people?" he asked slowly, rhetorically. "Do you know there are people who can afford heroin? They don't have to steal money to buy it. They live quite contented lives. The people who die usually die from infection, because they use dirty needles."

"What about the people who don't have money?"

Martel considered. "They sometimes do terrible things in order to get the money. You are right in that. But you must understand, heroin addicts are not really human beings. They are the ones mostly unable to endure frustration. That means they are unable to endure the world. They are the defective ones, unable really without drugs shot into their arms . . . or their feet or their tongues or anywhere . . . to exist as human beings. They are better off as dropouts from life. When they die, it is no loss at all to anybody."

This cheerful little philosophy frankly turned my stomach. I remembered the parents of a seventeen-year-old boy I knew. They woke up one night at the sound of a thump and found that their son had fallen out of his bed, and then realized that he was deathly ill. He had taken an overdose of heroin and died before morning. His parents, maybe their fault in part, I don't know, had not had a clue that their only son was into narcotics at all.

"The reason it should be run as a business," the Congressman offered, "is that otherwise there are tragic situations, just tragic. I knew two young men, both fine young men, who tried to smuggle some drugs, not a great amount, into the country. They each filled a rubber contraceptive with . . . oh, probably no more than half a pound of heroin, and swallowed it, thinking they would fly into New York and then pass that curious container through their bowels the next day. In both cases, the rubber material burst and both died. Just horrible. And all because there is a problem of availability of good heroin."

"And what you're doing is a service, planning to make it more readily available," I said, the sound of my own voice sounding distant and strange. The Congressman nodded.

I couldn't stand much more talk, thinking again of the little boy in the red baseball cap, and the day that he might be persuaded by an older schoolmate to try out the big H.

I kicked the Congressman in the balls, or near to it. He twisted and dodged and half managed to protect himself, but his yell was satisfying.

With one hand I flipped the little lever on the cigarette case and tossed it into the middle of the room, and with the other shoved at the crewman sitting next to me, just to get him out of the way for a second.

Jean and Martel were moving out of their chairs, as I leaped and grabbed at the Congressman and pushed him toward the other two men and dodged for the door.

I got the door open, but the bloody Congressman's falling body was half blocking it and I was just trying to jump around him enough to squeeze through the door when the long, muscular arm snaked around my neck and locked.

It was the crewman I had pushed, and I would have kept on struggling with the arm, but at the same time he put the point of a knife blade into my throat, literally into my throat, not trying to kill me obviously but pressing it in so that it broke the skin and felt sharp and painful.

I stopped struggling.

Where the hell was the goddamned tear gas?

There wasn't any tear gas. The crewman pressed me slowly back into the chair where I had been sitting, still holding the knife against my neck. I could see the cigarette case on the floor, just sitting there.

Martel reached and picked it up.

"What did you expect this to do?" he asked, frowning, then handed it to Jean. "You better throw this over the side," he said. "No telling what it is."

Jean got up swiftly and went out the door of the study, pulling it closed silently behind him.

Martel was back in his chair, that ironic, gentle smile on his face again, relaxed, his leg once more draped over the arm of the chair. The Congressman got up slowly, rubbing his genitals and glaring at me.

"You might as well cut his throat now," he said flatly.

I suppose I came in that second close to having my throat slit, but just at that moment there was a huge yell and a voice sputtering in French and the door to the study crashed open.

The crewman with the knife at my throat let me go, and the man suddenly looming in the doorway was firing the .38 pistol in his hand. The roar filled the room and echoed and the fire and smoke from the pistol looked to me like a forest fire. I'm not accustomed to having a firearm cut loose inches away from my face.

It was Stroud, for God's sake, looking tanned of face and husky and maybe a little drawn, as if he'd been sick, but not very much like a man who had been stabbed to death early that morning.

There was too much happening to worry about Stroud being dead or alive.

As I reconstructed it later, when Stroud jumped through the door the crewman behind me had let my neck go and lifted the knife and started to throw it. Stroud shot him in the heart, just as he started to release the knife.

The knife fell, rather than being thrown, and would you believe it, landed sticking up in the Congressman's leg, who shouted out a terrible string of obscenities.

Martel started up from his chair while this was happening and Stroud whirled and shot him in the left leg, a shot that threw Martel back sprawling into his chair.

About this time everything seemed to be going on at once. The Congressman pulled the knife out of his leg . . . it wasn't a very serious wound . . . and jabbed it at Stroud. It missed but it made Stroud jump to avoid the stabbing gesture.

I wanted to dive for the Congressman's arm, the one with the knife in it, but it would have thrown me between Stroud and Martel, and that seemed a bad move, since from somewhere Martel had produced a small, deadly-looking pistol of his own and was bringing it around to bear on Stroud, just as Stroud was trying to dodge the knife in the Congressman's hand.

I reached desperately around behind me on the table, looking for something to throw, and managed only to put my hand right in the swelling pool of blood from the young crewman slumped over the table.

Martel was going to kill Stroud, a glint in his eye as if to say, *you fool, you had the chance and shot me in the leg.*

Stroud was jumping and in the air, literally, and I don't know how he did it but he got his pistol aimed down at Martel and fired and this time the bullet hit right in the man's stomach.

Lieutenant Vitu was standing in the doorway, his pistol drawn and aiming carefully with the barrel on his left forearm, and he had expertly put a bullet through Martel's hand, the one with the small pistol in it, just at about the second that Stroud shot Martel in the belly.

After firing the one shot, Vitu reached down and slugged the Congressman back of the ear with his pistol and leaned down and picked up the knife.

Everything suddenly got very quiet.

"I wish you hadn't shot him," Vitu said grumblingly to Stroud, pointing to Martel, whose glazed eyes had the drifting-away look of a man not long with us. "I wanted him alive."

Stroud glared at Vitu.

"I wasn't going to let him shoot you," Vitu said, pointing, proudly I thought, at Martel's wounded hand.

Stroud glared some more. "You try making that kind of decision when you're spinning up in the air and one man is trying to get you with a knife and the other guy wants to shoot you."

Nobody had said a word to me yet and, in truth, I felt in a kind of shock.

Stroud put away his pistol and suddenly leaned over and gave me his hand. "Nice to see you again, Roundtree," he said.

It was the first time I ever shook hands with a dead man.

26 Martinique Connection

"I guess I owe you an apology, Colonel," I said to Henry Winston as we sat on the wide patio by the swimming pool back at the hotel.

Winston's lean, tanned, aging face crinkled into a small grin. "No apologies," he said. *"I owe you one."* He gestured at Stroud, sitting on my other side. "It was my suggestion that he twist your arm."

I sighed and peered at Stroud, who grinned at me good-naturedly. I had a small Band-Aid on my neck, where the knife had been poked at me, and after one tall, cold gin and tonic I was feeling a bit better but I hadn't quite sorted it all out yet. Except that obviously Stroud wasn't dead, and Vitu had told me that for his own reasons.

"Why didn't you just call me yourself, Henry, and ask me to come back to Troup-Kincaid, at least long enough to come to Martinique? I would have come."

"Would you?" Henry said, eager to believe me, seemingly delighted that we were friends again. He shook his head. "I suppose you would, but you know how damned stubborn you are sometimes, and I couldn't be sure. I didn't know enough then to give you a good reason for coming. I only knew I needed your help. I thought if Stroud threatened you and tried to scare you off . . . forgive me, Jim, it was the one way I thought to make you angry enough to come."

"Stroud was very convincing," I muttered sourly, rubbing my shoulder. This gesture cheered Stroud immensely and he ordered another round of drinks and looked again, for about the fifth time, toward the hotel, hoping to see Lieutenant Vitu come along, Vitu having promised to join us as soon as he made his official report at police headquarters.

Hank's information was accurate about the Washington tie-in between Stroud and Henry Winston. Stroud had been an investigator for a congressional committee while Winston was there for a year as staff counsel. And Winston had thought of Stroud almost immediately after Helen Wexler came to him.

Of course Winston and Stroud, between them, had never told me more than five or six words of truth, as I pointed out to both of them.

Ah, well. It is possible that Henry might have been right, that I might not have come to Martinique unless someone had made me angry. The thought that that could be true, well *that* made me angry too.

But to get back to it. Helen Wexler, God love her, had gone in fear and desperation to Henry Winston after her daughter, Susan, had been arrested and Bill had gotten the phone calls.

At that point only Helen and Bill Wexler and Henry knew that the curious things happening at the Troup-Kincaid offices, the notes and dead ducks and Cornelius Martin's death in California and all the rest could conceivably have something to do with pressure for getting the hotel project approved.

But they didn't know why. They didn't know for sure even that Martel was behind it.

Henry had first counseled that Helen and Bill go to

Wexler Senior and tell him the whole story, but Bill wouldn't hear of it, suggesting, probably rightly, that Wexler the older would blow his top at the hint of such blackmail pressures, that he might even move immediately to cancel the entire hotel venture in Martinique. That might endanger Susan.

But Wexler Senior and Medlock were already stirred up enough about the curious things happening, so it was easy for Henry to work my name into the conversation and help Wexler decide that I would be the perfect trouble-shooter to bring down to Martinique just to nose around and see what I could learn.

"One thing I don't understand is why you're not dead," I said to Stroud.

"I almost was," he said.

Stroud had been nosing around too, of course, trying to find out what he could. He had been going through the Frenchman's room, Roger Pirdeaux's room, when Jean and Pirdeaux returned unexpectedly. They had had a small container of heroin in the room, probably, Stroud guessed, to show to the Congressman as an indication of the quality and purity of the heroin they were already accumulating for the big shipment. Probably, suggested Stroud, the Congressman was being asked to persuade some of his connections in New York and New Jersey to put up some of the millions of dollars in front money Martel and his group needed.

Jean and Pirdeaux had decided, on the spur of the moment, to use that sample heroin to kill Stroud.

"Pirdeaux rather liked the idea. He had the notion, I think, that it would seem perfectly ordinary to the police on Martinique for a tourist to die through an accidental over-dose of the stuff."

Stroud said that he had pretended to pass out almost as soon as they started shooting the heroin into his vein, then he had broken loose and managed to floor Jean and then hit Pirdeaux one sharp, stunning blow on the head, the blow that finished him.

"You killed him with your hand," I said.

He shrugged. "I didn't plan to kill him, I was just trying to get out of there. But the son-of-a-bitch still had the hypodermic needle that he'd been using on me in his hand, and I hit him pretty good. It wasn't planned but, let us say, I have no reason to regret his demise."

Stroud had struggled to stay conscious until he could get to the desk and to my room and then manage to give me the piece of paper from Pirdeaux's, the only thing he had found that seemed promising before they caught him.

Jean, after realizing that Pirdeaux was dying, had gotten one of the crewmen from Martel's ship to help and they had taken him to the swimming pool.

"Lieutenant, over here!" called Henry Winston, waving at Vitu.

Vitu looked happier and less weary than I'd ever seen him and his eyes sparkled in that round, dark brown face.

He hesitated when pressed to have a drink and then ordered a beer. Vitu and Stroud exchanged cheerful glances when I asked why he had lied to me about Stroud being killed.

"There was a man who tried to stab me," Stroud said. "He just didn't succeed."

Why the lie?

Well, Vitu said, phrasing it as politely as he could, he and Stroud pooled their information as soon as it became apparent that Stroud had not been given anywhere near a lethal overdose of heroin. They discovered, indeed, that they had a mutual friend in Washington, and they in some cases had had similar police-investigation backgrounds.

"Mr. Stroud persuaded me that we both brought a professional point of view to these matters," said Vitu, "but that you were a talented amateur and that you might accomplish more if we did not tell you everything."

"Bull in the China shop is the way I put it, I think," said the grinning Stroud.

My gin and tonic was restoring my good humor, and I had only one other question, what in hell had happened to my cigarette case full of tear gas which didn't work worth a damn?

Vitu now looked embarrassed, and it was Stroud who answered.

"There wasn't any tear gas, you fool," he said, chuckling, absolutely delighted with himself. "There was a small electronic device in the case. We were recording everything that was said in the room. We have Martel and the Congressman on tape talking about the biggest shipment of smuggled heroin ever planned. It's beautiful."

There was only one question in my mind, only one decision, whether to hit Stroud in the mouth or not.

I sighed, thinking how fine the son-of-a-bitch had looked when he had plunged through the door with that pistol in his hand and undoubtedly saved my life.

"I have a program worked out," I said, finishing my drink and raising my hand to signal the steward. I touched the Band Aid on my neck, where the crewman had held the knife. "My wound is very painful. I think I will sit here and look out at the bay and sip gin and tonic very slowly until the pain goes away. I hope you will all join me."

This produced general approval and agreement.

"Then," I said, "I am going to eat dinner and I am going to bed. Now the best part starts tomorrow. Lieutenant, I would like to go to a black beach where you can sit in the shallow water and let the fish come up close enough to nibble on you. Can that be arranged?"

Vitu nodded, his face split by that quick, gay smile. "There is a girl, a charming, beautiful girl, a friend of my wife's. If you like, I will invite her and we will make it a picnic."

That produced more general approval and agreement from me. But after all, after Vitu let me play phony James Bond without any real tear gas . . . why, it was the least he could do.